PROMISES MADE
AND BROKEN

Books *by* Christine Matthews

PROMISES MADE AND BROKEN

Books *by* Robert J. Randisi and Christine Matthews

MURDER IS THE DEAL OF THE DAY
THE MASKS OF AUNTIE LAVEAU
SAME TIME, SAME MURDER

Available from PERFECT CRIME BOOKS

Christine Matthews

PROMISES MADE AND BROKEN

13 Stories

With an Introduction by Ed Gorman

PERFECT CRIME BOOKS

Printed in the United States of America.
Perfect Crime Books™ is a registered Trademark.

This book is a work of fiction. The characters, entities and institutions are products of the Author's imagination and do not refer to actual persons, entities, or institutions.

Library of Congress Cataloging-in-Publication Data
Matthews, Christine
Promises Kept and Broken / Christine Matthews
ISBN: 978-1-935797-55-5

First Edition: April 2014

CONTENTS

INTRODUCTION

Christine Matthews: Inside Outside

- The woman who hires a hitman to frame her father
- The shrink who categorizes his patients by genre type—mystery, western, science fiction, etc.
- An otherwise decent Las Vegas casino worker who felt close to the old man who just died but convinces herself to steal his winning ticket and cash it in
- A woman helps the daughter of the sister who despises her by committing the ultimate crime

I need to begin this with the fact that before she began to write genre fiction Christine Matthews was an accomplished playwright and poet. I mention this because the influences of both can readily be seen (and heard) in her crime fiction.

She writes ear-perfect dialogue and her prose is as clear and resonant as good poetry. The cool clean writing of her stories and books offer readers great pleasure. Combine with that her enormous skills as a storyteller and you'll see why she's appeared six times (close to a record) in the Year's Best anthologies I've edited with the late Martin H. Greenberg.

To date she's published four novels, one collection and more than seventy-five short stories. In addition she's edited several anthologies of note.

But whatever she chooses to write she's long been one of my favorite authors because she does what so few others do.

I've always particularly admired crime writers who played against the inherent melodrama of the form. The past master of this approach was the late Donald E. Westlake. In a number of his best novels he would set up his story with a familiar trope and then undermine that trope with black humor and writing that is more literary than genre.

Christine Matthews does the same thing in many of the stories you're about to read. The lead story is a fine example.

Give four crime writers the same plot and ask them to write their version of it and you'll get four very different stories. But plot is only what you hang everything on—character, mood, pace and structure. If one of those writers is Christine you'll likely get a story that is not only different from the others, you'll likely get a story that subverts not only the plot but the integrity of the various tropes involved.

"Gentle Insanities" begins with a wild card set-up. A private detective is on a TV show where theme of this episode is: "Daring People—Exciting Occupations."

She goes through the drill about real P.I. life not being at all like fictional P.I. life. Her biggest concern seems to be if the camera really does add ten pounds to her hips.

This is how we meet her. Now many private eye stories would have her get involved with a murder on the set; or get herself a stalker who saw her on the show; or get herself hired by a larger and better known firm than the one she works for.

Her first assignment for said firm would be to body guard a film star only to realize too late that she's been hired to be killed (the star's manager wants an assassination to get the star the kind of publicity that will get her back on top—and her bodyguard getting rubbed out will do it). Done with solid craft any one of these storylines could be turned into decent reading; maybe even more than that.

But Christine would push beyond that. She would use familiar characters but turn them into humans you'd never met before. And the same for motives. Several stories hinge on motives that Roald Dahl might have come up with. Even in the middle of a blackly comedic scene she can break your heart. Or maybe I have that backwards. Even in the middle of breaking your heart she can make you laugh.

The writer Joe Hill recently commented that the search for something new is not as important as finding a new way to approach and attack a familiar idea. I agree. Too many times what appears to be a "new" idea is like a one trick pony. As soon as the idea becomes familiar to the reader (say around page forty) you begin to find that the thrill is gone.

For two summers I taught at a writing workshop. I wish I'd had a couple of Christine's stories to use. Everything in these pieces here have what I call "echoes." You keep hearing them long after you set them down. Maybe it's one of the characters; maybe it's the ironic way Christine has set up a moral dilemma; or maybe it's the way the twists and turns of the storyline have taken up permanent residence in the back of your mind.

I'll make you a bet. As soon as you finish this collection you'll be on the immediate lookout for more work from this powerful, hilarious, sad and stunningly wise writer.

ED GORMAN

GENTLE INSANITIES

"They hired me because I'm a crazy lady." I squinted into the camera. Was my eye shadow smeared? Please, don't let me sweat through this new blouse—it's silk. God, I was enjoying my fifteen minutes of fame.

"A crazy lady? Is that what it takes to be a private investigator in Omaha?"

"It can't hurt."

The audience laughed.

The topic of today's *Donahue* was: Daring People—Exciting Occupations. I do admit I'm more exciting than the fire-eater sitting stage left. What does it take to douse a flame? Lots of practice and some sort of protective coating gargled inside your mouth. But I don't think I'm as daring as the eighty-seven-year-old skydiving great-grandmother. Now that takes real guts.

"Have you ever had to use that?" He pointed to the .32. I didn't have the heart to tell him I'd worn it because the leather shoulder holster matched my skirt.

"Once." I hung my head, as though the memory was too sad to discuss.

Questions from the audience were coming in spurts: "I've read that being a private investigator is boring, lots of routine, paperwork, photographs of cracks in sidewalks . . . you know."

"The agency I work for specializes in people, not pavement. We track down deadbeats who owe child support, runaway kids . . . that kind of thing. And I've only been licensed a year; guess I haven't had enough time to get bored."

The next question dealt with the great-grandmother's sex life and I zoned off wondering if it was true that the camera would add an additional ten pounds to my hips.

When I got to the office the day after the show ran on TV, Jan and Ken stood beside their desks and applauded.

I smiled, took a slow bow, and blew them each a kiss, "Please, be seated. I'll walk among you common folk and sign autographs later."

"Roberta," Harry called from his office.

"Robbie," I shouted. I hate the name Roberta, especially the way my boss, Harry Winsted, says it.

I sat across from Harry, eased into the leather chair, crossed my legs, and waited for him to tell me how lousy I was on *Donahue*. The more shit Harry gives me, the better I know I'm doing.

"Saw you on *Donahue*. That number about your little ale .32. Great stuff. Makes us look like big time."

"Just doin' my job, boss."

"Yeah, well it's back to the real world, kid. I got a job that needs your special touch." He picked up a folder from the table behind him. "Name's James Tanner. Seems the bastard skipped town with his three-year-old son, and the wife's not getting enough help from the police to suit her." He tossed the file at me.

I reached out, caught it without looking away from Harry's beady little eyes. "Anything else?"

"Yeah. You look fat on TV."

"Love you, too." I made a point to slam the glass door as I exited Harry's office. The glass rumbles; he always flinches. With my back turned, I waved over my shoulder.

After reading through the file, I found that James Lucias Tanner was all of twenty years old. He'd gotten married when he was seventeen, to a pregnant sixteen-year-old from the right side of the tracks. It was that family money paying for this investigation. After a series of bad career moves, James finally landed work as a manager at the Touchless Car Wash over on Dodge.

I made a note to check out Kevin Tanner's preschool.

The next day I drove out to La Petite Academy, in Millard. I expected to see rows of toddlers all dressed in red uniforms. Good soldiers with teeny, tiny swords tucked inside Pampers and baggy coveralls. Instead, I found a neat room full of partitioned activities. The smell of paste and warm milk reminded me of my own kindergarten class. I'd called ahead for an appointment with Kevin's teacher and made my way to her office, located in the back of the main room.

"Ms. Kelly?" I extended my hand.

"Ms. Stanton. I saw you yesterday on *Donahue*."

A fan. "That was taped weeks ago." I assumed a modest smile.

"Well, I enjoyed it a lot. Is being a private investigator really exciting?"

I shrugged, surveyed the room cluttered with Nerf balls and blocks. "I do get to go to some very exotic locales."

She laughed.

But her smile curved downward into a sad pout when I asked about Kevin Tanner.

"Oh, Kevin's such a sweetie. All the children and teachers miss him. But that father of his . . . what a creep. Always came in here dirty and mean. He had such a mouth on him. Tattoos all over his arms, and a green and black snake on one hand spelled out the name 'Donna.' Kevin's mother is Lynn. The man's a pig."

Good, she was a real talker. All I had to do was sit back, nod, and wait for recess.

Ms. Kelly told me, down to the rip in his seams, what James Tanner had been wearing the day he kidnapped Kevin. She described how the backseat of Tanner's car was littered with Burger King and Taco Bell wrappers. But best of all, Ms. Kelly's anal-retentive memory recalled a bumper sticker. A Mary Kay pink design telling every tailgater that inside was a representative. And the pink coffee mug Ms. Kelly saw stuck to the dashboard was stenciled with the name AMY.

By the time I got back to my apartment it was eight o'clock. The red light winked at me from the answering machine. I punched the gray button. The tape rewound, then replayed. My father's voice shouted from inside the machine, frantic.

"It's your mother. Jesus, she almost died! We're at the hospital. What am I going to . . ." His sobs were cut off by the infernal beep.

The next message started. It was Dad again. "For God's sake, it's five. Your mother's in radiation. I'm at Christ Community; they've assigned a specialist. I don't know what . . ."

The beep disconnected his agony and before I could call information for the number in Chicago, the phone rang.

I grabbed the receiver, startled. "Hello?"

"Thank God! Where the hell have you been, I've called twice . . ."

"Dad, I just got home."

"We were having lunch; all of a sudden she couldn't breathe, she grabbed her chest, turned an awful color, and just crumpled. I got her in the car and rushed to the Emergency Room. She almost died." He choked on his fear. "I can't lose her."

I maintained an artificial calm, not even allowing the idea of my mother's death to seep into my brain. "Could it be pneumonia?"

"Haven't you understood a word I've said? She's in radiation. The X-rays show there's a spot on her lung. But the technician said we caught it in time and your mother's so strong. You know how strong she is. Robbie?"

Cancer.

"Yes, Dad. I know." Thirty-five years had taught me well. Agree and listen. That's all Dad ever required of me. Nod, smile, be Daddy's little girl. I played the part so well that sometimes I lost my adult self in the charade.

"Oh God, what am I going to do?"

"I'll come up and . . ."

"No, we'll be fine. We're fine."

"Have you called Delia?"

"I'll do that now, while I'm waiting. Talk to you later." The connection broke.

Tears welled behind my eyes refusing to roll down my cheeks. Mother always said she'd live to be one hundred.

"I'm holding you to that promise," I whispered to her from five hundred miles away.

After staring at my scuffed floor tiles for half an hour I couldn't wait any longer. I called my sister.

She sniffed. "Dad just called."

"Well, what should we do?"

"I couldn't go up there even if I wanted to. The shop's busy. With Halloween coming, I'm swamped with fittings and special orders. Then there's Homecoming gowns."

"And I just started a new case, but if I can wrap it up, I'll go see what's happening."

"That'd be great. You know how Daddy gets. He blows everything out of proportion. Maybe it's not that bad."

"Maybe." I hoped, but deep inside I knew the truth.

The leaves seemed particularly vivid as I walked to my car. The apartment complex I live in offers covered parking, for an additional fee, of course. While my car is protected from the rain and ice, birds love to poop on it as they huddle above on steel beams supporting the ceiling. I cursed the black and white blobs covering my blue paint job and crunched dried leaves beneath my feet. The morning was mild and I could smell burning leaves. Someone dared defy the law and I applauded them. What was autumn without that toasty aroma clinging to orange and yellow leaves?

Ken was using the computer when I entered the office. He glanced up and grinned. "Get any last night?"

"Why do you ask me that stupid question every single morning?"

"Because I want to know if you got any."

"Sleazeball." I punched his arm as I walked to my desk.

"If you call me names, I won't show you a new program we just got in."

I admit it, I'm computer unfriendly. I admit, too, I've depended upon the knowledge of others when accessing or exiting a screen. I still needed to pick Ken's brain.

"I'm sorry. You're not a sleazeball. You're just scum. Better?"

"I knew you'd come around. Take a look. This is great."

Reluctantly, I stood behind him as he pushed keys with the artistry of Liberace. "All we have to do is punch in a last name and we practically get a pint of blood."

"Could you try 'Tanner' and see what comes up?"

Before I could turn for the file, the screen displayed twelve Tanners in the Omaha metropolitan area.

"First name?" Ken asked.

"James L."

"Bingo! We got your credit ratings, places of employment, marital status, number of children, pets, even a ring size from a recent purchase at Zales."

"Can you print it out for me?"

"No," he scolded. "I showed you how to print something. So do it yourself."

"Kenny." I pulled his ear. He loves it when I pull his ear. "Kenny, sweetheart, you're right there, in front of the thing. Please?"

"Just this once. This is the last time." He pushed some more keys and the printer started to life.

"Thank you very much," I said in my best Shirley Temple voice. He also loves it when I talk like a little girl. Hell, if it'll get the computer work done, I'll talk like Donald Duck.

I sat up straight behind my cheap desk and studied the printout. In between reviewing blue and white lines of tedious, boring statistics, I suddenly remembered Amy and let my feet do the walking to the yellow pages. I flipped to "Cosmetics." There were four "Independent Sales

Directors" listed. One of them was named Amy Schaefer. I jotted down her number and address and stood to return the book to its shelf. Passing Ken's desk, I poked his shoulder. "I bet I crack this case and don't even have to use a computer. Brains, ole bean. Human brains beat your computer friend any day."

"God, you're the most bullheaded broa—"

"Careful," I warned.

"—woman I've ever known. You belong back in the dark age."

"Where men were men . . ."

"Careful," he warned right back.

Omaha has a small-town feel to it. Tractors frequent busy streets, cowboys visit from out west when there's a cattle auction or rodeo. People are friendly and move in second gear instead of third. But with a population of half a million, a symphony, ballet company, museums, and great shopping, it also has a big-city mix.

I turned onto "L" Street and took it to Seventy-second. Making a right onto Grover, I found the apartment complex where Amy Schaefer lived. I backtracked to the Holiday Inn and dialed her number from a phone in the lobby.

After three rings a timid voice answered.

"Amy Schaefer?"

"Yes. Who's calling?" She was a regular church mouse.

"Let's just say I'm a special friend of James."

"Oh? Where do you know Jimmy from?"

"We've been friends a long time, met at . . ." Think, think. I looked across the street and saw a sign for a lounge named Jodhpurs. ". . . Jodhpurs. It was twofer night, ladies were free. You know how cheap he is." Was she buying any of this? From all the fast-food wrappers in his car, I figured the guy was not a big spender.

"Why are you telling me all this?"

"Well, Jimmy's been begging me to come back to him but after he told me about you . . ."

"You know so much about me and I don't even know your name." She waited.

"Oh, I'm sorry. It's Donna."

Suddenly her schoolmarm act exploded across the phone. "That son of a bitch!"

"Now, calm down. The way I figure it, us wome . . . broads should stick together."

My head felt as though it had been fired at, close range, when she slammed down the receiver. She was hot! Hell hath no fury and all that jazz.

I dashed to my car and swung back onto Grover. Parking across from the Grover Square Apartments, I saw a woman come stamping across the lot toward a pink Cadillac. I followed as she screeched into traffic, flooring the accelerator as the light turned yellow. I raced after her.

Then a Trailways bus pulled out of the McDonald's parking lot. Amy swerved, the car between us rammed into her rear bumper, and I jerked my steering wheel to the right, hoping no cars were in that lane or riding my tail. Last thing I saw as I passed the accident was one screaming woman, a busload of Japanese tourists snapping pictures, and a salesman-type man calling the police from his car phone. I hate those things.

"Damn," I hissed, rubbernecking as I passed the scene. I was hungry, frustrated, and had a headache that wouldn't quit.

While I hate the plastic trappings of twentieth-century life, I do love the simple pleasures. Like mail for instance. And as I poked through my mailbox and found only an ad for a new beauty salon, I felt cheated.

The apartment seemed cold; I hiked up the heat. Rummaging through the refrigerator, I looked for the chili left over from last night. The bowl had worked itself to the back of the middle shelf. I scooped a heaping portion into a smaller bowl and put my lunch into the microwave.

The microwave is another of those simple pleasures I referred to. I know, it also fits under the category of "twentieth-century conveniences." Oh well, I use it anyway but each time give thanks that I don't get contaminated from the radiation or whatever flies around in there to produce heat. And, if I should one day wake up to find all microwaves have disappeared, I'd survive. See, I don't depend on the convenience. That's the difference: the mind-set. I enjoy the convenience while knowing full well that one power outage will not upset my life. Dad taught us that. Don't depend on anything or anyone and you'll never be disappointed.

Dad.

I looked across the room. The answering machine was blinking. As I programmed the time into the oven, I realized my headache was fierce and went for some aspirin before listening to messages.

After gulping the last swig of water, I reluctantly pressed the gray button.

Beep.

"This is Mrs. Calhoun from American Express. Your account is now two months' past due and we were wondering if a payment had been made. Please call me at 800-555-9100."

Beep.

"Ro-ber-ta," Harry whined. "Some guy, says he's your father. He's been calling every fifteen minutes. Sounds weird. Give me a call, okay? Roberta?"

Beep.

"Just got a frantic call from Dad." It was Delia. "He's kidnapping Mother from the hospital. Call me!"

Beep. Rewind.

I pulled the phone over to the table, set my place for lunch, then poured a Coke over lots of ice. I dialed Delia's number. She answered on the first ring.

"Are you okay?" I asked.

"Oh, Robbie, thank God. I don't know what's going on. I talked with Mother's nurse—the doctor wasn't available. She said when Dad brought Mother in, she was barely breathing. They thought they'd lose her right there. What the hell have they been doing all this time? I've called and called and no one's home. I'm scared."

"Calm down," I advised with my mouth full. "If the doctor let her go home, she wasn't kidnapped. I'll talk to him and call you back."

"I think one of us should go up there." She was suddenly the frightened little sister and I knew which one of us would be going to Chicago.

"Your father needs help, Miss Stanton." That's the first thing Dr. Blair said after I'd identified myself.

"I've known that for a long time." I bet he thought I was kidding. "But right now I'm more concerned about my mother."

"I can appreciate your position. Well, your mother's a heavy smoker. Maybe if she'd come in sooner." He took a breath then dove right in. "Your mother has cancer . . . lung cancer."

"Should she be home now?"

"She responded very well to treatment and your father understands how important it is she come in twice a week for it. When she regains some of her strength, we can start her on chemotherapy."

"And then? After the chemo?" I really didn't want to hear his answer.

"Six months, a year. A year and a half—tops."

I had to hang up, quickly. "Thank you."

I ran to the bathroom unsure if I was going to cry or collapse but feeling the bathroom was the direction to head. I ended up sitting on the edge of the tub, holding my head in my hands, rocking back and forth until the panic passed. I thought I was going to die.

Delia took the news better than I had, or maybe she just pretended. It's hard to figure her out sometimes. While she stands five feet seven, I barely reach five feet four inches. She has dark hair—I'm light. She explodes over situations I find amusing and laughs when I want to scream.

We had agreed that I would fly to Chicago; I'd have to be the eyes and ears for both of us now.

I called Harry and told him about my near-miss with Amy Schaefer. He grumbled until I added in the news about my mother.

"Geez, kid," he sighed. "You just do what has to be done. Family comes first, that's what I always say. I'll sit on this Tanner case until you get back."

"Thanks, Harry. Thanks a lot."

"Hey, no skin off my ass."

I couldn't tell if Dad was happy to see me. He'd always made me feel as though I was intruding. Most times he looked annoyed.

"What are you doing here?" He stood behind the storm door, talked through the screen.

"Can I come in?"

"Well, sure." He held the door open. "It's just this is such a surprise."

I set my suitcase down and wrapped my arms around him. He felt thinner, bony. I whispered into his ear, "How's Mother?"

Tears welled in his eyes. "Not too good today."

I held him at arm's length, surprised at how old he looked.

"Let me go tell her you're here."

He walked away from me, went down the hall, and I stood waiting, feeling like a salesman calling on the lady of the house. Then I followed him.

"Hi," I said softly. She lay on her side, on top of the bedspread. She was wearing a pink sweat suit, her feet tucked inside a pair of white cotton socks. She didn't turn to look at me. I walked to her side of the bed and knelt down.

And then she whimpered.

I threw myself on top of her and we hugged.

When my eyes adjusted to the light, I saw how swollen and misshapen her face was. She reminded me of one of those Betty Boop dolls.

"Why didn't you call me? Or Delia."

"What could you do?" she asked, puzzled.

What could I do? Love you. Comfort you. What does a family do for one another? I knew then that she hadn't the slightest idea.

I couldn't get any information out of them and for two days watched my father dole out vitamins, steroids, and antibiotics. He cooked; he helped her up; he helped her down. I was in the way most of the time.

When I asked about Dr. Blair, I received mixed reviews. So I decided to check out Blair for myself. Telling my folks I was going shopping, I headed for Christ Community Hospital and the two o'clock meeting I'd set up the day before.

He looked like Elton John. Dark hair cut in bangs across his forehead, a toothy grin and oversized glasses. I agreed with Mother; I liked him.

"Her mental attitude is wonderful. And your father takes excellent care of her." His compassion assured me he wanted Mother to be well as much as I did. But doctors can't guarantee miracles.

I called Delia from a pay phone in the hospital lobby. She seemed relieved and encouraged. I felt better about the relieved part but cautious about the encouragement.

I packed my suitcase as my father trailed behind me. He walked in a clipped step and waved his arms as his voice rose. "How dare you."

I folded a blouse, keeping my back to him. "I'm her daughter. I have the right."

Words came in slow, deliberate syllables. "You're trying to turn your mother against me. We were doing fine until you came."

Hot, angry tears dripped down my face. I bent over the suitcase, quickly fastened the clasps, and turned to get my coat.

"Now what are you crying about? I can't say two words to you without you bawling. You're too goddamned sensitive, Robbie. Always have been. We're just having a conversation and you get hysterical."

"I gotta go." My eyes scanned the carpet as I walked toward Mother's room. I crept in and kissed her cheek. She breathed slowly, never acknowledging my presence. Confrontations were not her forte.

My father followed me to the front door, all the time telling me how I didn't understand, how selfish I'd always been.

I called a cab from the store across the street and waited, staring out the window.

❄ ❄ ❄

It was worth one more try. I dialed Amy Schaefer's number. Timid as ever she asked, "Hello?"

"Amy. Just thought you'd like to know we're taking Kevin and going to Disneyland for Christmas." That seemed like the kind of thing Tanner would do. At least I hoped it was. "Sorry if that screws up your holiday, doll."

"You're full of shit! Jimmy ain't going nowhere."

"Jingle bells, jingle bells, jingle all the . . ."

Slam.

I dashed out of the Holiday Inn and got in my car. Sure enough, after a ten-minute wait, Amy Schaefer came out of her apartment and this time she carried two shirt boxes wrapped in Christmas paper, tied with red ribbons.

I giggled. "Oh, goody, someone's gonna get their Christmas presents early."

Once again we headed up 72nd Street. Turning west on Dodge, we passed the Touchless Car Wash. She made a right on 120th and turned into an apartment complex. Amy got out of her pink car, and opened the door of apartment number forty-nine with her own key.

I knew I'd have to sit and wait. And I admit, okay, it would have been nice to have a phone in the car.

I checked my watch against the bank's huge read-out. My watch showed two-ten; the bank displayed two-twenty. I decided to compromise. It was two-fifteen.

Around three o'clock the door of number forty-nine burst open and I saw those two Christmas packages come flying across the parking lot. Amy Schaefer dashed for her car, followed by a short guy with dirty hair. I'd seen his driver's license photo and recognized James Tanner.

I called the police from the Taco Bell across the street, identified myself, and gave them the address where they could pick up James Tanner.

Within ten minutes a squad car pulled in behind me. They'd kept the siren off as I'd advised, but Tanner spotted the car just the same. He ran for the apartment while Amy stood screaming after him, "Run! You lying son of a bitch. I wish I would have called the cops myself. Coward!"

The police knocked at number forty-nine until Tanner answered. By that time several neighbors had gathered and traffic slowed to catch a glimpse of the action. I waited while an officer escorted James out. A female officer went inside and after a few minutes came out holding a frightened little boy in her arms. She patted his back, talking softly into his ear. The boy clung to her.

I opened my car door. I just couldn't resist.

"Amy?"

She spun around, relieved to see I wasn't wearing a uniform. "What? How'd you know my name?"

"Santa told me, said you'd been a real good girl. Jingle bells, jingle bells, jingle all the way." I kept singing as I returned to my car. "Thanks for all your help. We couldn't have done it without you."

"You bitch!" the timid church mouse screamed. "You fuckin' bitch!"

Some days are like that . . . you get no appreciation.

"Here you go." I dropped the papers onto Harry's desk. "All wrapped up, neat and tidy. Tanner's in custody, Kevin's being reunited with his mother as we speak, and Amy Schaefer is selling Passionate Pink blusher with a heavy, yet cheerful heart. Life just keeps—"

"Your mother died this morning."

It took me a minute. "What did you say?"

He stood as I fell into the chair. Coming around his desk he bent to touch my shoulder. "Roberta . . . Robbie, I'm so sorry."

"But I just saw her." I was angry. No, I was upset. I was going to cry. No, I was going to faint. Don't let go. Hang on.

"Your sister's been trying to get you all day. She broke down, couldn't say another word after she told me. I offered to break the news . . . I didn't want you to feel, you know . . . alone."

My grief started slowly and built into deep gulping sobs. Harry knelt in front of me, hugging me against his chest.

As the funeral procession wove down the street my parents had lived on for the past eighteen years, I noticed the Christmas decorations. A brick house on the end of the block had a life-sized wooden Santa, painted a hideous red and white. I hated it. The tree lights twinkling around doorways and windows seemed to accentuate our sadness.

Dad stood by himself at the cemetery. Bitter. He told anyone who would listen that now he had no family. Friends reminded him he had two lovely daughters. But he didn't hear. He repeatedly told Delia and me that he was alone and no one had ever loved him but my mother. I was too empty to fill him with reassurance.

❋ ❋ ❋

"We've gotten through Easter, Mother's Day, Father's Day. I really don't think he should be alone for his birthday," Delia worried. "We'll make a cake, bring some presents."

It was August, and once again I found myself back in Chicago. The birthday party had been a good idea. But the pressure of having a normal celebration had tired us all. Delia had gone to bed early. I sat in the living room, rocking and watched a *Fawlty Towers* rerun. John Cleese always made me laugh.

Dad walked into the room, grunting.

"What's so funny?" Before I could answer, he attacked. "How can you laugh? Your mother's dead! You know, come to think of it, I haven't seen you or your sister cry."

"We've cried a lot." My agony was all that would comfort him now.

"Well, I've never seen it."

I stared at the TV.

When he realized he wasn't going to get me to play, he changed tactics. Reclining in his chair, he sighed. I glanced sideways at him and he smiled. When I turned to look him full on, he smirked.

"I've got to tell you something." He leaned forward, confiding. "This is just between us."

"What?"

"I hired someone . . . to kill the doctor."

This had to be one of his lies. The kind he took back later claiming he had only been kidding.

"Your mother's doctor. That cocksucker, Blair."

"A hitman?"

"Yes." He sat back, satisfied his announcement had knocked the laughter out of me. "Money can buy anything, Robbie. That bastard is to die on the anniversary of your mother's death. At exactly eleven-ten in the morning. And if he's not alone, his wife or children, whoever's with him, are to die, too. Slowly, in agony. I want them to suffer like I have—like your mother did."

"Mother told me she was never in any pain."

"That's beside the point," he almost shouted.

"But what about Delia? And me? You could ruin our lives—our futures. There'd be headlines, reporters, we'd be humiliated. You'd end up in prison."

"It'll be done right."

"Don't you care about any of us?"

"He killed your mother. You expect me to let him get away with that?"

I walked over to him. Softly I tried to reason. "No one killed Mother. She had cancer . . . and she died."

"She didn't have cancer. She was getting better. You heard what they said. It was that doctor; he killed her. And I'm going to kill him."

"I can't talk to you now." I walked down the hall and went to the room I shared with Delia. In the morning I'd tell my sister that our father was crazy. She'd laugh and say, "So tell me something I don't already know."

By the time I returned to Omaha, it was late. The nine-hour car ride had allowed time for lots of thinking. I called Delia.

"I really think we should take Dad's threat seriously."

"Me too." She offered no resistance.

"Before we do anything, I've got to be sure. I'll try to trip him up or get him to admit he lied."

"Do it now. Please," Delia asked. "I can't sleep until you do."

"Right now."

I made a cup of tea to warm my hands, spirit, and mood. All the time wondering when things would get back to normal. But as Delia had said at the funeral, "Normal will never be normal again."

Finally I placed the call.

Dad spoke in a calm and serious tone. "I meant every word. Everything's been taken care of, there's nothing you can do now."

Then I lost it. All of it: my composure, my logic, my last shred of loyalty. "How can you do this?" I screamed hysterically. "How can you do this to us?"

Slowly, he explained, "Nothing will go wrong. No one will ever know. Just forget about it; it doesn't concern you."

"Please," I was crying now, "please . . ."

"You don't owe this man anything. He's a murderer."

"No . . ." I stopped. And that proverbial straw, the one that broke the camel's back, had finally been hoisted upon my own. I hung up the phone.

"From here on out," I later told Delia, "we're taking care of ourselves because no one else will. I'll go see a guy I know—a criminal lawyer. I'll pick his brain."

"You're the mother now," she said. "Please. Don't let Daddy hurt us."

"I won't," I said, and swore silently to protect us both. Our lives had suddenly taken on a soap opera quality and I did not like being cast in the role of victim.

✣ ✣ ✣

Bradley Johnson has this great office located in the Old Market area. A bricked passageway, flanked on one side by restaurants and on the other by shops, is illuminated by large skylights. Bradley's office is at the top of four flights of wooden stairs.

His secretary, Lucy, sits behind a small desk and greets clients with a cup of coffee.

"I heard your mother died. Harry told me. I'm so sorry." She buzzed Bradley.

"Thanks."

Brad escorted me into the large room that serves as his office, meeting room, and lounge. We sat next to the tall windows he prefers to keep free from draperies. He shifted his legs and leaned back in an overstuffed chair.

I confided everything. Bradley reacted with a raised eyebrow.

"Legally, there isn't a thing you can do, Robbie. It's your word against his."

"What I wanted, I guess, was more of a favor. I thought maybe you could contact my father, tell him we've talked. That might scare him enough to call everything off—if there really is a hitman. This way I'd be covered, the doctor would be safe, and my father would have to forget about all this."

"My advice is to call Dr. Blair yourself. Explain the situation, see what he suggests. That's the best you can do. But, Robbie?"

"Yeah?"

"None of this is your fault. You know that, don't you?"

"I guess. It's just that I feel so . . . dirty. It's hard to explain."

The hospital receptionist said Dr. Blair was with a patient and would get back to me. I knew he kept late hours and told her I'd wait up for his call, no matter what the time.

Around ten o'clock he called.

He was kind and my hands immediately started to shake. I finally worked the conversation around to where it should have started.

"My father told me he holds you responsible for my mother's death."

"Your father has been through a lot. Your mother and he were married forty-some years. It's only natural he misses her."

"I know. But . . . Doctor?" Nothing would ever be as difficult as this moment. "My father told me he's hired someone to have you killed."

Silence.

"Let me take this call on my private line, Ms. Stanton. Hold on a minute."

When he came back, his tone was hushed. "You don't really think he's serious?"

"Yes I do. It's to be done in four months, on the anniversary of my mother's death." My voice trembled. I felt sorrier for all of us having to go through this than I ever could for my father.

Dr. Blair said he wanted to think about things. He'd get back to me.

Sergeant Danta of the Oak Lawn Police Department contacted me two days later. Dr. Blair had filed a complaint.

I'd talked with police before. Lots of times. But this was about me . . . my life. I repeated my story for what seemed like the hundredth time and for the hundredth time I didn't believe it myself.

"We'll have to proceed with this as if it were truth. But tell me, Ms. Stanton . . . would you be willing to testify against your father in a court of law?"

I thought about all the years I'd worked for Dad's approval. I thought about all the agony Delia and I were going through so soon after losing our mother. And I answered.

"No."

"Call on line two. Pick it up, Roberta," Harry barked.

"Miss Stanton? I'm Detective Carter, with the Chicago Police Department. A report has been filed with us concerning your father."

"I've already been through this with Sergeant Danta."

"Danta's out of Oak Lawn, where the hospital is located. We need something filed in your father's precinct."

"Oh." I repeated my story from the day before.

"I have to tell you, Miss Stanton, when he first opened the door—"

"Wait a minute. You spoke to my father? You confronted him? In person? What did he say about Dr. Blair?"

"We had to get his statement. He said he thought the doctor killed your mother."

I suddenly felt as though I'd been strapped into a roller-coaster and was slowly being hauled up to the top of Anxiety Mountain. I could hear the gears clicking. And I prayed I wouldn't crack before Christmas reared its holy head.

"Your father's in bad shape."

"We all are."

"There's nothing else we can do."

"I know."

Detective Carter apologized and promised there would be no need to disturb my father again.

"Get any last night?" Ken asked as I walked through the door.

I punched him on the shoulder. "Scum."

"You may think I like it when you call me that, but I don't," he complained.

"Sorry. I had an awful night, didn't sleep at all."

He waited for the punch line and when none came, he shrugged and sat down at the computer.

Harry came banging in from outside and a frigid gust slammed the door. "Roberta. In my office. Now."

I followed behind, a little spaniel, and watched as his boots tracked wet black prints along the dirty carpet.

"Close the door." Harry pulled his gloves off and stuffed them into his pockets. Without removing the snowflaked overcoat, he abruptly turned.

"The body of one Dr. Blair, practicing out of Christ Community Hospital, in Oak Lawn, Illinois, was found this morning in the trunk of his car. The car was parked in the doctor's reserved space in the hospital lot. He had been beaten to death. They think it was one of those aluminum baseball bats. Very sloppy. I spoke with Sergeant Danta. He said it definitely was not a professional hit."

Click . . . click . . . hang on.

"Your father's in custody."

"Was anyone else with the doctor?"

"No."

I turned and we just looked at each other for a minute.

"What do I do?"

"Go home. The police will be calling you."

"Don't tell anyone. I feel so ashamed."

"It'll be all over the news soon enough." Harry shook his head in disbelief. "Go on, get your butt out of here."

After talking with the police, I booked a flight into St. Louis.

Delia was in shock when I told her. "Oh God, oh God, oh God," she repeated. "He really did it. Oh God."

"Will you meet me at the St. Louis airport at ten-thirty tonight?"

Springfield was only a few hours away and I knew the distraction would be good for her.

"I guess. But why St. Louis?"

I didn't want to scare her, to tell her that soon reporters and television crews would be camped out on her front lawn. "We need to be together now," I said.

When my flight finally landed, I spotted Delia standing by a fat man in a blue sweat suit. I could tell she'd been crying, I smiled a hello.

We walked silently to the baggage claim and then she said, "Oh, I almost forgot. Your office called. Ken somebody. He wants you to call him tonight. Here's his number."

After we registered and fought over who got which bed, I called Ken from the hotel.

"You lose our bet."

"What bet? What are you talking about?"

"Computers versus brains," He sounded so sad. "That was months ago. The Tanner case."

"No, now . . . the Stanton case."

"I'm tired and . . ."

"The computer. I was playing around with it today and punched in your name, Robbie. It showed all your credit card charges for the past year."

"And?"

"There was this code number that looked familiar. When I cross-referenced with the police computer, we came up with 'Freedom, Inc.' They offer a very unique personal service. Geez, you can buy anything with a Visa card. It's really disgusting."

Click . . . click . . . click . . .

"We plugged into the airline computer and know you're in St. Louis. Even the phone number you're calling from is being recorded. . . . Why'd you do it, Robbie? Your own father?"

"Ken . . . Kenny." I know he loves it when I talk in my little girl voice. Daddy always did. "I had to protect all of us. Delia and I don't want Daddy to bully us anymore. And this way, he won't be alone. Maybe the doctors can help him now."

It's those gentle insanities that bring such clear insight. The huge problems only come once in a while. They're easy to fix. But the small, everyday, constant, infuriating irritations drop you over the edge.

Click . . . click . . . click.

PROMISES MADE AND BROKEN

Crazy sure ain't what it used to be.

Remember all those old movies glamorizing insanity? They usually starred Loretta Young, who played the beautiful wife of a highly respected physician. Some terrible trauma befalls her perfect life and she crumbles . . . ever so daintily into a beautiful heap. Reclining on a velvet settee, holding the back of one hand to her brow, she clutches a frilly hanky in the other. Her eyes plead into the camera and then she sighs, retreating into her private world. The lens stays fixed on those beautiful eyes so filled with pain. A violin section orchestrates her breakdown.

Fade to black.

But that was then, and these are the nineties. Your modern-day crazy lady is a whole different breed. Therapy sessions, work schedules, exercise programs. No swooning allowed. Busy, busy. No time to apply makeup or even have my hair done. Work hard and melt back into society. But I wasn't the wife of a wealthy anybody.

When my extension rang, I jumped. I hadn't had a phone within arm's reach in a year.

"Ms. Stanton?"

"Yes, who's this?"

"You probably don't remember me; we met last year during your interview for the *Donahue* show. I'm the associate producer, Julie Wilson."

"Sure, I remember you." The other guests and I used to joke that Ms. Wilson was so uptight her suit creaked.

"Good. Well, we're doing an update show. You know, what ever happened to so-and-so? It's been a year since your segment: 'Daring People— Exciting Occupations.' I've managed to track down . . ."

"Wait a minute. You want me to go back on television? Don't you think that's a little . . ." I was trying to figure out how I felt.

"Exciting!"

"For who? Look, I came on the show originally to talk about being a female P.I. I did not, nor do I, intend to talk about my personal life." I realized I felt put-upon and it made me angry.

"But, but our viewers feel so . . . connected to you. First they see you on the show, a respected professional. Then they read about a doctor in Chicago getting murdered right after your father threatened to kill him. The news reports you hired a hitman and tried to frame your own father for the murder. *A Current Affair* does a whole hour on your troubled childhood, your father's abusive behavior toward you and your sister. Next comes a trial and the insanity verdict. We get letters wanting to know about you every day."

"Gee, I'm a celebrity." Neither one of us laughed.

"Maybe. But you could be such an inspiration to our viewers." She was trying to appeal to my altruism. Right now that tank was empty.

"I'm sorry, Ms. Wilson, but I don't want to inspire anyone. I just want to figure out where I'm going to live at the end of the week. I lost my apartment; my things are in storage somewhere and I can't even afford to get them out should I find someplace to live. I'm tired and lonely . . ." I stopped, hearing how pathetic I sounded. I wanted to hang the phone up and treat myself to a cry. Then a hot fudge sundae.

"Look, Julie, I didn't mean to dump all this on you. The truth is, I don't think my appearance would be very inspiring. I think your viewers would watch with the same curiosity that would make them slow down to gawk at an accident. And when it was over, they'd give thanks they weren't me."

She released a long sigh. "I understand. I won't press you. But, I do have a message from one of the other guests. Do you remember Hazel Franklin?"

"The eighty-seven-year-old, skydiving great-grandmother?" What a character. We'd had lunch the day of the taping and never stopped talking.

"Yes. She asked for your phone number or an address. We keep that information confidential. But I told her I'd be calling you today, and she asked that I give you her number. She said it was important. Do you want to take it down?"

I sat up and grabbed the hotel pen and small notepad lying by the phone. "Okay, I'm ready."

Julie repeated each number clearly and carefully. She would have made a great operator. "Hazel lives outside of Nashville. And while you're at it, here's my number, in case you change your mind."

❦ ❦ ❦

The urge to cry disappeared but the need for ice cream and chocolate persisted. Neither stress nor joy affected my appetite. I liked hospital food, airplane snacks, school lunches as well as haute cuisine.

While I calculated how many calories would be expended walking across the parking lot to Denny's, my hands patted my hips. I bent to touch my toes, then scanned my tight Levis on the way back up. Not bad. Could be better, but then everything could stand some improvement. I decided to call Hazel and wait out the craving for extra whipped cream.

She answered on the third ring. "KPRM: Home of Country Music."

Hesitating, I asked. "Hazel Franklin?"

"That's me. Did I win anything?"

"No, Hazel, it's Roberta Stanton."

"Oh, Robbie darlin', you must think I'm crazy. There's this contest on one of the radio stations; the grand prize is a week in Cancun. You just have to answer the phone with their slogan. I'll be glad when the fool thing's over with."

If there was such a thing as reincarnation, and I loved to believe there was, then I'd known Hazel in another life. And I'm certain she made me laugh the same way back then.

"Julie Wilson from the *Donahue* show told me you were trying to get in touch. Are you okay?"

"You're still the same sweet thing. Askin' me about my ole troubles when your life has been a livin' hell. I swear, honey, you make me want to cry."

I plopped down on the bed, getting comfortable. She wanted to know all my news, and I was surprised that I wanted to tell her everything.

We'd been talking for about twenty minutes when she asked, "So, where do you go from here? I mean, there . . . in Omaha. Are you back in your old place or gonna stay with your sister?"

"I'm at a Hampton Inn for now. My father died right after the trial. His insurance money went to Delia; everything went to her. She insists on giving me part of it, but she's still dealing with a lot of anger and guilt. I don't know . . ."

"You're comin' down here! I have this big ole place all to myself."

"You're very generous . . ."

"Generous, hell, I'm lonely and need your help with somethin'."

The change in Hazel's tone intrigued me. "What?"

"Just say you'll come down and I'll tell you the whole story."

I'd never been comfortable spending even one night in someone else's house. Never liked slumber parties when I was a kid. But now I tried imagining myself in Hazel's home. The fact that we'd gotten along so well, in such a short period of time, did make the prospect very inviting. There would only be the two of us; I could relax. A warm friendly environment, time to spend with this funny lady, it all made me promise to fly to Nashville.

It had taken two weeks, but I'd gotten a good price on a round-trip ticket and now sat in the Nashville airport waiting for Hazel Franklin to pick me up. I fidgeted and watched the people whose cameras gave their tourist status away. A video ran continually, urging travelers to come visit Opryland. Elvis souvenirs and Music City T-shirts filled the window of a nearby gift shop.

I had just noticed a petite woman in white who I swore was Dolly Parton, when Hazel tapped me on the shoulder. "Robbie! Sweetie pie!" She hugged me and I could smell her lilac perfume.

"Hazel. You look wonderful."

Her denim jacket matched the stone-washed shade of her jeans and was embellished with silver studs. Her hair, colored a chestnut brown, was sprayed and pinned on top of her head in a bouquet of curls. A white scarf camouflaged the loose skin of her neck. Her makeup had been applied a little extravagantly to cover wrinkles beneath her eyes. But all things considered, this eighty-eight-year-old woman could easily have passed for a girl of seventy.

"Sorry for bein' late. There was a limo blockin' things up. I heard someone say it belonged to Dolly Parton."

I knew it.

"We'll just get your suitcase and we're outta here."

I held up a large carry-on bag. "This is it."

"Travelin' light these days, huh?" Her smile told me she understood my need to simplify my life now. "The car's right out front. Another five minutes and the cops'll ticket 'er. Well, that's what they threaten to do until I go into my old lady routine." She started down the corridor and I hurried behind.

It took an hour to get from Nashville to Shelbyville. Signs posted near the city limits declared it "The Walking Horse Capital." It was after midnight and as we circled the square, only a full moon lit the way.

"Just round the bend here." Hazel pointed. "The big one, third from the corner." She pulled her car into the driveway of number forty-nine.

The three-story house was painted white with slate blue trim. Lace curtains covered each window and a warm yellow light glowed from inside. As I reached in the backseat for my bag, I felt an immediate calm.

Hazel slammed her door and walked over to my side of the car. "You okay, honey? Are you tired?"

"I feel great. Must be the Tennessee air."

"Good. I was hopin' you weren't one of those early to bed, earlier to risers. I've always loved the night. Get twice as much done after the sun sets."

Inside the Franklin house was what I'd expected . . . sort of. Crocheted doilies were pinned to the back of an overstuffed couch and chair, but the far wall of the living room was covered with a large-screen television set. An entertainment center took up another wall.

"Come on, I'll show you your room. It used to be Alice's, my youngest."

We walked up a small staircase to the second floor. The narrow hallway led to three bedrooms; Hazel stopped at the last door and turned the knob.

"Alice had scads of shows at the Thornwell Gallery in Memphis. Even got a scholarship to study in France. Each time she'd come home, she'd bring a print by some artist she admired or a new paintin' of her own. I thought you'd enjoy how excitin' this room is. It's reelin' with energy."

Colors bombarded my eyes then my brain. I had never seen paintings hung floor to ceiling; there had to have been at least one hundred frames.

"It's . . . very unusual."

"Glad you like it. Now, how 'bout some coffee? Tea? I've got soda or beer. You name it."

I grabbed at any excuse to shut the door on Alice's Gallery. "Tea. I'd love a cup."

The kitchen was cozy and painted pale yellow. A large wooden table sat in the middle of the room, covered with a yellow and white embroidered tablecloth. Its simplicity was complemented by a teapot collection that filled shelves, corner countertops, and windowsills. It instantly became my favorite room.

Hazel poured water into a copper teakettle and I finally asked, "What's wrong? Why do you need my help?"

Arranging cookies on a china plate she spoke with her back to me. "Do me a favor, Robbie, will ya?" She turned and set the plate on the table. "Never get old."

"I'll try. Real hard." I laughed and patted her hand.

"I've always been lucky, ya know? Had my health and my brain is sharper than ever. But the way some folks treat me brings on old age."

Hazel got out two mugs, dropped a tea bag in each, and poured the boiling water. She deposited the mugs on the table and herself into the chair next to me.

"For eight years now I've belonged to this skydivin' club—The Screamin' Seniors. That's where I met Tucker." Her smile gave all her feelings away. "Tuck was so handsome, probably the finest man I've ever known. We never ran out of words. There was talkin' and laughin' from start to finish."

For the second time, Hazel used the word "was." Past tense.

I shoved a cookie in my mouth. She didn't say a word while I chewed. Finally I swallowed and asked, "What happened to Tucker?"

Staring into her tea, she said, "I'm supposed to believe it was an accident. That his chute just didn't open. Over and out. The end."

"Hazel, I'm so sorry, but . . ."

"Tuck had been a paratrooper durin' the war and after that an instructor. He'd kid me all the time that he was born with wings."

". . . accidents happen even to the best people," I finished.

Ignoring my wise observation, Hazel eagerly continued. "I went straight to the airfield and cornered Pete, he runs the place. I asked him if he could tell me about Tucker's accident. He knew Tuck and I had been datin'. He was all sweet and sorry till I wanted to see the logbook and anythin' else filled out for the FAA. Then ole Pete started treatin' me like a senile biddy. Once he got past his cooin' and carin' he tells me I wouldn't understand the forms, they were too complicated, and I shouldn't worry myself with all the details. Even went so far as to take me by the hand and walk me to my car. Damn little snot ass." She slammed her hands on the table and stood up.

"I need you, Robbie. I need you to do the runnin' and talkin'. Look at yourself. You're smart an' young; you know all the right things to ask. It's your job."

"Was my job," I corrected. "I'll probably never get licensed again."

"Pish. What the hell does a piece of ole paper mean? If you don't have a birth certificate that don't mean you ain't been born. You have what counts: common sense and good instincts. I remember you tellin' me about some of the cases you worked on. You were good then you'll be good now."

"Thank you," was all I got out before I heard something drag across the floor upstairs. A loud moan followed.

"What's that?" I held my breath.

Hazel grinned. "Oh, it's just Tucker. Don't get scared or nothin'. He hasn't quite adjusted to bein' dead yet. An' when he promised he'd never leave me, he meant it. Tuck was known for bein' a man of his word." She offered me another cookie.

✦ ✦ ✦

As I lay in bed, staring at the pink cherubs painted on Alice's ceiling, I rationalized that this was an old house. Old houses settle. It was February and the cold evenings could warp wood or loosen things. Hazel was almost ninety, certainly entitled to imagine or forget things.

And I guess I was just too tired. Fear would have to be put on hold until I'd had some sleep.

When I stumbled down to the kitchen it was eleven o'clock. Hazel had left a note saying there was coffee in the pot, biscuits and gravy in the refrigerator, and she was at a church meeting down the street. Several newspaper articles concerning Tucker's accident were on the counter along with keys to her car. I poured some coffee, vetoed the biscuits and gravy, and popped two pieces of bread into the toaster. As I spread butter onto my breakfast, I read through the clippings.

Finishing up in the bathroom, I heard a door slam. "Hazel? I'm up here."

Footsteps dragged across the living room floor; the door at the bottom of the staircase opened.

"I was just getting ready to leave. Thought I'd start at the airport."

Slow, heavy feet walked the stairs and stopped outside the bathroom.

I opened the door. "I think it would be best if . . ."

The hallway was empty.

I dashed across the floor, setting a new record for stair sprinting. The kitchen was unoccupied as were the dining room and living room. I could feel my heart throbbing clear up into my ears.

My intellect screamed that I should stay put. But involuntary reactions dragged me back up the stairs, pushing me from room to room, making my hands open doors and flip on light switches.

As I was tapping the wall, feeling silly but hoping to find another entrance, the front door slammed. Again.

This time I leaped down the stairs, colliding with the chair and then Hazel in under thirty seconds.

"God Almighty! What is the matter? You scared the life outta me!"

"I heard someone . . . the door opened," I wheezed. "Then they walked up the stairs. No one was there . . ."

" 'Cept for Tucker." Hazel nodded.

I couldn't think of a comeback.

"Now, tell me what you're up to today." She stood in front of me, smiling, waiting for my grand plan to unfold.

I took a minute to calm myself. "I was going to start at the airport. I think it's best I go alone."

"Whatever you say, you're the darin' P.I." She said it with a straight face and sincere heart. "There's a map in the car; I marked all the important spots for you. The name of our instructor is Pete Hooper. You'll see him cumin'; he's a hunk."

"Looks like I have everything. Don't wait dinner for me."

"Oh, tonight's bingo. You'll have to fend for yourself."

Hazel was right. Peter Hooper was a hunk. A well-dressed, tanned, blue-eyed, I-think-I'm-in-love kinda hunk.

"So, this will be your first time?" He was asking me about skydiving. I'd decided to pose as a prospective student.

"Yes." Looking down at the release form, I tried holding back my blush.

"It's pretty standard. We need verification, for our files, that you're of age or"—he winked—"have the consent of your parents or guardian. There's also the danger factor; it's not like you were walking in the park. But we go by the book and our equipment is inspected daily."

"There's no chance that something will go wrong?"

"Oh, it's like anything else, you have to know what you're doing and don't take unnecessary risks." He smiled and my stomach fluttered.

"It's just that I came across a story in the paper a few weeks ago about a man who was killed when his chute didn't open."

"Tucker James."

"You knew him?" I asked in mock surprise.

"He belonged to our seniors' group; Tucker was their leader."

"What a shame. Did he take unnecessary risks?" I looked back at the form, didn't want to seem anxious.

"No. He was just stubborn."

"What do you mean?"

"The guy knew his stuff; he'd been jumping since way before any of us were born. But he was bullheaded, refused to admit he was sick. They get like that, my grandmother was the same way."

"Sick? What was wrong with him?"

"Alzheimer's. When Tuck first told me, I insisted on talking to his doctor. The doc assured me the disease was in its early stage and he'd keep me posted. Also said that because Tucker had been jumping for so many years, it was kinda all reflex to him now anyway."

"But you said he died because he was stubborn?"

"The silly old fool insisted on packing his own chute. That should have been reflex too, I suppose, but apparently he got ahold of one of the old ones we use for a target."

"God, how awful."

"Tell me about it; I was the one who found him. Out there." He pointed to a patch of field by the highway.

"Was he . . . ?"

"Sometimes a person can fall from a great height and end up lookin' like he's asleep. Sort of peaceful. But I knew better than to touch him. Called the police right away."

I'd finished filling out the form and handed it to Peter. "That was all you could do."

"Well, everything looks good. We ask you to watch a short film. Would you like to do that now?"

I hated to leave. Peter Hooper's khaki shirt was unbuttoned just enough, revealing soft curly hairs on his chest. "No. I'll have to come back next week. I just wanted to check out schedules and prices."

"Okay then. You have our brochure, the phone number and hours are on the back. Give me a call when you're ready."

Boy, was I ready!

I sat in Hazel's car at the A&W, eating a hot dog, drinking root beer from a frosty mug. February had never been like this in Omaha. The sun reflected off a large white house across the street. I wished for a pair of sunglasses while trying to verify lettering on a small sign stuck in the front lawn. HUFFMAN BROTHERS COLONIAL CHAPEL.

Returning my unfinished lunch to the tray, I rummaged through my purse for the newspaper articles. Tucker James had been laid out at the chapel three days after his accident.

I honked for the carhop.

It was cool inside. I looked for a ladies' room, hoping no one would intercept me until I'd figured out what to say. The air was saturated with the scent of carnations and roses; my stomach tightened.

Sobbing came from the last stall. I assumed tears were the norm here. I headed for an end sink; the crier was now using one in the middle.

"Are you all right?"

"Me? Sure."

"Sorry. I didn't mean to intrude."

We now stood in front of the lighted mirror and talked to each other's reflection.

"No, no, it just gets to me."

I spoke in a soft, hopefully comforting voice, "Who did you lose?"

"No one in particular. I work here; this is my father's business. Today they brought in a little boy—he drowned. It's just too sad sometimes."

"I bet."

"Are you here to see Mrs. Russell? She's in the Magnolia Suite."

"No. I'm here . . . a little late. I was out of the country when my uncle, Tucker James, died. The only thing I know for sure is that he had an accident and was brought here." She was buying it and moved a little closer.

"I prepared Mr. James. If there's anything I can tell you . . ."

"Did he have an open casket? He was so claustrophobic. Hated tight spaces. It probably sounds silly, but I just need to know he was . . . okay." I was spreading it on too thick and bit my bottom lip as a reminder to shut up.

"Well, he did fall from an airplane. His parachute malfunctioned; I did my best, but we had to have a closed casket. Just about every bone in his body was broken. If it's any comfort, he didn't suffer."

"I read that sometimes the victim of a fall can come through the whole thing without any obvious signs. That he just looks like he's asleep."

"True, I've seen a few like that. Unfortunately, Tucker looked pretty bad."

"Was there anything else?"

Her pretty long curls fanned out around her head when she turned her full attention on me. "Like what?"

Wishing to restore the chatty mood and alleviate her suspicions I did what I could to throw her off. I cried. "I don't know. I'm just so upset."

She offered me a tissue. "Of course you are. And here I go on and on about broken bones and caskets. I'm so sorry. But we have a close relationship with the police department. Very close. I've been dating a sergeant for two years." She hoped her little joke would make me laugh, but I decided tears were working better and added a few more sniffles.

"My boyfriend knew Tuck; he filled out the reports himself. The hospital did an autopsy, and I worked on . . . sorry . . . prepared your uncle. His injuries were typical for what I've seen in these types of accidents."

"It's just that I miss him terribly."

"You said you were Tucker's niece?"

I let out a nice long sob. Inching toward the door, I couldn't help noticing the large diamond on her left hand as she handed me another tissue.

"My name's Elizabeth Huffman; call if you need anything."

Finally I stood with my hand on the door. "Thank you for your help. I feel much better now."

"Sure you're all right?"

"Fine."

I left the way I'd come.

The sun was setting when I pulled up in front of forty-nine. Stooping to look at red tulips poking through dirt on either side of the front steps, I wondered where I'd be living next spring. A terrible crash came from the second floor, and I darted up the front steps. Fearing something had happened to Hazel I dug my key into the lock, turned the knob to have it pulled out of my hand as a man came running out onto the porch.

"Hold it!" I screamed, clutching my purse.

Slamming the door, he shouted, "Who the hell are you? And why do you have a key to my grandmother's house?"

"I'm staying with Hazel. Roberta Stanton." I offered my hand.

"Sorry, but you scared the shit outta me. I'm Clay Bowman, her grandson."

"Hazel's at bingo. I assumed that was a regular thing with her."

"It is, I just stopped by to drop off some groceries. She'll go days just eating cookies." He grinned, and I wondered why he held a grocery bag if he'd dropped off things inside.

"Clay! Robbie!" Hazel waved as she got out of a car.

Clay shifted the brown paper bag and waved back. "Hey, Granny!" He appeared to be in his twenties, but I remembered Hazel saying he was thirty-two. His black cowboy hat swallowed up most of his hair except for the blond sideburns.

Hazel ran up the stairs and hugged him. "Doll baby, you look great! Come in and meet Robbie."

Clay looked uncomfortable. "We met. Just now."

"Well, come inside anyway; it's gettin' cold."

We ended up in the kitchen and I surveyed countertops for any sign of the groceries Clay had mentioned.

"Sit! Sit yourselves down. I'm fairly bustin'—tonight I won me fifty bucks. Clay, darlin', take off that ole coat. I'll make some cocoa."

Hazel flew around the kitchen like a bird. Pecking and landing long enough to tell us she was out of cocoa. "Hon, would you remember to pick some up next time you stop by the market?"

Clay hung his jacket over the back of a kitchen chair. "Granny hates the grocery store. Says it's crowded with old people takin' too long an' sample ladies shovin' pizza in your face."

Hazel came up behind her grandson and snatched off his hat. "So my big strong policeman here does the shoppin' for his sweet granny."

"Policeman?"

"Oh, didn't I tell you my Clay is a sergeant?" Hazel tossed the cowboy hat. While mussing his hair she bragged, "Clay graduated at the top of his class, received a commendation last year. He's got himself a condo on the other side of town and is engaged to a beautiful girl."

Clay's expression went from bored to delighted. "Me and Beth have been goin' together for twenty-three months now."

"Elizabeth's a cosmetologist; works for her daddy."

Knowing, but asking anyway, I said, "What's the family do?"

Clay answered, "They own and operate the Huffman Mortuary."

Hazel slowly lowered herself into a chair. "Tucker was laid out there."

Clay stood, snatching the bag from the floor. "Talkin' of Beth reminds me I'm supposed to pick her up in a while." He kissed Hazel goodbye. "It was nice meetin' you, Roberta. Hope to see you again."

He had made it as far as the porch when Hazel noticed the jacket left behind.

"I'll catch him." He was on the sidewalk when I dashed outside. Careful to shut the door behind me. I called to him. "Clay, you forgot this."

When we were both out of Hazel's hearing range, I spoke honestly. "Why were you really here today? There weren't any groceries. What's going on?"

"Look, I don't think it's any business of yours what I do in my grandmother's house."

Even though my license had been suspended, I still had a Photostat of the document. Withdrawing it from my wallet, I held it close to his face. "I'm a private investigator. Your grandmother asked me to look into the death of Tucker James."

He chuckled. "What a gal. A P.I.! I love it!"

I stood with the license still in my hand. "Today I found out you worked on the case."

He took his jacket from me. "Look, Pete called me, said there'd been an accident. It took me five, maybe six minutes to get out there. Poor Tuck was broke up real bad. The parachute was lyin' all around him, shredded to pieces. I took a report from Pete. There was an autopsy. It was ruled an accident."

"It was that simple?"

"Tuck was a great guy. He made Granny very happy. But I guess it was just his time to go."

"I guess. Thanks. Look, if I upset you I'm sorry, but please, don't tell your grandmother you know why I'm here. She wanted this handled discreetly."

"Sure."

When I returned to the kitchen, Hazel was gone. I started for my room and met her on her way down. "You just missed Tucker."

"Hazel, we've got to talk about this . . . this . . . ghost thing."

"I know, sugar. I've been waitin' for you to start in about the house bein' old and the noises comin' from plain ole wood and rust rather than the great beyond."

"Well . . ."

"And you must have been wonderin' about me. We haven't known each other all that long. It's only natural you'd be uneasy. Probably figure my elevator isn't goin' all the way to the top floor."

I had to laugh at her. "No, it's not that."

"Then if the idea of Tucker comin' back, even for a little while, comforts me, what's the harm?"

I felt embarrassed. "I'm sorry."

"No need for apologies, sweetie. If there's one thing I've learned in this lifetime, it's to be kind to myself. I'm tryin' to get through this god-awful loneliness right now. And if talkin' to a ghost helps, so be it."

I hugged her tight. "So be it."

I decided to pay another visit to Peter Hooper. It was an easy decision to make. I took great care dressing the next morning, even spritzed myself with the last of my vanilla perfume.

A twin engine buzzed the field; it was a gorgeous day, temperatures had to be in the high seventies. I parked the car next to a small hangar made of corrugated metal. A gravel trail led right to Peter Hooper's office.

He flashed a smile that could reinvent the swoon. "You're back!"

A slight breeze ruffled my long skirt and I felt pretty. I could hear Bette Davis repeating, "Peetah, Peetah, Peetah," but my own voice said, "Yes, I am."

"Have a seat, I'll get that film set up for you."

I stood in front of his desk, preferring the superior stance. "I'm not here for that."

He straightened in his chair. "Oh? Why are you here then?"

"For more information about Tucker James and his accident. Hazel Franklin hired me. I'm a private investigator." We stared at each other for a minute.

"I don't believe this! Why won't Hazel let it go? I told you everything yesterday."

"You were very kind." That blush crept over my cheeks again. "But there were a few details that don't fit."

"Such as?"

"You were the first to find Tucker?"

"Check."

"And you said he looked like he was asleep."

"Check."

"Then why did Sergeant Bowman tell me Tucker looked pretty bad when he arrived on the scene?"

Peter shifted in his chair then stood. He came around the desk and guided me by my elbow. "This'll take a drink to tell."

The small room served as a lunchroom. Three vending machines offered drinks, sandwiches, and candy. A ceiling fan stirred the air, and we sat at one of the four tables in the empty room.

"I'll be right back."

He returned with a bottle of tequila and two glasses. He poured the drinks and we toasted, "To honesty."

The liquor went down hot. "Why are we drinking tequila at eleven in the morning? What happened?"

"I didn't lie. Tucker was sick. He did pack the wrong chute. I was the first to find him in that field. And he did look untouched. God, how is that possible?"

"So," I prodded, "what did you lie about?"

"Tuck was alive when I got there. He was lying on his back, moaning, in such horrific pain. I have dreams about him crying to me for help. It was awful."

I finished my drink.

"He begged. Have you ever heard anyone beg from the pit of their soul? He begged me to finish him. The pain was that great. He tried getting up and that's when I saw he'd landed on a rock and the back of his head was caved in."

"What did you do?"

"I ran like hell to call the police and when I got back, Tuck was still beggin'."

My attraction for this man was now overshadowed by my compassion.

"I kept tryin' to get him to stay still. He grabbed me, asked me to promise that he wouldn't have to go to the hospital. He moaned and begged and before I knew it I picked up that rock and hit him. Just once."

"And when Sergeant Bowman got there, Tucker was dead."

"Yes."

I didn't know what to say. If Peter Hooper had pulled a plug and never bloodied his hands, would he be considered more humane? Tucker James was dying. If not immediately from a fall, then slowly from an illness. He had enjoyed a full life and died doing what he loved best.

"Do you believe in ghosts?" I finally asked. "Homemade ones?"

"We did drink to honesty . . . and I've come this far. Yes. Clay—Sergeant Bowman—and I cooked up the hauntin' to comfort Hazel. Clay was worried about her mental state and asked that I help. He gave me a key. We take turns. Hazel's fit but she's not fast. So far I've been able to make a few noises, move some furniture. We started doin' it every night, now we're down to every other night. Clay says after she's adjusted we'll stop altogether."

The chair squeaked as I stood. "Thanks. I'd better go have a talk with Hazel."

"You're not gonna tell her about the ghost, are you?"

"No. She just needs to be reassured Tucker died from an accident."

"Tuck was a real gentleman. I respected him greatly. I know he would have helped me the way I . . . helped him."

"Yes, I knew he was sick. But he had a lot of good years in him. And I wanted some of them to be spent with me."

"I know." I wanted to comfort her. "He must want to spend time with you if he keeps coming back at night. You were the love of his life."

"I was, wasn't I?"

"You're lucky, you know. I still haven't found my great love. I envy you."

Grandmother hormones clicked in. "You will, Robbie, you will. When you've been around as long as I have, you see life rolls forward like a wheel. Repeatin' itself. Old is new, new is old, lost is found, and found is . . . lost forever."

"I'd give anything if I could bring Tucker back. But, he had an accident.

There are people all over this town who miss him. You're very lucky to have known him."

"You're right, hon, I know you're right." Hazel Franklin lifted her glasses and dabbed at the corners of her eyes. "Look at me, you've come all this way and done exactly what I asked. You've put your life on hold and now I guess you have to get on with it. Have you thought about where you're goin'?"

Before I could answer, a chair skidded across the floor upstairs. Every night since my arrival, the ghost of Tucker James had visited Hazel. Peter Hooper told me the hauntings were rescheduled to occur every other night.

I ran for the steps.

"Robbie, you'll never see Tucker, he vanishes before even I can catch a glimpse."

By the time I got to the bedroom, Clay Bowman was halfway out the window.

I ran to assure him I knew about his arrangement. "Clay, it's okay, Peter told me everything."

He threw something wrapped in brown paper down to the front lawn. Startled, he came back inside the room. "Is Granny downstairs?"

"Yes, but don't worry. She won't come up. What did you throw out the window?"

"Nothin'."

"You're lying. You lied last night about dropping groceries off. You were taking something out of this house. And now I find you taking something else. What's going on? Do you want me to ask Hazel?"

"No! I've been all through it with her. This is the only way."

"What is?"

"These are mine." He motioned to the paintings in Alice's room. "Mom told me they would go to me when she died. She promised! But after she passed away, I asked Granny if I could have them. Do you have any idea what these are worth?"

"Sorry, no."

He pointed to a small canvas. "That's a genuine Benton, and that red one, a Warhol. I told Granny, Mom promised I could have the collection. And I wanted them now."

"Hazel would never treat you unfairly; she loves you."

"Oh, she knows the collection is mine, but she wants to keep it around her, a memory of Alice, she says. Even offered to give me some money instead. Granny doesn't even know what she's got here. It's all just sentimental, not cash value to her. I've been takin' pieces outta here for months now and she hasn't missed one thing."

"Do you intend to take all of them? Leave Hazel with nothing?"

"Granny's got Tucker's life insurance money, and still has some of Granddaddy's money socked away. Besides, she gets social security, and this house has been free and clear for years. What more does she need?"

"Clayton! Get your butt out of there!"

Startled, I looked over Clay's shoulder to see Elizabeth Huffman's head sticking through the half-opened window.

"Hurry up before that old lady finds you. Oh, I thought you were alone."

Annoyed, Clay turned and scolded her in a loud whisper, "Didn't I tell you to wait by the car? You're gonna ruin everything."

Ignoring him, Elizabeth pushed the window the rest of the way up and climbed into the bedroom. I couldn't figure out if it was jealousy or that inbred Southern hospitality, but she walked right over to me and extended a hand. "I'm Clayton's fiancée, Elizabeth. Have we met?"

The candlestick lamp produced more shadows than light. I lifted my chin, offering her a better look. "Yes. Yesterday. At the chapel. In the ladies' room."

"Oh, you're Tucker's niece. I don't believe I caught your name."

"She lied to you. Her name's Roberta Stanton and she's a private investigator. Granny hired her."

Elizabeth looked frightened. "I told you she wouldn't buy the idea of a ghost. I knew she'd miss the paintings. I told you. I told you!"

"Shut up for a minute, will you! Granny hired her to investigate Tucker's death. She's never said a word about the paintings? Has she?"

"No."

"Then we're okay. Right?" Elizabeth looked to Clay for a nod.

"As long as Nancy Drew here keeps quiet about all this."

"You will, won't you?" Elizabeth Huffman seemed more little girl right now than grown-up lady. "We're only takin' what belongs to us . . . him, I mean. The old lady doesn't even miss 'em."

"No matter how you juggle this around in your brain, it's stealing. I can't keep something like this from Hazel: she's my friend. And for God's sake, Clay, she's your grandmother."

"I knew we couldn't expect her to understand." Clay reached inside his jacket and pulled out a police revolver. He pointed it at me while ordering Elizabeth back to the car.

"I'm not leavin' you now." The tension seemed to excite her.

"Suit yourself but stay out of my way."

I stood with my hands at my sides. I'd imagined this moment for years. How I had avoided other guns in other cases always amazed me. And now as I faced this desperate man I stepped outside myself and instead of the victim, became the witness. Dim light, hundreds of eyes staring from inside their frames, it all seemed unreal. I had to say something to snap us out of this scene.

"You're not going to kill anyone. You're a coward and a thief, but not a murderer. Now let's just go downstairs."

"You don't know shit about me! First it was my mother. The artist! The oddball! Now the whole town's talkin' about my grandmother. Skydivin', datin' younger men. The guys at the station laugh. It's embarrassin'. Now along comes her crazy friend."

"Crazy?" There was that awful word again.

"I did my own investigatin', Ms. Stanton. It wasn't hard to track you from Omaha to the nuthouse. You have a police record, remember? Jesus, what a pair you and the old lady make. Who in their right mind would listen to either one of you? Besides, I'd only be doin' my duty if I killed me a crazy woman caught stealin' Granny's precious paintin's."

"I don't know what is goin' on here but could we please hurry?" Elizabeth stopped pacing in front of a small canvas. Removing it from the wall she brought it closer to the light; admired the work of art.

"You're right, honey, we ain't got all night." Clay raised the gun level with my nose.

Fear unexpectedly released itself inside my head like a waterfall; my ears flooded with panic. "Wait a minute."

"I'm tired of waitin'!" His hand shook but his eyes never left mine.

We stood, frozen, for a few seconds until Elizabeth Huffman interrupted the quiet with a startled gasp. The painting she held seemed to jerk from her hand. I can't explain how, but I swear the canvas flew at least six feet through the air before chopping Clayton squarely across the forehead. Elizabeth exhaled her surprise. Clay grabbed his head, blood dripping down to his nose as he wailed in pain.

Hazel called from the foot of the stairs. "Robbie? Are you okay?"

I maneuvered a nice kick and the gun went flying across the floor.

Out of the corner of my eye, I saw Elizabeth trip, fall, then scurry for the ladder. I grabbed the gun from the corner where it had landed and called to Hazel, "I'm fine. I'll be right down."

✿ ✿ ✿

The video for Opryland was still playing as Hazel and I sat in the Nashville airport. "I want to thank you for everythin'. I have your payment right here."

"No, I couldn't." I desperately needed the money but taking it from Hazel seemed wrong. She'd already had so much taken from her.

"You did a job, you get paid." She pulled a small package from her huge shoulder bag. Untying a piece of string and spreading back the brown paper, Hazel held up a small painting. It was a pale blue pond strewn with water lilies. It was also the same Monet Elizabeth Huffman had admired two nights ago.

"I can't accept this, Hazel. It's worth . . ."

"Not nearly as much as you are, Robbie, darlin'." She wrapped the treasure back up in its plain wrapper and handed it to me. "Hang it on your wall and think of beautiful things. Or, if it'll help more, sell it. Either way, get some enjoyment."

I hugged her and kissed her soft cheek. "Thank you."

"That grandson of mine is after me all the time to sell his mother's collection. That's all he sees when he looks at those beautiful paintin's: money. Poor Clayton. He thinks I don't know he's been takin' a few at a time." She shook her head. "I fooled him, though, hid my favorites in the closet, way in the back. Close as I can figure, he's got enough now to buy that house Elizabeth's naggin' him for. Well, he can consider it a weddin' present from his mother and me. And when he settles down a bit, maybe after he has a baby of his own, I'll give him the rest."

My flight was announced and I stood to get in the boarding line. "I'm still worried about you. You could have been hurt . . ."

"Clayton's all the time talkin' big, but the truth is he's just a traffic cop. Wanted to be assigned to a desk, but they needed him out on the street. Why, up until the other night, he'd never had cause to pull a gun on anyone. They scare the daylights outta him. I know for a fact, the first thing he does when he's off duty is unload his revolver. Thanks for not pressin' charges, sugar, but you were never in any real danger."

The situation between Hazel and Clayton was a family matter. It didn't concern me. Professionally. I struggled to separate my feelings. But I couldn't help voicing my concern. "Just because the gun wasn't loaded doesn't mean he won't hurt someone."

"Pish, darlin', Tucker's around to protect me. He took care of you, didn't he?"

I had to agree with Hazel, even though it sounded crazy. "Yes, he did."

CHARACTER FLAW

If it hadn't been for the blood matted in her hair, I would have noticed Skye Cahill's turquoise eyes first.

"Miss Stanton?" she asked in such a calm voice. "Are you the Roberta Stanton? The one from TV?"

"Yes."

"I just killed someone—well, not just someone . . . I'm pretty sure he was my father."

I stood back from the door. "Get out of the hall." I let her into my apartment so easily. I wasn't the least bit frightened. Not even after noticing the gun in her right hand.

I guess I was at that raw patch in my life. There didn't seem to be a clean spot left on my body or psyche that hadn't been hurt. It felt like I'd been frightened for years. Then one day I just got pissed off. But the terror returned. In tidal waves. Then suddenly . . . it passed. All of it—the good and the bad. Nothing mattered. And it was at that point in my life I let a frightened stranger enter my apartment.

She stood in the middle of the kitchen, unsure where to turn. Like a dog circling until he finally plops down for a nap.

I pointed to a dining room chair. "Why don't you sit there?"

"Yeah. Okay. I'll do that . . . I'll . . ."

"How about if I take this?" I reached for the gun hanging from her limp hand.

"Okay." No struggle. She let me take it and then eased herself onto the stiff chair. "Could I have some coffee? A Coke? I need caffeine. All the way over here I felt so tired, like I was going to fall asleep. Isn't that crazy?" She looked at me, realizing how her last word stung and quickly added, "Sorry."

I laid the gun on the counter, in plain sight, but closer to me just in case I needed to go for it. Then I poured last night's coffee into a clean mug and set it in the microwave. "Well, I did spend time in a mental hospital."

She took the coffee from me and shrugged. "So you hired a hitman, big deal. If I had the money I wouldn't have had to kill my father myself."

"But I was messed up back then . . ."

"That's why I came to you. I remembered reading all about your trouble growing up, how they took your license away, and how you finally got out last year. I knew you—of all people—would understand how I feel."

I sat down across from her, folding my hands on top of the table. "Understand what?"

"That it was his fault, not mine."

Before we got any deeper into our new relationship, I thought it best to tell her, "I have to call the police, you know. If what you're saying is true and you killed a man?"

She looked at me like I was an idiot. "Of course. But I came to hire you first."

I picked up my cordless, curious to see her reaction. "I make the call first and then we talk while we wait."

"Fine." She gulped the hot coffee down; I wondered how she managed without burning her throat. "Call."

"I figure we've got at least ten minutes—tops," I told her after hanging up.

"It won't even take that long," she said, reaching for her purse.

I jumped for the gun then, and she grinned like I'd fallen for the punch line of a tired old joke. While I held it on her, she groped around in her tote bag.

"I made this on the way over here." She handed me a cassette tape.

I took it with my free hand. Turning it over, I asked, "What is it?"

"Details. I thought it was important you have my side of the story before you go investigate."

"So you're hiring me to establish the fact that you killed your father? I don't get it." I put the gun back on the table, feeling foolish pointing the thing at her that way.

"No, I want you to check out the man. You'll find his body at the address I wrote on the tape. I can stall the police for a while. You go there, look around . . . to make sure."

"He's dead, right?"

She nodded.

"Then I still don't get it."

Suddenly she was a little girl. "I need you to tell me that there is no doubt—whatsoever—he was my father."

Before I could ask any more questions, the police were knocking at my front door.

Reaching in her pocket, Skye pulled out two hundred-dollar bills. "Here"—she thrust them at me—"for gas, your time, whatever. Please."

I lied . . . so sue me. I managed to convince the police that Skye Cahill and I had been friends for years, explaining we were practically sisters. I handed over the gun, and they took her in for questioning. Then I promised to come down after I could arrange bail. Another lie? It all depended on what I found at the address she'd written on the tape.

Elkhorn is a small town about twenty minutes outside of Omaha. The only thing I had ever heard about the place concerned its strip clubs. Since time was definitely not on my side, I decided the quickest and straightest shot would be Maple Road, which I steered toward while listening to Skye's voice coming out of my cheap car speakers.

> My name is Skye Louise Cahill, I'm twenty-five years old. I'm a filmmaker and I live in Los Angeles in the Valley. The only way I know how to do this effectively is to pretend this recorder is a camera. Maybe if I distance myself, you can understand better.

Her voice took on a tone that was both detached and informative. I felt as though I was listening to a documentary.

> The trailer sits by itself in a vacant lot. There are no trees for shade, not one blade of grass for color. It's gray now, but she assumed it used to be silver.

I was taken by surprise when she referred to herself in the third person but soon got used to it . . .

> A small window on the side that faced her had a box pushed against it, blocking anyone from looking inside. The only thing adhering to the structure was dirt. No antennas, no paint, not even an address.
>
> She stood a few feet from the door, kicking a large dirt clump, watching it crumble into the air. Trying unsuccessfully to walk a few feet without stepping into a hole, she made her way to the side, to an entrance. It took her a few more minutes before she knocked.

"Yeah? What do you want?" a man yelled.

"I'm looking for Edward Blevins. Is this number three-twenty-nine?"

She could feel him on the other side of the door, could hear him shift his weight. If he thought making her wait would discourage her, he was very wrong. She sat down on the wooden box which served as a stair.

He couldn't leave without her seeing him. She'd circled the lot several times and knew for a fact there was only one door. He couldn't even move around inside without jostling the trailer. The late afternoon sun was at her back, and she could feel her blouse sticking to her damp neck.

"Is this three-twenty-nine Oak or isn't it?"

"Who wants to know?"

The immediate response startled her enough to make her stand. Facing the door, she shouted, "I do!"

Only silence filtered from inside the trailer. She hoped he was spying on her, searching to make sure she was alone, or harmless — worth the effort to answer. She had turned to sit down again when the door suddenly opened.

"Get your ass off my property. I don't know who the hell you are, what you're selling, or what church you're collectin' for, and I don't give a damn—"

"I'm not collecting or selling anything! I just came to talk to Edward Blevins. Is that you or not! Just tell me so we can both stop yelling!"

The heavy-set man stepped out onto his wooden step and slammed the door behind him. Easing onto the ground, he forced her back a few steps. "So what if I am?"

"I'd look you straight in the eye and tell you I'm your daughter."

"Helena's kid?"

"Yes."

"How the hell is she?" he asked without smiling or softening his face in any way.

"I wouldn't know. We've never met."

"What the hell you talkin' about, girl?"

"She put me up for adoption."

"Then how do I know you're Helena's . . . and mine? What the shit you trying to pull here?"

She shoved the birth certificate in his face. "Here. It says you're my father."

"Look, it's too goddamn hot to stand around. I guess it would be all right if you came inside. Just till I get a good look at that."

It was roomier than she expected. Dark, except for one lamp in the corner, by the kitchen area. A bit of sunlight managed to filter through the skylight between dirty streaks and bird shit.

He pointed her toward a folding chair teetering against a wall while he threw himself onto a stained sofa. "Says here you was born in May of seventy-four."

"In Ardmore, Oklahoma."

"I can read," he snapped. "Suppose I am this Edward Blevins. What do you want? It sure don't look like you suffered none. I bet you had real nice folks an' a pretty little room all to yourself. Your mama done the right thing, givin' you away."

"How long did you know her?"

"A few months was all. But that don't mean shit. Lots of guys knew Helena." He laughed.

"And you got her pregnant?"

"Hell, sweetheart, I got six kids in town that I know of, if you get my meanin'?" He laughed again, and she thought she'd be sick. "Helena got herself knocked up if you so much as shook her hand. She already had four kids when I knew her. Workin' the hell outta welfare; she was really somethin'."

They stared at each other for a while before she asked, "Haven't you ever wondered about me? Even for one minute?"

"It might surprise you, girlie, sittin' there with your pink frills an' shiny shoes, but I got a lot more important things on my mind. Things ain't been all that easy for me."

She pulled her chair closer to him.

"What now?" he complained. "Lookin' for your roots ain't gonna make things easier for any of us. You came to see me—you seen me. Guess we're finished."

"Do you ever think about my mother?"

"Jesus H. Christ, give me a fuckin' break here." His voice rose as his face grew red. He lifted himself off the couch and took a few steps toward the small refrigerator. Pulling it open with the toe of his shoe, he groaned as he reached down for a beer. Returning to his seat, he twisted off the cap, tossed it onto the floor and took a swig.

She watched him.

"Is that all you think I got to do with my time? Sit and wonder about some whore I slept with once or twice? Shit. I got better things to do. Not like you."

"You can't begin to understand me."

He grunted. "Look, I'm just tryin' to survive out here. Takin' any job I can to keep the electricity on. Sure, I had some good times with your old lady. So what? I earned 'em. An' I had me a good job down at the lumber yard. Even a car. Then that load of two-by-fours fell on top of me. Now it's beggin' each month for comp checks those lousy bastards owe me. In case you ain't heard, baby, life ain't stinkin' fair." She watched him drink half his beer down in one long gulp and was glad he hadn't offered her one. Any act of kindness would have thrown her concentration off.

While I marveled at the dramatic flair Skye had for telling a story, the tape stopped. I waited for the cassette player to click to the other side. A semi came speeding past the passenger's side, splashing my car. That's when I realized what didn't feel right about the recording. Right before it started up again.

"I've had my problems, too."

He threw the bottle, and the remaining beer spattered across the wall behind her as well as on her clothes. But she never took her eyes off him. She could tell her defiance startled him.

"Now, just what kind of troubles do you have, Skye Blue? Just what the hell is it you have to worry about?"

Her eyes fogged over with rage, and she could hear it pulsing in her ears. "Why, just last year I was worrying about where I could go to get an abortion. I think it was just after my husband skipped town. And before that I was a little concerned about a vacation I was planning. Just a few weeks to myself to get away from the beatings, some time to let the bruises heal. I worry about a lot of things, Mr. Blevins. I try to imagine what kind of a tramp my mother was and could my father possibly be the asshole I imagine? I can feel you inside me, and I wonder if I just sit here quietly and listen to you, will this anger go away? Ever?"

He sneered. "Well, lookin's free. But I ain't never said if I is or I ain't your daddy. Even though I do see my likeness a little around your mouth. Whooo boy, what your mama could do with her mouth."

"I've wondered about you on Father's Day, birthdays, and at Christmas. Especially while I was cleaning up the broken glass from all those happy family gatherings. And while I was pushing slop down the disposal, I wondered what kind of scum could spawn a piece of garbage like me. Because, dear father, I enjoyed it. I actually enjoyed pushing everyone around me. It didn't matter how much they said they loved me or how kind they were. I pushed until they had no choice but to fight."

"Good God, I do believe you are my daugher." He smiled. "Now get outta here." He worked his way up to a standing position.

She slid the small revolver out of the pocket of her jacket and into his gut. "For years and years, more years than I can remember, I've thought about this. I've thought that if you were dead, maybe . . ."

He grabbed her hand, squeezed it inside his large meaty paw and pushed the gun deeper into his belly. "Do it, then."

There wasn't a struggle, it was more of a standoff. He glaring down at her, she glaring back.

"Are you deaf and stupid? I said do it!"

There was a slight hesitation. Then her voice changed.

I pulled the trigger. His stomach exploded. The small room echoed. God, it was loud. Then I pulled the trigger over and over. It felt wonderful.

"I guess that's all of it, Miss Stanton. There's no question I killed someone. I just need to know if he was really my father. I'd hate to have gone through all this for the wrong person. I'm sure you know how I feel, after what you did to your own father—framing him for a murder you arranged, setting him up like that. But somehow I don't think it was a fair trade-off considering you got put away and he just had to suffer a little bad press. They never get what they deserve, do they?"

I waited for more, but the rest of the tape was blank.

I knew Elkhorn wasn't large enough for me to get lost too badly. But just to save time, I pulled into a gas station. I was directed toward West Papillion

Creek where it intersected with the Old Lincoln Highway. After that it was just a few turns before I found myself on Oak.

I checked the address again. Three-twenty-nine was a blue split-level colonial house on a freshly mowed lot. It sat on the edge of a cul-de-sac, and as I stood there rechecking my directions and the address on the tape, I can't really say I was surprised. Puzzled would have been a more accurate way to describe my feelings.

"Beep! Comin' through!" a little boy warned as he peddled close to my toes on his Big Wheel.

"Do you know who lives in this house?" I asked before realizing he shouldn't be talking to a stranger.

"My girlfriend, Tiffany Thompson." And he was off, beeping a man mowing his lawn.

I started back to my car but hesitated. How many times had I stopped for directions only to find out the thing I was seeking had been right in front of me? I turned back toward the blue house and walked up the flagstone path to the front door.

A teenage boy answered the bell, "Yeah?"

I flashed my suspended license. "My name is Roberta Stanton, I'm a private investigator."

"Look, the cops already been here. My dad told them all he knows. Which ain't much."

"Can I speak to your father, then?"

"He's watching a game now, and if I interrupt him, he'll get pissed. Why don't you just go ask the cops about that crazy lady?"

The word "crazy" flew out of his mouth and slapped me in my ego. For two years I had been trying to get on with my life, all the while being labeled crazy by the press. And at that moment I knew why I was standing in front of that door in a small town asking a snotty kid for help. Skye Cahill and I had this very tiny character flaw in common. Maybe I had felt sympathy for her from the start. But I knew one thing for sure. I wasn't crazy. Now I had to find out about her.

"Is Tiffany your little sister?" I tried a different angle.

He rolled his eyes. "No. She's my mother."

"Can I talk to her?" I tried returning his sarcastic tone. "Or is she watching a game, too?"

"Wait here," he said, and slammed the door.

Not even a full minute passed before Tiffany Thompson came to the door. She was petite and very pretty with auburn hair pinned up on her head. She waved her hands, trying to dry her long purple nails. "Yes? My son said you wanted to ask me some questions."

I opened my mouth to start, but she talked right over me.

"My husband told the police everything he knows. I don't appreciate you coming here and bothering us. We've lived in this house for almost five years now. I remember the day we first saw it. We were out driving around, and I told my husband—well, he wasn't my husband then—I said Jack, this is my dream house. This is the place—"

"Mrs. Thompson, I'm not with the police. I'm a private investigator." She stopped waving her nails, and I knew now that I had her attention, I had to keep talking and not come up for air until I was finished.

After my brief chat with Mrs. Thompson, I realized there was nothing for me to uncover at 329 Oak. And when Mr. Thompson came to the door looking for his wife, I was more convinced than ever.

Jack Thompson must have stood all of five feet five inches tall and weighed in at considerably less than I did. No way could he have been the Edward Blevins Skye had described.

Driving back toward Omaha, I caught sight of the gas station I had stopped at on my way through. Suddenly craving a candy bar, I thought it wouldn't be a bad idea to call the police.

While I waited for the phone to be answered, I peeled back the silver paper covering the Hershey bar. Its dark brown texture brightened my spirits. The detective who had given me his card after he'd cuffed Skye picked up on the fifth ring. After inquiring about the case, I was told she had been released.

"What about the blood in her hair?" I asked.

"There was a deep gash right at the hairline, over her left eye."

"And the gun?"

"It was registered in her name—she had all the papers with her. There was no sign of it having been fired," he added.

"You checked out the address she gave you?" I asked, already knowing the answer.

"Yes." A heavy sigh. "Yes, Miss Stanton, we checked it all out."

"So where is Ms. Cahill now?"

"She was escorted to Douglas County to have her wound stitched up, and then she'll be evaluated."

I knew he couldn't tell me how long any of it would take. "Thanks."

He hung up.

A breeze came up; I felt a chill on the back of my neck and along my arms. Wishing I'd thrown on a jacket, I was again struck with another inconsistency in Skye's tape. She'd said how dry and hot it had been outside the trailer. Even inside. I remembered thinking how it sounded like she was somewhere in the desert. Maybe she had become disoriented and was talking about an Oak Street in California; that's where she'd said she was from. And the sun shining so brightly had rung a false note. The closer I'd gotten to Elkhorn, the wetter the ground had appeared. It had obviously rained earlier that day.

I tossed the candy bar wrapper into a trash can, licked my fingers clean and brushed a few stray slivers from the front of my khakis. Before getting back into my car, I scanned the directory chained to the phone for the name Blevins. There was no listing.

As I shifted into third gear, I slid the tape into the player to listen to Skye Cahill's story another time.

When I was first released from the state psychiatric facility, I lived in a hotel. Being surrounded by generic paintings, lamps, and furniture, I could logically assess my situation while not being influenced by anything familiar. My sister had put my things in storage, and I didn't even know if I wanted to remain in Omaha after the tabloids got through with me.

But the public does indeed have a short memory, and I managed to lay low, finally settling into a small apartment on Q Street. I found comfort in once again having my own things in my own place.

I made a cup of tea and was wondering what to do next, or even if I should do something, when the phone rang.

"Miss Stanton? This is Dr. Paige at Douglas County. Miss Cahill asked me to call to let you know we'll be keeping her overnight for observation."

"How's she's doing, Doctor?"

"Well, calmer than her previous visits. I think she's finally starting to resolve some issues."

Now I was surprised. "You've seen her before?"

"Oh yes, I was working with her in group until we found Ann."

"Who's she?" I held my breath.

"Her second personality. Why, I assumed you knew. Aren't you Roberta Stanton? The one from TV?"

"Yes. But I don't understand what that has to do with this."

"Miss Stanton, I was under the impression you were somehow related to

Miss Cahill." I could hear him shuffling papers. "Yes, here it is. She has you listed as her next of kin, a cousin . . . on your father's side."

It took me a minute to mentally climb up and down my family tree. "I think there's been a mistake here, Dr. Paige. And even if it were true, why haven't you notified me before this if you thought I was a relative?"

"Miss Cahill has sessions twice a week with me. She is well over the age of twenty-one, and there have never been any problems. Besides, if I remember correctly, you were 'out of town' for about a year?"

He was diplomatic, I gave Dr. Paige credit for that. "Sorry, Doctor, but Ms. Cahill and I just met this morning. We are not related in any way. And the only reason we met at all is because she came to hire me. . . ." Suddenly I decided I was saying too much about a woman I hardly knew to a man I wasn't sure actually was who he claimed to be.

"Hired you to do what?" he calmly asked.

"That's confidential. Sorry."

"Well, Skye asked me to give you a message and I've delivered it. I guess that's it, then. Have a good evening."

"You, too." I hung up before he could. That always made me feel just a little superior, and after getting the runaround all day, I needed the boost.

Walking back into the living room, I plopped myself on the couch. Holding the hot cup of tea between my hands, I studied the mug painted with tiny brown teddy bears, then stared at the blank screen of the television, and I started planning what I would do tomorrow.

Maybe it's true what they say. That if you think about a problem before going to bed, you'll wake up with the solution. Because while I brushed my teeth, I suddenly knew. I had to go to Ardmore, Oklahoma.

Skye Cahill had mentioned being born in Ardmore. No mention of where she was raised. I could have gone on-line, I guess. But no matter how proficient I became on my new computer, it was still a piece of plastic. Like the phone, I considered it just an impersonal tool. Something told me that if I looked up Skye's past, actually smelled the Oklahoma air, I'd learn something.

After checking my trusty Rand McNally, I figured it was about 570 miles from my front door to Ardmore. With the two hundred-dollar bills my client had paid me still folded in my wallet, I stuffed clean underwear and a few T-shirts into a small suitcase and felt excited at the idea of a road trip.

My Toyota was starting to show its age. A tire on the passenger's side was missing its hubcap. The faux leather interior was split in spots where the sun had baked it during last summer's excruciating heat. But for now I couldn't even think about replacing the blue Tercel. Besides, it ran like it had just glided off the showroom floor. And the best part—it was paid for.

Before heading out of town, I stopped by the hospital. It took a while, but I managed to snag a nurse.

"It's very important Ms. Cahill gets this," I said for the second time and then handed her the letter I'd written that morning.

"She'll get it, don't worry." She looked at me with such pity. "We're all professionals here; we operate very efficiently."

It took every bit of self-control I could muster not to respond sarcastically. From clerks who couldn't make change to doctors who prescribed the wrong medication even after I told them repeatedly about my allergy to penicillin. The older I got, the more it became clear to me that very few "professionals" did their job the way I thought it should be done.

"Okay then, I guess I'll be going." I started to walk away, knowing in my gut that something would happen to my letter. "Remember . . ." I started.

"I know, I know. I'll give this to Miss Cahill." The nurse shoved it deep into her pocket and waved me goodbye.

My first impulse had been to distance myself from Skye, at least until I knew a little more about her situation. That went for Dr. Paige, too. In the letter I assured her I was working on her behalf and would return in a few days. Attached was my card with all sorts of numbers where I could be reached. I then pulled out of the hospital parking lot and got on the highway with a clear conscience.

The trip was an easy, uneventful one. Turning on the radio, I caught up on world events, switching stations as soon as one faded out and another came in clearer. Country music and sermons seemed easiest to find the farther south I got. It was technically winter, mid-January. But other than the trees looking scratchy and bare, that day was a clone for one in early spring or fall. I had gotten by for months with a light fleece jacket, and now had to pull my sunglasses out of the glove compartment as the glare from other cars reflected into my eyes.

After hearing the tinny twang of one too many soulful guitars, I slipped Skye's cassette into the tape deck and listened to it for the fifth time in two days.

It took about eight hours to get to Ardmore, and I was pooped when I crashed onto my bed in the Okay Motel off Highway 35.

✶ ✶ ✶

I slept for ten hours straight. Waking up early the next morning, I walked next door for breakfast and got into an easy conversation with the waitress. Between snapping her gum and scratching her head, Fern finally remembered the Blevins family.

"Lived here my whole life. But can't say as how I remember an Edward. There was Doreen, her twin boys Joe and Beau. Over to the other side of town was Fat Gator and his mama, Beatrice."

"Fat Gator?" I asked, trying not to be rude.

"Called him that on account of his summer jobs down at Disney . . . on the Jungle Ride. An' him also bein' a bit . . . oversized."

I stirred the grits around on my plate, wondering who ever thought to serve the white mush like it was real food. "What was Gator's legal name?" I asked.

"How 'bout that. I don't know. Hey, Dot!" she shouted to the hostess with the sixties hairdo. "You know what Fat Gator's Christian name might be?"

"Edward," she shouted back.

I couldn't believe my luck. What were the odds of coming up with a hit first time out? I quickly thanked the cosmos and pushed for a little more. "I don't suppose you'd know where he lives." When she cocked a suspicious eyebrow at me, I added, "I'm a friend of his daughter's."

"That man did have a passel of kids. But you're not gonna find ole Gator home, I'm afraid."

"Oh?" I looked up from my breakfast.

"He got hisself killed 'bout ten years back. Yeah, it was right about the time I started workin' here."

I had dreaded a day schlepping myself around from newspaper office to library to county records, and here all had been eliminated while I talked to Fern. She knew everybody's business and wasn't afraid to tell what she knew. Praise the Lord and pass the information!

By the time the lunch crowd started showing up, I had a map sketched on a paper napkin giving me detailed directions to the murder scene. Fern couldn't remember ever meeting Skye. But as she told me many times, Fat Gator was a "genuine lady's man." When I smirked, she assured me, "Gator could get real ornery, 'specially when he was drinkin'. But when that man was sober, he was a real sweetheart. He made a lady feel special, know what I mean?"

Blevins and Fern had gone all through grammar school together until Gator dropped out in the seventh grade. She wasn't sure what had become of his trailer or even if it was still hooked up on the lot outside town close to Enville, near Lake Murray.

Fern had also been kind enough to give me the name of the chief of police, his age, marital status, and year of graduation. She warned me he was a snot at eleven years of age and was still one. That I shouldn't expect much more out of him than a grunt. I checked in with him before driving the ten miles south toward the lake.

When I had heard the word "lake," my brain did a free association: speedboats, skiers, cottages, wooded areas, concession stands, motels. But those were summer images and this was winter, a weekday. The skiers were in school or at offices. The only thing lit up in front of motels were their vacancy signs.

After finding the dirt road, I drove for a few minutes hoping my tires wouldn't blow out. My body jiggled up and down on the seat while I held tightly to the steering wheel, forcing my car to stay in the deep ruts. Just when I was getting ready to find a clearing to turn around in, I saw a large silver mailbox leaning to one side from too many side swipes. The name, painted sloppily in red paint, read: BLEVINS. I made a hard left.

There was the trailer exactly the way Skye had described it. The only discrepancy was the rusted lawn chair sitting in front of the single step. I didn't see any vehicles parked in the area, and as I got out of my car I reexamined the copy of the newspaper story Chief Jackson had given me. Contrary to what Fern had said, the chief had been gracious and very helpful. I could tell the unsolved murder had haunted him for years.

As I put my hand on the dirty knob, the door was yanked out of my hand.

"What the hell do you think you're doin'?" a frightened woman wearing a floral printed house dress asked. "This here's private property. You cain't go prancin' up to someone's private home and walk in pretty as you please."

"I'm sorry." I fumbled in my purse. Flashing the suspended license, I said, "I'm a private investigator working for Miss Skye Cahill."

"Let me see that." The woman grabbed my ID and brought it closer to her face. "This here's no good, missy." After looking me up and down, she finally said, "But if you say Skye sent you, I guess I can hear ya out. Come on in here." She stood back and motioned impatiently for me to enter.

The inside of the trailer wasn't anything like Skye had described. But then, if Blevins had been murdered ten years ago, there had to be some changes made. Chief Jackson had gone on and on about what a bloody scene the trailer had been after the murder. My eyes scanned the floor for traces of scarlet. But, in sharp contrast to the disheveled woman wearing grimy tennis shoes, the interior was immaculate.

"Can I offer you a cup of coffee?" she asked.

"That would be nice."

While she filled two cups she asked my name.

"Roberta Stanton, I'm from Omaha."

"So how would you hook up with Skye, her livin' out in Los Angeles?"

I took the cup she handed me and seated myself on the leather sofa.

"Well, that's kind of a long story, Mrs. . . . ?"

"Sorry, I'm Beatrice."

I sat a little straighter. "Edward's mother?"

She slowly lowered herself onto a folding chair. "My only child."

"I'm so sorry; you have my sympathy."

"Honey"—she blew on the hot coffee—"it was the best thing for all of us. I only wish I'd never brought him into the world is all." She waited for my reaction. When it was obvious I didn't know what to say, she asked, "Ain't that a terrible thing for a mother to say?"

"A few years ago I would have said it was. But not now. Being related to someone doesn't mean you automatically love them."

"Amen!" She smiled at me, and I could see she didn't have any teeth. "Now, Miss Stanton, tell me what it is you came all this way to find out."

"Well, I understand your son fathered several children with various partners."

She cackled at my civility. "You're bein' very polite, but there ain't no need. Eddie was a pig. He poked anything and anybody. I know what they says about him havin' all these children, but the only one I ever seen was Skye. She was a beautiful baby . . . a real Kewpie doll."

"You saw her? I was under the impression your son never met his daughter."

"Far as I know, he never did."

"Mrs. Blevins, the reason Skye hired me was to find out if Edward Blevins was in fact her real father."

"Oh, he surely was."

"You're absolutely positive?" I asked.

"It took some convincin'. Even after I got a letter from Helena—that bitch. Thought she was just stirrin' up the shit like she always done. She said she wanted money for the baby and didn't care if it come from the family or some stranger in the gutter. She was gonna sell the poor little thing. There was a picture stuck inside the envelope. 'Course, I had to be sure if it was true or not. Called me a lawyer, the one in them TV commercials. He said he'd check it out."

"And you never told your son?"

The old woman seemed weary at the memory. "I tried. Brought the letter for him to see. I was livin' up at the house back then, it's 'bout a mile from here. That way he never got wind of my mail, liked to keep my private affairs away from him. But when I told Eddie, he didn't wanna hear nothin' 'bout no kid. He just laughed, went on how I should be proud that the ladies loved him so much. That kinda talk always made me sick."

"So what did the lawyer find out?"

"Took 'bout ten days, but they said it was all true. My grandbaby was livin' in back of some bar in El Paso. Said that the place was a real hole and I should try to get her outta there. But I was too old to care for a baby myself. An' I certainly did fear for her if Eddie got wind of the situation.

"So I cleaned out my savin's. All twenty thousand of it. Mr. Blevins left me a little and there was government checks. It took everything I had."

"What happened to Skye?"

"The lawyer gave Helena the money and arranged for the poor child to be adopted."

"Did you have any idea where she was living?"

Beatrice Blevins looked at me for a long moment, studied my brown boots, then the hems of my jeans. "I knew all along. I fixed it so the pastor and his wife down at the Methodist church who had just moved to California got her. What better people for parents than those God-fearin' Cahills? They was such a sweet couple."

"Did they turn out to be the perfect parents you thought they'd be?" I wondered out loud, not expecting an answer.

"I figured they was till some woman called me one day—oh, it must have been 'bout five years ago. She told me Skye was in danger and asked me to help."

"What kind of danger?" I asked.

"That's what I wanted to know. But she just kept goin' on, like she was a doctor or somethin'—real quiet and listin' off how she had been beat up an' hurt."

I did the math. "Five years ago Skye would have been twenty."

Beatrice scrunched up her face while she did her own calculations. "She was married by then. To some important guy in the movies. Not anyone famous, some big cheese that did all the dealin'. I thought for sure she struck it rich."

"Apparently not." I could hear Skye's own words replaying as she told her father about her unhappy marriage. That poor kid never had a chance, and I wondered how much worse off she would have been if Beatrice hadn't tried so hard to save her. "Did you help?"

"There wasn't nothin' I could do. She was an adult, with her own life to live, and I was stone broke. Had to sell the house an' move down here. Eddie was long gone, but even if he was still around, he wouldn't of done nothin'."

"You did your best." I leaned across and patted her hand.

"Don't stop me from feelin' bad. But now ya say Skye come to see you? How did she look?"

I remembered those turquoise eyes. "Beautiful," I told her.

I stood to leave. Beatrice walked me out to my car and asked that I give her granddaughter her regards.

I was buckling myself into the front seat when something made me ask, "Do you happen to remember the name of the woman who called you about Skye?"

"Sure. Have a hard time with faces, but names stick in there pretty good." She tapped her right temple. "It was Ann. Never did give me a last name."

Dr. Paige wouldn't give me Skye's home address, and since there was no message from her when I returned home, I was forced to plant myself in his waiting room.

"The doctor only sees patients with appointments," his pretentious receptionist told me. "And he never sees investigators. If you have a legal matter, we advise you to take it up with the police. In turn, we will be more than happy to cooperate with them."

After that speech I went out to get a hamburger, bringing it back to eat, loudly and slowly, while I waited. I was slurping at the bottom of the ice in my plastic cup when the doctor came out.

"Five minutes," Dr. Paige said as I slid into the chair across from his desk. "Please remember I'm seeing you only out of respect for Miss Cahill."

I checked my watch before asking, "When you called me the other evening, you said you've been seeing Skye for two years."

The jerk just stared at me and nodded.

"I assume that means she lives here, in Omaha?"

"Elkhorn."

Now it made sense why she'd sent me out there. Maybe seeing the street name had triggered off a repressed memory. "According to her grandmother, Skye was raised in Los Angeles?"

"Yes."

"Would it be breaking any great ethical code to tell me the last address you have for her in California?"

He rolled his eyes in such a way that made me want to harm him. "Miss Stanton . . ."

"Look, you can either cooperate with me now or later. Now will only take up"—I checked my watch again—"four minutes and thirty seconds. Later could take days. I'm a bullheaded German with free hours to spend haunting your office."

He pounded his fist down on the date book in front of him. "Yes! Of course I know her address!" He swiveled his chair angrily around and started punching numbers into his computer. When the screen was lit up with Skye Cahill's history, he read the address: "Three-twenty-nine Oak Street. She lived there with her husband for three and a half years." Then he closed the file and defiantly turned toward me. "What else?"

"Three minutes left for you to listen to a theory of mine."

He sat back nodding, at first bored and then stunned to hear that I suspected Skye Cahill of murdering her father, Edward Blevins, when she was sixteen years old.

"Miss Cahill is incapable of such a violent act."

"What about Ann?"

The doctor's ears perked up then, "Now, that's an interesting thought." I must have struck a nerve; all of a sudden he wanted to talk. I leaned back and listened.

"The personality of Ann is the idealized mother figure. She protects and loves Skye, unconditionally. I would suspect she is capable of doing whatever it takes to keep Skye safe. But if that was the case, why hadn't she struck out sooner, try to harm the unstable parent or abusive husband?"

"When was Ann . . . born?"

"As far back as Skye can remember," he said.

"Then wouldn't it make sense that the mother would blame the father for putting the child in danger?"

"Very good, Miss Stanton."

"How long did Skye know she was adopted?"

"As far back as she could remember. Yes, it all makes sense."

I picked up my purse and pulled out a copy of the original cassette Skye had given me. I started to stand, and the doctor looked disappointed. "You're not going so soon? Look, I apologize for my ad manners."

I tossed the tape at him. "Listen to this and see if you agree with me that Skye was confessing to protect Ann, the personality who actually pulled the trigger."

He was excited now. "Sit, we can listen together."

I started for the door. "Dr. Paige, I'm really not interested in helping you make a name for yourself by exploiting this young woman. The chief of police from Ardmore, Oklahoma, has also received a copy of that tape and will be contacting you, as will the detective who booked Skye here, in Omaha. I have no interest in the outcome of this case. That will be left to the three of you."

I hurried out of the door before he could say anything else. When the elevator doors opened, I thought I was home free until I saw those frightened eyes.

"Miss Stanton." Skye grabbed my arm and nudged me to a corner in the hall. "I've been waiting outside your apartment for hours. Where have you been?"

"Working on your case," I told her gently.

"So? What did you find out? Was that man my father?"

"Yes, Skye, he was." I watched her expression and it never changed. I wasn't sure if I was talking to Skye or Ann. I felt so sorry for her.

"I need to see Dr. Paige," she said, and walked away as if I had suddenly gone invisible.

"And I need to make a call," I said to myself, dialing the police.

Someone once told me that the second most important thing about doing a job is knowing when you are finished. As I forced myself back into my car, I kept telling myself I'd done only what Skye Cahill had hired me to do. My job was done. What happened to her as a result of my investigation was of no concern to me.

But still I felt guilty.

I'M A DIRTY GIRL

"I'm a flasher at heart. I'm a dirty girl."
... Deborah Harry

Guys never liked me. Why should they? I was always the scrawny kid. There I sat, in every damn class picture, third from the left, first row. Mousy hair, skinny arms stickin' out of homemade sleeves, buck teeth. Lookin' down at the floor cause I was always too shy or too scared to face the camera. They never took the time to know me—not even the girls--until I improved myself.

I took acting lessons while all the other girls were pissin' away their time in some snotty sorority house. And after they graduated and got forced into the real world, lookin' around all frantic for a job in their "chosen field," I took modeling classes. In between the classes and lessons I pulled double shifts tendin' bar at the VFW. But it wasn't until the night of my twenty-fifth birthday that my learned skills and natural talents all started workin' together for me.

One of my regulars, a guy named Petey Lindstrom, came up to me with a big box, all wrapped in shiny red paper.

"Petey," I said, "you didn't have to get me nothin'." I see the other guys laughin' and I figured it was one of them gag gifts and decided to play along. So after he goes on and on about how it's just a little somethin' he wants me to have, just a token, I said thanks and started unwrappin'.

When I lifted the lid off the big box, there was another box, and then another, until I got down to the last one. Finally, after all the paper's off, what did I spy but one of them Wonder Bras, black lace.

Well, the guys all howled so I played along and acted like I was embarrassed. They got a big charge out of the whole thing, kept shoutin' for me to "Put it on! Put it on! PUT IT ON!"

"Jesus!" I shouted. "Okay, anything to shut you idiots up."

The mirror in the bathroom was cracked right across the middle but I could see I looked hot. The bar went ape shit when I sashayed out with my T-shirt tied tight under that push-up bra. And it was at that exact moment I realized the time was as right as it was ever gonna be for me to get my boobs done.

Oh, I know, it takes a hell of a lot more than a pair of 38Ds and a tight ass to make it big. And you better believe I intend on makin' it bigger than big. Gigantic even. Cause I know the secret; I know it's all in timin' and preparation. You gotta know when to be flashy or classy. When to coo and when to howl.

Well, Doctor Roseman said I should take a few days off to recuperate. TV got boring, so I cleaned out some closets. I read all the *Cosmos* that had been layin' around for months. There were lots of hours to think about what I'd done. All of a sudden I found myself with the bod and the talent but not the cash to get me to New York, to one of those fancy modeling agencies. I had to come up with somethin' to feed my bank account if that was ever gonna happen.

That's where Jess came in.

About a year ago my friend Jess moved to this po-dunk town outside of Omaha over on the Iowa side, near the river. The place's crawlin' with porn shops, and strip clubs. She called out of the blue (see what I mean about timin'?) and while I went on and on 'bout my surgery and how I didn't have no money, she told me the real reason she'd called—her old man had split. Then she had one of her brainstorms, said that I should come out there an' we could get a great place, rents were dirt cheap. Hell they should be, in the middle of who knows where. An' she could get me a job at the club she worked at. Well, it was time to take my girls out for a test run and I figured why not?

So I moved into the Riverview apartment complex. River view my ass! You gotta drive half a mile just to see some water and before you even see it, you smell it. But who needs a view anyway, I figured, as long as the place was cheap. But it wasn't. It seemed every day I spent at the Riverview, I found one more lie I had to swallow.

Like for instance, the "gentlemen's club" turned out to be a joint called "Tit-illations." Get it? Tits? Jess thinks it's real clever and that I'm stupid or somethin' when I don't bust a gut every time she laughs at the cleverness.

And the money sucks. Oh, on a good night, a Saturday, I can pull in four, maybe five hundred, but the rest of the time I'm prancin' 'round up there on that joke of a stage for a few drunks. Leon, the owner, he's tryin' to get a lunch crowd but as long as I been there—four and a half weeks—there's never much of a line in front of Leon's Chinese buffet. Buffet, that's another lie. I think you need to have more than one gigantic big bowl of rice, some Chop Suey an' egg rolls to consider what he puts out to be a buffet.

I was bitchin' to Jess one night, complainin' that things just weren't turnin' out the way I expected. She said that I had to give it more time.

"It?" I asked her, "Which *it* are you referrin' to? The rent *it*, the pissy job *it*, or the shitheads that come in here *it*?"

"All of *it*!" she said in that scolding way that made me really mad.

"One more month an' I'm outta here. End of conversation."

"You're just pissed because you're lonely. So stop taking it out on me because you need a man." Then she flipped that long blond hair of hers.

We were sittin' in the back room at the Tit, waitin' for our next set. My chair was wicker and I knew it was gonna leave those criss-cross marks all along the back of my thighs, but I didn't give a shit. I leaned down to pull the sags out of my fishnets; if I looked at her face I'd puke.

"I can have any man I want—whenever I want, I just happen to have certain requirements. Unlike you who'll sleep with anything."

"A girl, such as yourself, is gonna get very lonely each night, all alone with her precious requirements."

I could hear my music startin' up; I stood and yanked at that ugly spangled bra Leon made me wear. An' then I said the only thing I could in a situation like that, "Up yours, Jess."

When opportunity knocks you right in the head, you gotta answer . . . or at least take notice. So when I walked out onto the stage that night, it wasn't the three burned out bulbs my eyes kept starin' at but the guy at a back table. His hair was styled with just the right amount of gel. He wasn't wearin' any jewelry, not even a pinkie ring like most all of Leon's friends, even Leon himself wore. An' the very best thing about that guy was that killer suit of his. Some kind of tweedy stuff like from one of them fancy shops in England. He didn't smoke; didn't even have a beer bottle in front of him. He just sat there, eyein' me like I was bein' interviewed for a job instead of grindin' my bare ass against a brass pole.

As the last few notes of "I Will Survive" screeched out of the monster speakers, I bent down to pick up my clothes, real slow, gave the guys one last good look while I watched that dude out of the corner of my eye. Before I got backstage, Leon came up to me, grabbed my arm, and told me that Killer Suit wanted a lap dance.

"Let me go put on my Daisy Dukes first."

"He said now, he has an appointment and can't wait."

Leon was holdin' my arm real tight so I jerked away from him, gave him that look of mine. The one that said if he touched me again I'd knock those gold teeth right out of his mouth.

I walked slow. Sashayed my hips as I went. It don't matter what a girl's wearin', it's how she carries herself that really counts. But clothes do help and I snapped that bra back on just so I had somethin' to take off.

Before I could introduce myself, the guy holds out his hand. I didn't want to embarrass the poor sap so I shook it but I could feel he was tryin' to keep me away from him.

"My name's John," he said.

"An' I bet your last name's Doe, or maybe Jones?" I laughed.

"Neither."

"Well, John, I'm Mandy. Did my boss tell ya it's twenty bucks? An' no touchin' my tits."

"That's fine."

I dumped my things on top of the table next to him an' sat down. "The next song should start up in a minute. You want to get your money's worth. If I start now you only get five minutes instead of ten."

"Five minutes should do it," he said, so serious.

"Fine with me, John." I stood up. "Night Train" was playin'. I moved the table away from him so I could get closer and started runnin' my hands across his shoulders. He looked me square in the eyes, sized me up. I leaned over and shook my 38s in his face and he glanced down at 'em, sizin' them up. I turned around, unhooked my bra and lowered myself nice and ladylike into John's lap. The music was slow an' moody; I closed my eyes, feelin' the beat drivin' down my spine and nuzzled his face along my neck. When I leaned back John pushed me away an' started takin' somethin' out of his wallet. I guessed it was my money but instead of cash, he slapped a business card down on the table. An' that's when his face lit up, not from anything I done.

"You're perfect."

"Well . . . I've been told . . ."

"I'd like to offer you a job."

"What the hell do you think I'm doin' here?" He was pissin' me off, treatin' me like that.

"Sit there." He pulled a chair over for me. "I'm an investigator, I specialize in matrimonial discord cases."

"Matrimonial what?"

"When a wife, or husband—mostly wives—have a suspicion that their spouse is cheating on them, they hire me. I send out a decoy, who tries to nail the guy, or gal, in the act."

"Wait a minute. I don't take money to let guys . . ."

"No contact will ever be made. What we do is wire you up and send you out to entice . . . make the guy ask you out on a date. Then you inquire if he's married. He'll say no . . ."

"But you told me these were married guys."

"They always say no. Then you arrange to meet him and get as much on tape as you can. We deliver the evidence to the missus all neat and clean. No fuss, no mauling, no problem."

"And how much do I get paid for bein' a prick teaser?"

He tried to hide his grin by lookin' down into his lap a minute. Then he looked back at me all serious like. "A hundred a job."

"I'll have to think about it," I told him as I scooped up his card an' then my stuff. "Don't call me, I'll call you."

The guy's card said that he was really named John. But his last name wasn't as simple. It was long an' Polish, started with a D, had three i's an' seemed to run for miles along the top of the card. First thing I did, as soon as I got home that night, was call the number printed in big red letters, in the bottom right hand corner. I figured there would be some sort of answerin' machine hooked up to the other end an' I wanted to hear how professional it sounded. After five rings I got this woman an' she told me she was the agency's "service." I made up some phony name an' hung up.

The next day I decided to call the Better Business Bureau. They said John had a license registered but they didn't have any complaints against him so they couldn't tell me much more. That afternoon I drove down to check out the address on his card. Sure enough there was this dinky place stuck between Scotties Market an' Blockbusters with his name painted on the door.

When I told Jess all about it that night, in the back room of the Tit, she practically exploded all over the place.

"A hundred bucks? Just for flirting with some schmuck? That's all you gotta do?" Then she got this scared look, leaned closer in to me an' said in a quiet voice, "Are ya sure there won't be any danger to yourself?"

"How dangerous can it be? We'll be sittin' in a public place. Hell, it sounds safer than most the dates I been on." I thought about it all that night, through all my sets. When I spotted Leon I asked him about John. All he knew for sure was that the guy wasn't a regular. But after all my thinkin' an' checkin' the thing that cinched it for me appeared in the newspaper like a sign from God.

It was another one of them price wars. Fares to New York were cheaper than I had ever seen before. With the money I made strippin' an' the extra I could make decoyin' I figured I could be in the Big Apple inside a month. So I booked myself a one-way from Omaha (the biggest airport near Council Bluffs) to New York City. The very next day I called John and told him to "sign me up." He promised there'd be at least two jobs a week. It took some jugglin' but by Thursday night, my regular day off, I was workin' my first decoy job.

Like I said before, a girl's got to know when to be flashy and when to be classy. I been in the lounge at the Best Western, over by the dog track, before. And as I stood in front of my closet, trying to decide the perfect outfit to wear for my new job, I knew the leopard print spandex would work. The top's cut low and my black lace bra peeks just a little bit out of the sides. John looked me over real good when I got there. We met at the bar for a drink.

"Maybe next time you could wear something more conservative?" He frowned but I didn't give a shit what he thought so I acted as though I couldn't hear him with all the talkin' the room. "Now don't think this is the way it'll go down before each job. Because tonight's your first time out, I thought you might be a little nervous so I'm here for you."

I crossed my legs, ran my hand up the shiny black hose on my right leg. "Need I remind you what I do for a living?"

"Need I remind you," he said shooting me such an attitude, "that stripping for a bunch of drunks who know they can't touch you, with bouncers in every corner of the room, ain't exactly the same as being out on your own without any protection?"

I poked my finger down inside my bra. Even though the microphone he'd taped to me was the tiniest thing I'd ever seen, I kept thinkin' it would cause some trouble.

"Okay, okay, I'll watch myself."

"Good." John tossed back what was left of his Scotch, slammed the glass down on the bar an' said, "Now, slap me."

"What?"

"Your mark, Albert Coral, just arrived. He's standing by the door, watching us. Make a scene so we can get his attention."

The actress in me kicked in. "You son of a bitch!" I screamed. Then I slapped John so hard even I was surprised. "I can't believe you did this to me! Get outta here! You make me sick."

He wasn't bad himself, as far as actin' ability goes. He looked real hurt, rubbed his cheek a little, stood up an' threw a ten at me. "It's been real." Then he walked outta there like we'd just had a real lover's spat.

I didn't turn to see if anyone was watchin' me, just swiveled my stool back to face the bartender who was askin', "You okay lady? Anything I can do?"

"Yeah, how about another drink." I slid my empty glass across to him.

"Sure thing." He hurried off, glad that I hadn't asked him to do somethin' more difficult.

I admired my nails while I waited. I'd splurged on one of them fancy manicures. I had the girl press little gold stars into the red polish, right on the tip of each nail. I clicked them on the bar as I looked up to watch Mr. Coral in the mirror.

"Hey, you okay?" A young kid, probably just old enough to get his ass into the place, plopped down next to me.

"Yeah, I'm fine." I never made eye contact, didn't want him thinkin' I was invitin' him to get any closer.

He straightened the Cornhusker cap on his head, I saw the shine of a big class ring on his fat finger. "Well, I'm glad to hear it. A gorgeous redhead like you shouldn't be sitting here . . ."

"Go away." I didn't have time to dick around.

"Pardon me?"

"Look, kid, go away now while you can still move. Because if you don't haul your flabby ass offa that stool, I will stab you."

He got that look on his face, sorta like he wanted to laugh but didn't cause he wasn't sure he heard me right. "You'll what?"

I picked up my purse and reached inside. "I will stab you with my nail file; it's very sharp. An' it's so dark in here. What if I missed your leg on account of I'm so upset? I'm sure a stud like you plans on havin' some kids someday."

"You're one crazy bitch," he said right before he walked away.

Albert was still standin' by the door. I had to do somethin' to get him to move.

"There you go." The bartender was back. "One screwdriver for the pretty lady. That'll be three fifty."

I handed him the ten John had given me and asked, "Could you please have the waitress take a martini over to that guy by the door? With my compliments."

The bartender grinned. "You mean Bert? Sure."

John had filled me in on this Mr. Coral. He owned a small jewelry store in town. Mrs. Coral told John that her husband wanted to expand, open another store at the big mall in Omaha. But what he really wanted to do with his life was sing. So he came to the Best Western every Monday and Thursday night cause that's when they had Karaoke competitions. He even had a followin', she said. And oh how he loved martinis.

I watched as Mr. Coral took his drink from the waitress and saw him talkin' to her, no doubt askin' who it was from. She pointed across the room to me. I stared straight ahead, watchin' it all in the mirror. When he waved to me, I looked down, like I didn't see. Ignore a guy and he's yours. It always works. Treat 'em like shit, he'll never leave.

"Ahh, Miss?" Albert Coral tapped me on the shoulder.

I swiveled around, brought my bodacious self right up into clear view. "Yes?" I tossed back my head like Jess does.

"I'd like to thank you for the drink."

"My pleasure," I said it with such fuckin' sincerity I almost made myself sick.

"Mind if I join you?"

I patted the stool next to me. "Please do."

"I couldn't help but notice the guy you were with."

"The asshole I smacked or the jerky kid?"

"The asshole." He twirled the olive speared to a toothpick around in his drink and a diamond ring sparkled on his right hand. It was just big enough to be tasteful lookin'.

He wasn't bad. Medium height, longish straight, dark hair, just brushed his collar in the back. He was wearin' black jeans, a white shirt, a black suede vest an' he smelled great. His face was nice—not too friendly, in that phony way—with just the right amount of teeth so's he didn't look horsey. His eyes were dark and he spoke kinda slow, like he was makin' sure I would catch each word, like it was real important. That's the way he listened, too.

The usual amount of crap got flung around. I told him I was an actress and model. What a coincidence, he said, he was an entertainer. "Really?" I said, all impressed and breathless. "By the way, I didn't catch your name." I held out my hand all dainty like. "I'm Mandy. Mandy Monroe."

"Extremely nice to meet you, Mandy." He kissed my fingers. "I'm Bert Coral."

I had to give the bastard credit. He looked me straight in the eye and told me his real name. I'd really expected an alias, like in the movies. Either the guy was too lame to think of somethin' more excitin' or thought he was too slick to get caught. Some guys are like that, think they're wearin' some kinda protective coatin'.

"So, what kind of entertainin' do you do?"

He smiled, so full of himself. "Guess."

Seein' as how I already knew the answer and didn't feel like wastin' too much time, my second guess was, "Singer?"

Typical man, he was really pumped that the conversation revolved around him and his dreams and his talent. I nodded an' smiled, tryin' not to yawn while he went on an' on an' fuckin' on. How he wanted to get a singin' contract but first had to sell off some property. I guessed he meant his store. How he had to get to L.A., out where the music industry was. He talked about half an hour, non-stop, until ten o'clock when some guy announced that the Karaoke would begin.

Bert asked me what my favorite song was.

"Oh, gee, I like 'em all."

"No," he insisted, rubbin' his hands together, "your all time favorite."

"'New York, New York.'" I waited for him to ask why, but he didn't. He was suddenly hoppin' off the bar stool an' dashin' up to some DJ guy.

"First up tonight is a favorite here at the Bluffs Run Best Western, Bert Coral!" The microphone gave out with a shrill screech. "Bert's gonna do 'New York, New York' for us."

The lights got dimmer and the stage got brighter. Bert walked up there like a real pro. He held the microphone in his right hand and the cord in the other, just like I seen Dean Martin do it. He pointed toward me and said, "This one's for the lovely Mandy."

The music switched on an' Bert started off real soft an' gentle. He never took his eyes off me; I could feel all the women there were wishin' they was me. He looked handsome in that light. It was a nice picture: him singin' an' all of us admirin' him up there. By the time he got to the middle part, he got a little louder. I could see why he had some fans, he knew how to work the crowd, just like I do when I dance. By the end, he was beltin' those words out. Each time he got to the New York part it all seemed new an' excitin'. I knew then that he had every freakin' one of us in the palm of his hand. It was truly a breathtaking experience.

The applause went on forever. The DJ had to hold the next singer back awhile until Bert finished takin' a few more bows. As he made his way to me, people slapped his shoulder, tellin' him how great he was.

"Well? What did you think?" he asked, as if he had to ask.

"I am truly impressed." And I was.

"So then you'll have some dinner with me? To celebrate? After they announce the winner, that is."

John's only instructions had been that I shouldn't let the guy touch me, he didn't say nothin' about eatin' with him.

"Sure, why not."

The trophy sat on the table between us like a big gold centerpiece.

"How many of these things do you have?" I asked after we ordered our steaks.

"Twenty-four. But enough about me; we've been talking about me all night. What's your story?"

So I told him a few lies—little ones—but mostly I told him the truth.

"Why do you have to go to New York? I thought you said you were already into modeling."

"Small time. To make it big ya gotta be in New York, or Europe."

"Well, I'm sure you won't have one bit of trouble. I mean, just look at yourself."

"Oh, I ain't worried about my looks." I stretched a little, just enough to pull the front of my dress tighter. His eyes went right in the direction I wanted them to go. "It's gettin' noticed. It's gettin' some hot shot at some big-time agency interested."

"Don't worry. I've seen the toothpicks they have in those fashion magazines. I'll let you in on a secret. Men want something to grab onto, know what I mean? A woman with some womanly flesh on her bones." Then he brushed his fingers down my arm.

I thought the time was right so I straightened up an' asked, "So, Bert, tell me, are you married or what?"

"Why do you want to know?" He looked a little angry, kinda suspicious. I didn't want to blow it just when things were goin' so well.

"I just figured a gentleman like you would certainly have somebody."

"Yeah," he said, "I'm married."

I waited for him to add somethin' like . . . but we're separated, or we don't get along . . . some kind of bullshit excuse why he was sittin' at a table with me. But he didn't say another thing about it. Even though I admired his bein' so honest, I did have a job to do. So I figured I should play it like I was upset. Maybe it would force him to say somethin' incriminatin' into my cleavage.

"Then why the hell are you here with me?"

"Good question, I was asking myself the same thing. All I can tell you is that I don't have a good reason; I've never done this before. But I just couldn't resist you. And when you get right down to it, we're only having dinner. After I walk out of here, it's back to my wife. And you'll go back to . . . ?"

"Me? I ain't married."

"There isn't even a fiancé or boyfriend somewhere?"

"Nope, just me an' my roommate Jess in our shitty little apartment." I couldn't believe how goddamn pathetic I sounded. It made me embarrassed thinkin' that John was listenin', back in his office, to my sorry ass self. I could only hope he thought I was connin' the guy.

"Sometimes life sucks, doesn't it? But sometimes it's great, like right now." Mr. Albert Coral leaned over an' kissed me. Oh, I heard about those kinds of kisses in songs an' on *The Young and the Restless*. But that was the very first time I had one planted on my own lips. I know how sickening it sounds but it was like our souls melted down. The heat rushed through me an' made my heart throb an' my pants wet. I couldn't help myself from takin' a second one, an' then a third.

When our food finally came, my appetite was long gone. All I wanted to do was crawl into bed and then all over that sexy man. But instead I worked on my prime rib an' thought. So far Bert hadn't said nothin' that his wife could use. He hadn't lied about bein' married, even said how he was goin' home to her. So what if he told me he was a singer an' left out the jeweler part? There sat the trophy in front of us to prove he was honest about performin'. What had he done so wrong, I asked myself, 'cept have dinner with me? An' steal a few kisses. Why I bet that with all the noise around us the mike hadn't even picked the kissin' part up. We didn't moan or nothin'.

While I was thinkin' through it all Bert opened his mouth like he was gonna say somethin'. Before he could get a sound out, I said real quick, "Excuse me a sec." Then while he sat there lookin' all confused, I high tailed it to the Ladies Room. I didn't have a plan when I ran into that flowery room, but I sure as hell had one when I came out.

I stood there by the table with Bert lookin' me up an' down, his eyes finally stoppin' to check out the paper towels bunched in my hands. If I read him right, and I was pretty sure I had, he'd go along with me. If not, I knew it wouldn't take much to convince him.

After plantin' my butt, I laid down the piece of towel I had written on with my eye liner, in the bathroom. I watched as his lips mouthed: YOUR WIFE HIRED SOMEONE TO TAIL YOU. SHE WANTS THE JEWELRY STORE FOR HERSELF. OUR TABLE'S BUGGED. THE BALD GUY BY THE PHONE TOLD ME. READ WHAT I WRITE OUT LOUD. When he was done, Bert looked at me. I knew he believed it cause he hadn't told me about the store an' there was, in fact, a scary lookin' bald dude standin' by the phone, who I had picked just because he was there . . . convenient.

Then I started. "So, I guess there's no chance for us, huh? You bein' married an' all?"

I wrote frantic like and Bert read: "No, I'm sorry. I love my wife too much to ever hurt her." He did it real convincin'. But then I knew him bein' a spotlight junkie like me, he'd do good.

"You won't even meet me back here for one lousy drink tomorrow night?"

He read as I wrote. "No, I'm not gonna risk losing my store for a one night stand." When he saw those words his eyes got sad and he turned red.

"You're a real asshole ya know that?" I stood up, made a lot of noise so the mike in my bra would get it all. His hands reached over to grab me but he stopped himself. I smiled that I understood and it was okay. Then I told him, loudly, "You can't just invite me out an' insult me like this. I have feelin's ya know." Then I handed him a shred of paper with my phone number on it and a message: GIVE ME AN HOUR THEN CALL ME.

In the car, on the way home I talked to myself, like I forgot that John was listenin' to every word. I sniffed a little here an' there for realism. "That's it! I've had it! I don't need this shit; who the hell does he think he is?" I screamed into my breasts.

I was soakin' in the tub when the phone rang—just like I knew it would. I reached over an' picked up the cordless sittin' on the toilet. "Yeah?" I made my voice sound good an' pissed.

"Mandy, considering it was your first time out, you did just fine. But you gotta stop taking the whole thing so personal. Remember it's just a job."

"It's kinda hard on my ego, ya know? I thought you said these guys always say yes."

"Well," John sputtered like he was rennin' outta gas, "almost always. Who'd a thought you'd find the only saint in Iowa? Forget it. Stop by my office on Monday, I'll cut you a check and set you up with another job."

"Sure thing," I said and hung up.

I couldn't help laughin' as I dried off and got into my robe. "Gee, Johnny, a whole hundred bucks, all for myself. How 'bout you keep your chump change? I got me some serious money to worry about."

I was pourin' myself a vodka when the phone rang. Right on time. I picked up the receiver and cooed like a love bird. "Thank God you're okay, honey.

Yeah, your wife's out to get ya all right. But listen, I know just what we should do." If I said it once, I'll keep sayin' it forever—it's all in the timin'.

And the preparation . . . don't forget that part. Boy was I prepared to talk Albert Coral into blowin' that pop stand with me after we grabbed some of wifey's inventory, of course. She'd never be expectin' it an' I figured that good report she was gonna pay John for would keep her off our ass a few days. Then we could fly to New York an' get me interviewed at the Ford Modeling agency. After I signed a contract with them, we'd head for L.A. to get Bert an agent to work on his singin' career. We sure as hell both had more than our share of talent.

"What, honey? Yeah, I felt it too. We got somethin' special." He bought into the whole bad bald guy routine and I hung on the other end of his conversation smellin' like a rose. No one would ever be able to convince him I was really such a dirty girl.

BELATED REVENGE

"After she found her grandfather's body, Dana was never the same."

Rena Mancini scooped the tears from her eyeballs. I offered a tissue but she only shook her head. Her large hands continued to rub her eyes, then smoothed the wetness into her cheeks.

I hadn't seen her or her husband in over fifteen years and it would have been great visiting with them now if the circumstance weren't so depressing. But, you know that saying: "What goes around comes around"? I guess Dana ended up where she deserved to be and I can't say I was feeling badly for anyone except her poor mother.

As I waited for Mrs. Mancini to stop crying, I noticed Mr. Mancini was still quite dashing. My mother and I would wonder, between coffee and soap operas, what this handsome man saw in Mrs. Mancini.

She'd gotten even shorter over the years and her face lay in soft wrinkles like a silk dress in need of ironing. She was the gruffer of the pair and had a third grade education. Instead of complementing each other, they contradicted. But it had always been evident that Mr. Mancini adored his wife.

"Mrs. Mancini . . ."

"Rena," she corrected.

She'd been my second mother ever since I was five. I felt embarrassed confessing my inability to think of her now as a pal. So, I chose the easiest way around the situation and avoided calling her by any name.

"I don't understand why you came to me. I thought you retired to Phoenix."

"We did. Moved there right after you girls graduated from high school. But Dana stayed in Chicago. Got her real estate license and was making good money until she married that loser."

Dana and I had been best friends forever. We'd met our first day in kindergarten, played together after school almost every day, and talked on the phone when we were out of each other's sight.

I loved going over to Dana's house. She was a blond, blue eyed, pampered little girl and owned every toy imaginable. Mrs. Mancini would make spaghetti dinners, all the while telling us stories of coming to America on a big ship with her parents. She claimed that was the first time she'd had her teeth cleaned — while onboard. I still remember the gory details about how a dentist supposedly scraped tartar from her teeth with a knife. Sweet woman — awful teeth.

"Your mother and I kept in touch. She told me how you went on to college and married Jon. He was such a nice boy. Dana always liked him."

I bet she did. Jon was the reason I hadn't seen Dana since our senior year in high school. She'd made a play for him while I was away on vacation. I stood in my living room, holding a stupid souvenir from Mexico, listening to Dana tell me how Jon had taken advantage of her.

Later, Jon told his version and I believed him. We got married, then separated. People grow up, things change, but I'd never worked through my resentment for Dana.

So many plots I'd conjured to insure she suffer for stealing my trust. And after hearing news through friends of friends that Dana had married an alcoholic, divorced, and then taken to the bottle herself, I sadly admit, it made me feel vindicated.

But this?

"Paul reminded me you'd gone into investigation, Susan. He heard it from Mrs. Trama."

Chicago may be a big city, but like anywhere else, it's made up of neighborhoods that breed gossip.

Paul finally decided this was his cue and came to life.

"And since we were here to visit our oldest daughter, Arlene, we thought we'd look you up. What better person to help our Dana than her best friend from the old neighborhood."

Mrs. Mancini's body and head trembled in agreement.

"Where's Dana now?"

Mr. Mancini answered. "At a sanitarium, near Schaumburg. It's close to Arlene's house so she can visit whenever she wants. Dana's been there since last spring. Almost a year now."

"And what do you need from me?"

Paul set down his coffee mug. He stood and looked out the window. The view from my office, located in the spare bedroom of my apartment, looks out over the large parking lot of a discount furniture store. He watched a truck unloading sofa beds and then spoke.

"I'm sure you remember when the old man died? — well, Dana became depressed, withdrawn after that."

"We were about ten?" I asked.

Mrs. Mancini picked up the story as her husband continued watching the furniture truck. "Just barely. It was three days after Dana's tenth birthday. We'd gone shopping. When we came home I thought Papa was sleeping and sent Dana to wake him for supper. She got about halfway up the attic stairs when she saw her grandpa laying on the floor in his room. She screamed. It was too dark to really see anything. Thank God she was spared that."

Mr. Mancini walked to his wife's side and bent to offer comfort; my mind wandered back up Dana's attic stairs and to her wonderful train set.

The tracks were mounted on a piece of plywood that was the size of two large dining-room tabletops. Her father had painted it dark green and added a small village. Plastic evergreen trees dotted the landscape and tiny people stood waiting on a miniature platform. There was a tunnel, street lamps that lit up, and when the train came into the station you could press a button and the engine whistled and blew circles of white smoke. As much as I loved that train, Dana loved it more. She'd do anything to play with it. Even walk by the bedroom where her grandfather had killed himself.

Every time I came to visit, she'd point out the bullet hole and tell me how the slug had passed through his head and into the ceiling. Every time we wanted to play with the train she'd point and recite and never, never, even once did she let me work the controls of that train. Not even once would she let me hold the panel of buttons. Not even once did she let me blow the goddamn whistle. And still I came to that house and still I listened to her story.

Mr. Mancini shuffled back to his chair. "Her grades suffered. She cried a lot. We had to take her to the doctor for depression. And the migraines started."

"And now she's in Oak Hills. They started her on shock therapy last month." Mrs. Mancini sniffled.

"I still don't understand why you need me." I hoped I didn't sound rude.

"Because . . ." Mr. Mancini leaned forward, speaking slowly as if I was deaf and he wanted me to read his lips, ". . . because all the doctors in the world won't be able to free her from the guilt she's been stabbing herself with for over twenty years. Dana needs to be free of this, know that her grandfather's death had nothing to do with her, nothing at all."

I shifted my weight in the swivel chair behind my desk. "I didn't know she felt responsible; she never showed much emotion."

"Don't you remember the time she said her grandfather's ghost came to visit when she was taking a piano lesson?" her mother asked. "Dana had such a crush on that Edelman boy then."

"Stephen." I smiled. All the girls loved Stephen Edelman. Myself included.

"Yes. He's the one. Well, she was at the piano and said she was asking her grandfather how she could get this boy to like her. All of a sudden a key on the piano started playing. All by itself."

"She told me it was B natural," I said. "That her grandfather was telling her to just be herself and Stephen would like her."

"And it helped." Her father beamed. "She dated Stephen for quite a while after that. All the boys were crazy for Dana."

My resentment flared up again but I didn't tell them I'd been dating Stephen first. I found out about a year after he broke up with me that Darling Dana had been sharing all my confidential fears and gently stirring in a few of her own until Stephen figured I was more than he bargained for. But even after I'd found out the truth I refused to believe my best friend would do something so terrible to me.

"What Mr. Mancini and I need from you is proof. Something to convince Dana she was not responsible for her grandfather's death. He'd yelled at her earlier that morning. She'd left a toy or something on the floor and Papa almost fell. He was angry. But she needs to know that had nothing . . . nothing at all to do with his death." Mrs. Mancini was all business now. Her tears had dried, her shoulders stiffened and her hands were still, folded on her lap.

"How about the death certificate?"

"We had several copies but the insurance company and the funeral home and social security, they all needed one and we can't find another anywhere."

"I'll call the Hall of Records. It should take a few days to get a copy."

"We'll be in town for a month," Mr. Mancini said. "You can reach us at Arlene's."

"I'll see what I can find."

"Do you need something up front? A retainer?"

I patted her hand. "This is a favor for some dear friends."

"No, friendship and business do not mix." Mr. Mancini pulled out a brand new eelskin wallet. "Here. Is this enough?" He laid two one-hundred-dollar bills on my desk.

"That's fine." I picked up the money and put it inside a small drawer.

"Well," I said, standing, "let's hope this does some good."

"Oh, one thing more," Mrs. Mancini said as I followed her to the door. "Maybe you could find time to visit Dana at Oak Hills? I know she'd love to see you. I don't mean to mix business with friendship but . . ." She looked up at her husband sheepishly.

"That's for Susan to decide."

I hesitated. "I'll try."

I didn't try that hard. In fact . . . not at all. The first thing I did was exactly what I'd told the Mancinis I'd do. I called the Cook County Hall of Records and asked for a copy of the death certificate for Louie Grigoletti. There was a ten-dollar fee involved and the document would be sent out within the week.

Spring wasn't showing itself as quickly as previous years and I was suffering from cabin fever. I decided to visit the old neighborhood. It was only a thirty-minute drive and maybe a blast from the past would stir up some ideas.

I headed for Michigan Avenue. Not the section that cuts through downtown Chicago flanked by elegant stores, no, the end of Michigan Avenue that runs through the old neighborhood in Roseland.

As I drove down the street, I saw the bus unload three high school students. They stood in front of the Karamel Korn Shop. I couldn't believe it was still there. They shoved one another, then started to concentrate their bullying efforts on the smallest, a black boy who looked like a freshman. He saw me watching and embarrassed, started shouting.

"You got a problem, lady?"

I steered down the hill, away from the group, and hid my grin. Things change, I guess, but most often they stay the same. That was certainly true of the attitude on the south side of Chicago contained within these blocks where I'd walked, cruised, and just hung out.

I turned left at Palmer Park and went past the library until I came to Dana's street. Her house was the smaller of the two situated on one oblong lot and it skimmed a cluttered alley. I couldn't park my car in front because it was a bus route; parking was prohibited.

A vacant lot occupied the space where Dana's cousin had lived. I maneuvered between the broken glass and stray pieces of wire and parked. Locking the door, I realized the sun was casting my shadow at a 3:30, after-school angle. And I was ten years old for that half block walk, avoiding the cracks in the sidewalk, careful not to break my mother's back by stepping on any.

I swear it was the same metal gate that hung on two rusty hinges. I remembered swinging back and forth on it, chanting: "in came the doctor, in came the nurse, in came the lady with the alligator purse."

Then I was standing in front of the weathered old house. Badly in need of paint, it had always looked haunted. I'd never once seen Mr. Mancini do any work on the place. The lawn was laced with ruts where bicycles made their summertime journey from the back door to the front gate. A kid started screaming, "Mommy! Mommy! There's a lady in our yard! Should I call nine one one?"

A young woman came to the back door; it opened onto the side of the house and she held the screen shut as she shouted.

"You lookin' for something?"

"Sorry," I apologized weakly, "I didn't mean to scare your daughter."

"Never mind her."

I walked closer to meet the woman's eyes.

"I'm Susan Elliott."

She waved a damp dish towel at my extended hand. "Yeah, fine, so what do you want?"

I cut the preliminaries. It was obvious this lady meant business. "I'm a private investigator and I'm working on a case for the family who used to live in this house. It's very important that I look around—take a few notes for the police."

Even though the police would never become involved, and it really wasn't necessary I look around, a few intimidating words thrown in at the right time usually stuck to the brain of those standing in the way. The scowl covering her pimpled face turned to a smirk. She'd surely heard the words "police" and "private investigator" but wasn't convinced enough to let me enter.

"You got ID?"

"Sure." I climbed the bottom two steps, digging through my purse until I found my wallet. "Here."

She moved her lips as she read to herself. "Can't be too careful," then held the door open for me.

The house smelled of baby poop. Cabinets were spotted with handprints, the floor sticky with something red, probably Kool-Aid, and when she offered me a seat, I told her I'd only be a few minutes and just needed to walk through the house.

"Well, I'll take the kids out front so's you can concentrate." She scurried out the door with a baby in one arm, a toddler in the other and a girl of about five, hanging onto her mama's dirty shirttail.

"Thanks."

You always hear how people return to a childhood scene and things seem smaller. There's always that rare exception. This house felt just as large and empty as it had all those years ago. The floor creaked and not one hint of welcome showed itself. The woman out in the front yard must have threatened her kids with sure death if they disturbed "the law." Except for the ticking of a clock in the front bedroom, the place was shrouded in silence.

After I'd walked through each room and delayed myself downstairs as long as I could, I backtracked to the kitchen and opened the door leading upstairs to the attic.

Automatically my hand went to the cord hanging above my head and a low-wattage bulb lit the uncarpeted, steep stairs. I counted six steps and stopped. Because there was no wall, to my left, enclosing the staircase, my eyes were level with the floor. I could see the door of the small bedroom. The view was exactly as it had been that evening when Dana discovered her grandfather's body.

I continued up the stairs, ducking as I neared the pitch in the ceiling. I went straight to the bedroom and opened the door. Expecting to find it as I had found everything so far—the same. It was startling to see the walls had been painted black, decorated with Day-Glo posters of Guns N Roses and Ozzy Osbourne.

The ceiling was also painted a matte black and if there had been a leftover bullet hole, by now it surely had been patched over. I dragged a red plastic milk crate out of a corner and stood to poke my fingers across the low, cob-webbed ceiling.

Near the light fixture, my nail caught and inserted an entire index finger into the hole. Then I got off the crate and stood over where Grandpa Louie's bed had been. Holding my hand to my head, I cocked a thumb and aimed at my temple. One clean shot entering the right side of the head, exiting the left and the bullet would have planted itself in . . . the wall.

Strange.

There was no way the bullet could have lodged itself into the ceiling unless the old man had been lying down. I bent myself into several positions and couldn't come up with one that the arthritic man could have managed.

I distinctly remembered the funeral director talking to us explaining how lucky for everyone that "Grandpa still looked like himself." My nightmares had been narrated by that soft-spoken undertaker for years. Always patting my hand, and when he put that alabaster figurine into my small hands he said, "This is what death feels like. Cold and hard."

Each time Dana took me upstairs we followed our routine. She'd tell me the story of finding her grandfather and point out the bullet hole in the ceiling. She'd explain how there hadn't been much blood. I'd ask a new question and then we'd slam the door and run over to watch the miniature village light up and the signalman wait for the next train.

A child's memory, of course, is questionable. And all those years in between have adjusted my recollections. But when something is reinforced the way each visit to Dana's imprinted the tragedy into my impressionable brain, I grew up never questioning that Louie Grigoletti had shot himself in the head. But if the bullet had entered Louis Grigoletti's head at an angle required to penetrate the ceiling near that light, then part of the top of his head had to have been splattered on that ceiling.

I was curious now. More curious than when I was ten years old. Suddenly all the hazy moments were almost coming into a sharp focus and I wanted to see Dana again. I wondered how much she had changed. Would she be glad to see me? Was she a bona fide nut case and would she even recognize me? I decided to check in with her parents first.

Mr. Mancini answered the phone. He told me his daughter Arlene and Mrs. Mancini were out shopping.

"I just wanted to tell you I visited your old house. It felt odd going back . . ."

"I don't like to remember that place. Rena wanted to stay. It was the only home she'd ever known. With the war, coming to America when she was so young. Then when her two older brothers joined the rest of the family . . . That house, that neighborhood, it all meant security to her."

"You're not even a little bit curious about how it looks?"

"No."

I knew this line of questioning was leading to a dead end.

"Well, if you can tell me where Oak Hills Sanitarium is, I think I'll visit Dana tomorrow."

"That's good of you, Susan." Mr. Mancini seemed genuinely happy. "Dana loves to have visitors. Just take Meachum Road for about three miles; it's right past the hospital."

"Is it a big white building, surrounded by a wrought-iron fence? I always thought that was a hotel."

Mr. Mancini laughed. "For what they charge it should be a first-class resort on the Riviera. Any word on the death certificate?"

"I called about it right after you left the other day. It should be here by Friday at the latest."

"Fine. I'll tell Rena you called. Oh, visiting hours are only from one o'clock until suppertime. Do you need any more money?"

"No, I've only made a few calls."

"Guess we'll wait to hear from you then. And, Susan . . ."

"Yes?"

"I want to thank you. I know you and Dana had some differences, your last year of school. She never told me the particulars but there was a definite change after graduation. Fathers aren't as dense as you might think."

At that moment I liked Mr. Mancini even more. "I never thought you were dense."

"I just wanted you to know I'm aware this might make you uncomfortable. Rena and I think of you as one of our own. And poor Dana needs a friend now."

The lobby of Oak Hills Sanitarium was tastefully decorated in varying shades of beige and green. Potted trees gave the large room an outdoorsy feel. The receptionist wore a linen suit and smiled through perfect white teeth as I approached her desk.

"You can wait over there." She pointed to a row of wicker chairs. "I'll page Ms. Mancini. She's expecting you?"

"No."

I turned and walked to seat myself on the chair nearest the door. Maybe I wanted to be close to the exit in case Dana got violent. After all, her mother had mentioned shock therapy. I fidgeted with the strap of my purse while reassuring myself this wasn't a mistake.

"Ms. Elliott." The receptionist waved for my attention. "Ms. Mancini will meet you on the veranda. Just go out those doors."

Veranda. I hadn't actually ever heard anyone say that word let alone sit on one. I thanked the woman and pushed open the French doors leading outside. At least twenty oversized rocking chairs lined the porch. The afternoon had turned into a full-blown spring day; the view was gorgeous. Apple trees were in blossom and the wide yard was planted with daffodils and tulips. A wind chime tinkled in the warm breeze. I settled into one of the rockers and with each push backward, my feet left the porch and my stomach jumped a little.

"You look good."

Her voice startled me and I stood up.

"So do you." I wasn't lying. There was no need to lie. Dana Mancini looked great. A few wrinkles around those big eyes but the teenager I remembered was still inside there and we hugged each other hello.

I could feel her heart pounding against my chest and a part of me was glad she felt uneasy. She'd earned so many uncomfortable moments I was glad I was there to watch.

Finally we held each other at arm's length and she silently nodded her approval. She stared at me for a few moments more and then broke free to sit in the rocker I had occupied. I sat to her left and we both faced toward the flower-spotted yard.

I finally broke the silence. "Long time no see."

She didn't laugh. "If my parents hadn't called you, I guess it would have been even longer."

"I've wondered about you a lot." Not with much affection and I still didn't feel any guilt about that.

"You could have picked up a phone anytime. You could have called Arlene."

"The phone works both ways, you know. My name hasn't changed and I've lived at the same address for . . ."

"Six years." Her head bobbed as she rocked slowly. Her voice hadn't betrayed one emotion and my irritation gave way to surprise.

"It'll be seven years in August." It seemed important I get in the last word.

She was weary and still avoiding my eyes asked, "Do you even remember what it was that we fought about?"

"Yes. It was the lies you told about Jon. It took me a long time to realize you'd deliberately set out to hurt me. And later, when I was willing to try and get past all that, I found out you'd lied about so many other things I just couldn't forgive you anymore."

I waited for Dana to argue and was again surprised when she didn't.

"I lied a lot back then. My therapist says it was to cover up my insecurities, my loneliness, blah, blah, blah . . . there's a million reasons why I did what I did. I don't blame you for not wanting to see me. There was a long period when I didn't want to see myself anymore either." She held out her arms, and showed me scars on both wrists.

"Why? You got anything you wanted; your parents adored you . . ."

"They pampered me, they protected me; I was their pet. I got everything they could afford and nothing they were free to give. I hated them. I still do."

"But . . ."

"Grandpa was different. He understood. We were so much alike."

Dana stuck both hands into the pockets of her white cardigan. I was startled when her voice rose. "I lied about that, too."

"About what?"

"Grandpa . . . he didn't kill himself."

Stunned, I turned back to the view. Dana wedged her feet under the rocker so her chair couldn't move.

"You shouldn't believe me. No one does. There's no way I can make anyone believe me and it's driving me totally . . ." She started rocking again and this time pushed herself back and forth at a more frantic speed. ". . . completely, forever insane."

I stood, bending down to grab the arms of her chair. "Why would you lie? You were only ten? I remember everything you told me, all those times, all the stories. I even went back to your old house and the bullet hole is still there, in the ceiling. Remember all the times you pointed it out to me? All the goddamn times you told me about finding your grandfather?"

Her sad eyes finally stared into mine. "I did it. They tried to make it look like suicide. Only I knew the truth but I was a spoiled selfish kid. Who'd believe me, right? Now I'm in here. Aren't you happy about that one? Rotten, bitchy Dana, she finally got what she deserved. Isn't that what you thought? What you've been thinking ever since my loving, adoring parents came to you for help?"

I leaned against the railing in front of Dana's chair. My breath seemed to have been sucked out of me and I needed support. Finally, after digesting the information she'd thrown out at me, I started in with my own questions.

"If this is true, why would your parents come to me, allow me to dig into the circumstances regarding your grandfather's death? Why would they risk anyone finding out? Why is their only concern in all this that you have some peace of mind?"

Dana rocked back and her mouth laughed up toward the sky until her eyes filled with tears.

"Peace of mind! There was never any peace in our house. Didn't you wonder why Arlene was never around? They fought all the time. Grandpa heard them; he wasn't deaf. He'd cry and I'd sit with him and I'd cry. Rena would get mad and Paul would get mad that Rena was picking on me, and on and on it went."

I'd forgotten Dana referred to her parents by their first names and her voice colored my black-and-white memories. "Until that afternoon you went shopping."

"We never left the house. Rena was so angry that day. Grandpa wanted meatballs for dinner and Rena said he'd get what he'd get. They fought and finally Grandpa went upstairs for a nap. On the way, he tripped over my Raggedy Ann. He kicked her out of his way and scolded me.

"Rena had always hated Grandpa. She blamed him for having to leave Italy when she was small. She blamed him for everything bad that ever happened to her. And when Grandma died and Grandpa had nowhere else to go, Rena let him come live with us but he had to stay out of her way.

"Paul just ignored Grandpa but every time Rena complained, Paul would shout that it was her father and she had a responsibility.

"Rena came upstairs about an hour later and woke Grandpa up. They started arguing all over again. I ran in to try and break them apart. Grandpa was crying, holding his cheek and asking how his own daughter could be so cruel. I ran and hugged him.

"That's when Rena went crazy, she started screaming that he'd stolen her little girl away from her and he couldn't have me. Grandpa got scared. He opened the top drawer of his dresser and I saw a gun. He only wanted to keep her off of him. He didn't even pick it up."

The image of Rena Mancini as a screaming banshee was one I would never be able to imagine. To me, she was the warm, loving mother. As I listened to Dana I rejected her crazy accusations that would force me to rethink my childhood and recast the good guys and bad guys. But she spoke with such sincerity . . .

"All of a sudden, Rena was pointing the gun at Grandpa, screaming how much she'd always hated him. He just sat on the bed."

The words started coming slower and we both needed a rest from the truth—at least as Dana perceived it. She rubbed her temples. My head pounded and my stomach clenched. I took a deep breath of the clean air scented with cut grass.

"So." I spoke slowly, still trying to sort through it all. "Your mother had the gun and your grandfather never fought for it? Touched it?"

"Not until later. Rena finally calmed down. She said she hated both of us for making her life unbearable. She said she wished we were both dead. That's when I got hysterical and Rena aimed the gun at herself.

"I screamed and grabbed for it the same time Grandpa did. But I was younger and quicker. I held tight, so afraid to let go. A shot went off. The stupid thing just exploded in my hand. Grandpa dropped to the floor.

"I killed him."

"This is all so hard to believe. Too hard. Everything's changed if what you say is true. It makes all my memories . . ."

"What about mine? I swear, Susan, you're the most selfish person I've ever known. How many things are exactly as you remember them? Tell me! How many?"

I answered without hesitation, "Your old house is exactly as I remembered it. Even the bullet hole in the ceiling."

"Yeah, well, I guess that was the only bit of truth in the whole story."

"So, if your parents altered the truth, why did they come to me to help you?"

"Stupid, stupid Susan. They know you believe the story almost as much as I did. And they also know you don't particularly like me anymore. You're their ally."

A recorded announcement instructed that visiting hours were over and would all visitors please leave through the east entrance.

Dana and I walked toward the front door, never touching each other with our hands or emotions. I still didn't like her and I could tell she hadn't grown any fonder of me.

"I'm expecting a copy of your grandfather's death certificate. Your parents didn't have one. Maybe that will have something that I can use as an opening and get them to explain all this. I'm still not sure what I believe."

"It doesn't matter what you believe, I know I've told the truth. Oh, could you give a message to my parents for me?"

"Sure. What is it?"

She politely held the door open. "Tell them not to come back here. I don't ever want to see either one of them again." She slammed the door with such force I thought the glass would break.

I spent the next few days sorting through what I believed to be true, what I knew to be true, and what I hoped would end up false. When Louie Grigoletti's death certificate arrived, I called Mr. Mancini right away.

"Could you and Mrs. Mancini come over to my place this afternoon?"

"Did you see Dana?" He didn't seem to hear what I'd just said.

"Yes. Wednesday afternoon."

"Did she say anything about us? Did you upset her?"

"Why don't you just drop by and I'll tell you everything."

"My wife can't come." Mr. Mancini started to sob. "She's in the hospital. After we tried visiting Dana and got turned away, Rena was so upset she started having chest pains. Her heart, it isn't strong. They're keeping her in for a few days to take some tests. Keep her quiet. This is upsetting her so."

"Are you okay?"

"I'm just hoping you can find something, some little something that will reassure Dana and help Rena relax, too."

"I'll come to you. How's two o'clock? I'll drive out to Arlene's; the death certificate arrived today. We can discuss what I found."

"Fine. I'll be here all day. I can't go to the hospital until later."

"Is there anything else I can do?" I felt helpless.

"No. I'll see you soon."

A middle-aged woman answered the door and I assumed it was Arlene. Because she was so much older than Dana and married at an early age, I'd never really known her.

"Susan?" She looked just like her mother.

"Arlene?"

We laughed and nodded and she let me into her large split level. Obviously she and her husband were doing very well.

"Dad's in the kitchen. But before you talk to him I'd like to know how Dana's doing?"

"I thought you went to visit her regularly. Your parents gave me the impression they put Dana in Oak Hills because it was close to you."

"Oh no, that was just a coincidence. Mom has a way of making things seem nicer than they actually are. Sit. We can talk awhile. Dad's having lunch and watching a baseball game. The Cubs, I think."

"You sure he won't hear us?"

"Positive. He doesn't even know I answered the door."

"Good, then tell me how your grandfather died. I need to hear your version."

Arlene looked confused. "My version? Well, I was eighteen and married. I would have done anything to get out of the house. Mom and Dad fought all the time. When Grandpa came to live with us, things really got unbearable."

"Then one night, Mom called and told me she'd been out shopping with Dana and when they came home, Dana went to call Grandpa for supper and found him dead. He'd had a heart attack."

"A heart attack? Did you go to the funeral?"

"Oh no. I hate things like that. I just couldn't go and Mom and Dad said it was better if I stayed home and didn't get everyone else upset."

"So you never saw your grandfather's body?"

"No."

"When's the last time you saw Dana?"

"Sometime before she went to Oak Hills. We're not close. Mom's always kept me up on Dana's news. She told me how Dana felt responsible for Grandpa's death because she'd had an argument with him that day. She's obsessed about it ever since. Mom and Dad never get any peace."

"Thanks. Do you think I can see your father now?"

"Sure." She stood and went to the kitchen, never looking back.

Mr. Mancini followed Arlene back into the room. She carried a tray set with coffee for two. "I'll just leave this and you can talk in private."

"No, I'd like you to stay."

"Pop, is that okay with you?"

Mr. Mancini nodded. "Fine." He smiled toward his daughter.

I pulled the document from my purse. "Mr. Mancini, this morning I received your father-in-law's death certificate. I think you should see it."

"My eyes aren't that good with these glasses. I need new ones. Why don't you just read it to me, tell me what you found."

"Well . . ." I looked to Arlene, watching her face for any change of expression. "According to this, Louie Grigoletti died from a self-inflicted wound to the heart, a gunshot wound."

"What?" Arlene looked shocked. "That's got to be a mistake. Grandpa died from a heart attack. Isn't that true, Pop?"

"No. That's the story we told you, sweetheart. And anyone else who would listen."

"What do you mean, the 'story'?"

"We were trying to protect Grandpa's memory. He killed himself, honey. And you know the church considers suicide a mortal sin."

"Are you aware that Dana thinks she killed her grandfather?" I directed my question to Arlene.

"Killed him? Why would she think that when he had a heart attack . . . no, you said he killed himself . . . so how could she think she had any part in this? Pop, explain this to me."

"Dana didn't have anything to do with it. Your mother and I have been trying to tell her that for too many years to count."

"When I spoke with her the other day," I said, "she told me there had been a gun, a struggle, and a shot was fired. She claims that her hand was on the trigger when a bullet entered Mr. Grigoletti's head and exited into the ceiling."

"What? Oh my God!" Arlene was hysterical now.

"Susan, Arlene, listen to me."

We both sat back and waited.

"Rena is not the easiest person to live with. You know how agitated your mother can get." He stared at Arlene until she nodded her agreement.

"Her papa used to know all the right buttons to push to make her crazy. Every time they had a fight, the old man would storm upstairs and threaten to kill himself. Well, this particular afternoon, Rena was too tired to plead and beg his forgiveness. When she didn't hear anything she assumed he'd fallen asleep. She went to check on him, he was awake, and the arguing started again. The crazy fool finally opened a drawer to show Rena he had a gun.

"Dana ran into the middle of the argument, they all ended up struggling for the gun. Rena still gets confused when she tells me about this part. I was at work so I have to believe her. Dana was too young to know any better and Louie was dead by the time I got home.

"After Rena made sure the old codger was alive, she ran down to get Dana and show her Grandpa was fine. She made her come back upstairs, but by then, the old man had come to, found the gun, and shot himself in the chest.

"Dana saw the blood and went into hysterics. Rena called me at work and I came home to that crazy house. Louie was already cold by the time we decided what we'd tell the police. We rehearsed Dana until she repeated our story."

"Don't you realize what you did to Dana?" I asked Mr. Mancini. "Can't you see the damage you and Mrs. Mancini have done?"

"But Louie couldn't have been buried in sacred ground if the church knew the truth. We had to think of his soul first."

Arlene left the room, disgusted.

"You understand, don't you, Susan?" Mr. Mancini still looked convinced he'd done the only thing he could in that terrible situation.

I wanted to make him feel better but my shock was too great. "I'm not a Catholic, Mr. Mancini. And even if I were, I think I'd have to take care of my little girl before anyone else."

"Rena and I did what we thought was right. It hasn't always been easy, but we've managed until yesterday when Rena broke down. Now I'll have to take care of things myself."

"I need to know one last thing." I was still curious. "Why did you hire me? Why didn't you just tell Dana the truth, show her the death certificate yourself?"

"She may be my daughter but I've never been able to get close to her. She's a strange kid. I thought she'd believe you because you don't like her either and she'd know you're not trying to make her feel better but just doing your job."

I tried calling Dana at the sanitarium—she wouldn't accept my calls. I tried visiting her but she wouldn't see me. I mailed a copy of the death certificate to Oak Hills, it came back unopened. Dana chooses to blame herself for her grandfather's death. I'm smart enough to know there isn't anything else I can do for her.

The Mancinis returned to Phoenix after Mrs. Mancini was well enough to travel. They phoned several times. I haven't returned their calls.

Arlene plans to try to see Dana and explain everything. I wished her luck.

Revenge is a strange thing. Once you get it, you're never sure what to do with it.

FOR BENEFIT OF MR. MEANS

YOU ARE CORDIALLY INVITED
TO JOIN LILY ARMSTRONG-SMITH
IN CELEBRATING HER TWENTY-FIFTH BIRTHDAY
ON THE FOURTH OF SEPTEMBER
ONE THOUSAND NINE HUNDRED and
TWENTY-SEVEN
EIGHT O'CLOCK IN THE EVENING
AT HER BENTON COVE ESTATE
NEWPORT, RHODE ISLAND

gifts required

"*If I told ya once,* I musta told ya fifty times—you'll be swell."

Irma bit her red fingernail. "But I don't know all the words. Not like Peggy does."

"If ya get into trouble, just give us a nod and we'll cover ya."

Cal turned toward Johnny Long and nodded a signal. Johnny reached up to straighten his bow tie and then played the first six notes solo before the rest of the band joined in.

Cal shoved Irma toward the microphone, "Just remember—smile!"

It was the caliber of people in the mansion that got the butterflies flapping in her stomach, not being up there on stage. She'd been singing most of her eighteen years . . . that was the easy part. And what God had cheated her out of in talent, He'd made up for by loading up the charm.

She sang the first three lines of the song and then hesitated for a moment. Raising her eyebrows and then her small hand, she waved as Harold Lloyd entered the room. Now, why had she done that? Like she knew the man, jeepers! But the guy was a real gentleman and bowed slightly, even waved back before continuing through the crowd. "The man I love . . ." Piece of cake, she thought. If I can just keep from going gaga every time one of them hot shots looks at me, I'll be fine.

"There's three of them. All perfectly matched. I heard Lillian had those chandeliers made in France. Mustn't be outdone by the Astors!"

The woman's companion looked up at the pale lavender ceiling, then inspected the crystal lights evenly spaced across the expanse of the great room.

"You can bet your Aunt Sally they cost more than Lillian's dearly departed father plus his father made in their entire lifetimes—even throwing in that haberdashery her brother runs up in Providence," he said.

"And just how would you know that, if I may ask?" she asked.

"I was her accountant years ago."

"Do I detect a tiny smidge of bitterness in your tone?"

He laughed.

A man with a grudge. The evening was going to be fun! "And now?" She leaned in closer. "You work for her in some other capacity?"

"No, she has an entire office—hand picked—just to handle her affairs." More bitterness. "Men highly qualified to run at the drop of her imported hat."

Now it was her turn to laugh. After composing herself, Zelda Fitzgerald pressed on. "'Twice divorced! That's our Lily. I bet that would require more than one lawyer indeed."

He gulped down his martini. "She's become quite an expert at the fine art of matrimony but when it comes to divorce, Madam Curie couldn't keep up!"

"Will you look at that carpet! Really look at it!" the newcomer said loudly as he interrupted the two guests. "Hand stitched. Custom made! Exquisite. Simply exquisite."

Before Zelda could get rid of the obnoxious intruder, her accountant friend walked away.

"Well?" Dorothy exhaled the word, slowly. Smoke from her second cigarette of the evening hung above her head in a halo. "Where is our birthday girl? Is she decent yet?"

"If she were, she wouldn't be giving herself another birthday party."

"Now, Bill—be nice."

He looked at her with disdain.

"You have to feel sorry for poor Lily. Three birthdays in one year. And twenty-five? How on earth did she come up with that laughable number? A bit eccentric or pathetic, I haven't quite figured it out yet," she said.

"Keep at it, old girl, I'm sure you'll come up with something."

This time it is was she who scowled.

"Why, you're W. C. Fields, aren't you?" A round, balding man stood in front of the group seated on a long divan covered in velvet the color of burnished pewter. "I've enjoyed you on Broadway . . . oh, and of course, the films. Yes, I've spent many enjoyable hours laughing at you and Chaplin . . ."

"*He*, sir, is not an actor. I'll thank you to never mention him in my presence."

The man looked puzzled.

Fields continued, "Chaplin is a goddamn ballet dancer, nothing more." Picking up the book that lay in his lap, he resumed his reading as if he were the only person in the room.

"Don't mind him," the woman said. "He's just a cantankerous old man."

The stranger shifted his weight, unsure how to proceed until his ego kicked in. "Allow me to introduce myself. My name is Means. Gaston Bullock Means." He waited a moment for some sort of reaction. When she didn't say anything he elaborated. "I'm the author of *The President's Daughter.*"

"Oh." She withdrew her hand. "Of course I've heard of you. Who hasn't?"

Fields huffed. "You, sir, are a hack—a gossip monger who happened to luck into a scandal. Now Mrs. Parker here is a writer."

Fields had enough of the boorish crowd and stood up. Without a nod backwards, he walked across the room to the bar.

"Gin. And keep pouring, my good man, until I pass out," he said to the bartender.

"Sure thing, Mr. Fields."

The band was getting ready to wrap up "Someone to Watch Over Me," as two couples danced slowly.

"Have you seen Miss Armstrong-Smith?" he asked the bartender.

"Gee, Mr. Fields, can't say as I have."

With a glass in each hand, the actor made his way to a large seating group in the middle of the room. The sweet young thing singing with the band caught his eye. He raised a glass and blew her a kiss.

She tried concentrating on the words, but he was W. C. Fields—in the flesh! She stopped to return his kiss and Cal leaned over.

His tuxedo didn't fit as well as it could have but the call to play for the party had come at the last minute, it being a Saturday and all. His regular suit was at the cleaners so he borrowed his brother's tux and scrambled to replace

Peggy with Irma. Irma Levine, what a mixed-up dame! But so far so good. And Mrs. Armstrong-Smith paid well, had a lot of parties at the Cove and he wanted to get in solid with her. Now, baton in hand, he tapped on the music stand propped in front of him and asked Irma, "Need some help?"

"What? Oh, sorry, no, I'm fine."

As she sang, she never lost eye contact with Fields. "I hope that he, turns out to be . . . someone to watch over . . ." Ramon Novarro walked into the room and she lost it again.

In contrast to the glamorous, inviting atmosphere downstairs, the air on the second floor was charged, like a storm ripping through a Kansas town.

"Where are Mrs. Smith's pearls?" the maid asked, panicky. "If we don't find them, there'll be hell to pay, I can guarantee you that! She's out for blood tonight."

"Alice!" Lily's voice boomed down the long hallway. "Hurry! Alice!"

"So, tell me my good man," Gaston Means said, "what is the source of your supply and will I die of alcohol poisoning later this evening?"

The bartender studied the pompous little man for a moment and then decided to take his comment as a joke. "Don't worry, sir, it will be a most pleasant death. Mrs. Armstrong-Smith only serves the best."

"Then I'll have a brandy." The man patted the bar, happy with his decision. "Yes, brandy."

After carefully pouring, the bartender slid the crystal glass toward the man. "There you go sir. Napoleon, the best we have. Enjoy."

He swirled the amber liquid around in the snifter. After a moment spent inhaling, he finally sipped. "Ahh, yes, excellent."

Truth be told, Mr. Means couldn't tell bad brandy from good, As he stood there, surveying the room, he watched the parade of celebrities pass by and felt confident he belonged. A gentleman came and stood beside him. Recognizing the voice, he turned. "Mr. Crosby." Means held out his hand. I'm a great fan of your trio, The Rhythm Boys. Allow me to introduce myself."

Bing Crosby started to shake hands until he heard the name Gaston Means, then quickly withdrew his hand. "Sorry, I don't associate with swindlers or spies."

"I beg your pardon?"

"You and your kind make me physically ill."

"But . . ."

"I've read all about you, Mr, Means. How you sold information on Allied shipping to the German embassy, were fired from the FBI, got yourself involved with that Ohio Gang scandal. Then without missing a beat, rolled around in the dirt with that Nan Britton woman."

"She hired me to investigate her husband . . ."

"*The President's Daughter*! You expect the American public to believe that a president of the United States fathered an illegitimate child?"

"He was a senator at the time . . ."

Crosby wasn't interested in anything Means had to say. "You, sir are a coward, benefiting from people's delusions . . ."

"But I assure you Miss Britton's claims are true!"

"Why don't you try doing something useful with your life?" After taking a minute to stare at Means with disgust, Crosby walked off.

It wasn't embarrassment that swirled around in Means's brain, no, it was disbelief. Hadn't H. L. Mencken written favorably about *The President's Daughter*? Right there in the Baltimore *Sun*? Who the hell was this Bing character anyway? What did some lousy crooner know about politics? Literature? Means shrugged and headed for the buffet table.

"Gee, Cal, when are we gonna get a break?" Irma asked. "My feet are killing me in these shoes." She pointed down to her new red satin pumps that had been custom-dyed to match the roses stitched across the black velvet of her chemise. While the band played, Irma fingered a spit curl which curlicued across her left cheek. "Come on, Cal, I need to sit down a minute," she whispered. "Be a pal, will ya?"

The last note of "Lady Be Good," ended when Cal brought his baton down. "Ladies and gentlemen, thank you for your enthusiasm. We're going to take a short break but don't worry, we'll be back to play more of your favorites in fifteen minutes."

A few people applauded but most seemed not to notice. "There, are ya happy?" he asked Irma.

"Yeah, thanks." It wasn't her feet that were hurting—it was her heart. She had to go meet Ramon Novarro. What a dream boat! As she hopped off this bandstand, her long string of pearls bounced in time with the matching earrings that hung almost to her shoulders.

✪ ✪ ✪

Judy McKeon hated her employer. If she could have gotten away with slitting the throat of that obnoxious cow, she would gladly have done so. But then she'd not only be out a big fat pay check each week, but have to clean up the mess as well.

"Juuudith! Come here this instant!"

Ordinarily, Judy would have run to help Lily (Mrs. Armstrong-Smith insisted she call her Lily). But this particular evening she wasn't feeling very helpful. As she rushed past the bedroom door she kept her eyes down and her mind set on escape. The party had started, the guests were sucking up the free hooch and one of the maids could surely tend to their demanding mistress.

"Gaston Bullock Means," he said as he shook the man's hand in almost a violent manner. He was sick and tired of being looked down on. "Author of *The President's Daughter*. You must have heard about the book. It's almost certain to become a bestseller."

The poor fellow had been in the middle of a conversation with the beautiful woman next to him when this imbecile interrupted him. His anger forced the truth to erupt from inside like a volcano. "I sir would never soil my hands let alone my intellect with such garbage. Besides, I thought that piece of trash was written by a woman."

"Well yes, Nan Britton and I did collaborate."

"Maybe you should mention that next time you introduce yourself. By saying you're the author gives the impression you had an original idea—did all the difficult work of writing yourself. Maybe next time . . ."

Means walked away.

A large man sat in the corner, alone. Means headed toward the loner to introduce himself. This time he would leave out the part about writing a book. All he wanted to do now was get drunk. The booze was free, the food exceptional. If he just kept his mouth shut he could have a good time.

After twenty minutes, Cal went looking for Irma. Aside from the ballroom and library, the first floor of the mansion was quiet. Walking through the French doors, he scanned the pergola which had been strung with red and gold lacquered Chinese lantern. A few couples stood admiring the view of Narragansett Bay. The air was cool and clean, the grass slightly damp. Even though an additional bar had been set up outside, the evening was too chilly to have many takers.

The bartender waved across the expansive lawn to the bandleader.

"You seen Irma anywheres?" Cal shouted.

The man pointed toward the water.

Cal walked across the lawn, wondering why on earth Irma would be out in the cold. He could hear water slapping against the rocks and as he wandered away from the artificial light of the lanterns, his pace slowed a bit while his eyes adjusted to the darkness beyond.

Finally, he was able to make out two figures. One, short—female, and one considerably larger—male. He stood there, conflicted. Not wanting to intrude, not wanting to walk any further in the dampness and dark. But even more anxious than ever to find his girl singer.

He started to shout out to the pair but was interrupted by the low bellowing from a nearby lighthouse. He waited, then shouted, "Irma!"

The female turned toward him. "Just a sec, Cal. I'm kinda busy here."

"No, Irma. You're on my time now, break's over!"

"Okay, okay!"

He turned and headed back to the house.

The crowd seemed to have grown considerably in the short time he had been outside. His men sat waiting impatiently for their instructions.

"Come on, Cal," the trumpet player complained. "Are we playin' or ain't we?"

"Quit your gripin'. You're gettin' paid, aren't ya? Whether you play or just sit back on your rented tails, you're gettin' paid."

Looking away, in the direction of the drums, Cal stood waiting for Irma, silently daring the musician to say another word.

The drummer, oblivious to the situation, stared out across the crowd.

"Fascinating Rhythm," Cal finally said. "And ah-one, ah-two." Bringing his baton down, he continued, "ah-three."

The band had only gotten a minute or so into the number when Irma appeared. Frantically, she scrambled across the small stage. Cal was too angry to notice the long tear in her dress.

"I'm sorry," she whispered.

Cal ignored her.

"Gee, give me a break, will ya?" she asked. "It was only a few minutes. So I got a little carried away. Come on, Cal, I said I was sorry. I promise it won't happen again."

Before he could respond, a woman pushed her way through the crowd.

The bandleader couldn't make out what she was shouting until she got closer.

"Mrs. Armstrong-Smith is missing!"

The musicians froze, conversations hung unfinished in the air.

"What do you mean by 'missing?'" W. C. Fields asked.

"I'm sure she's around here someplace," an older woman said, "You know how fond Lily is of surprises."

"She was upstairs in her bedroom just a moment ago."

"And who might you be?" Gaston Means asked.

The hysterical woman looked around, unsure who had asked the question and even more unsure if that person was speaking to her.

"Young woman," he started again, "calm down. And please, tell us just who in Sam Hill you think you are, coming in here shrieking like a banshee, ruining our—"

"Judith McKeon. I'm Mrs. Armstrong-Smith's personal secretary, sir, that's who the hell I am! And would you be so kind as to tell me why you're standing here wasting my time instead of helping me look for Mrs. Armstrong-Smith? She's vanished—maybe been kidnapped—or worse. We have to find her!"

Means approached the woman. "Surely your employer couldn't have just disappeared."

"But I saw her less than ten minutes ago. Well . . . I didn't see her . . . with my eyes. She was in her room, dressing and wanted her . . . ." That's when Judith's eyes settled on the sapphire clasp of Irma's pearls. Wide-eyed she pointed and screamed. "Those pearls! You stole them! They belong to Mrs. Armstrong-Smith!"

Irma was mortified. Clutching her throat she shook her head violently. "I didn't steal nothin'. These are mine!"

"What did she say?" someone asked.

"What's happening?" a lanky man sporting a pin striped suit wanted to know.

"Should we call the police?" one of the maids who had been serving hors d'oeuvres asked, after swallowing the small toast point and last bit of caviar she had swiped.

"No!" The large man standing near the French doors shouted, "No police!"

Everyone's attention turned. As he walked into the room, a unified gasp rose from the crowd.

"I can certainly understand your concern, Mr. Arbuckle," Judith began, "but I don't think . . . ."

"Fatty Arbuckle?" Gaston Means asked. "*The* Fatty Arbuckle? The man who killed that Rappé woman?"

"He was acquitted," Judith snapped.

"And if your memory is good enough to dredge up that poor woman's name after six years, then I'm sure you remember I was exonerated twice."

"Hey! He told me his name was William Goodrich," Irma explained to Cal. "He said he was a director."

Cal whistled through his teeth. "Yeah, honey, and I bet he told ya he could get ya in the moving pictures." As he spoke, Cal noticed the rip in Irma's dress. "Was he the one who did that?"

"Well . . . yes . . . but not like you . . ."

Cal walked to the microphone. "Miss McKeon, I suggest ya detain Mr. Arbuckle. He attacked my singer, here."

"What?"

"I did no such thing," the large man said. Sweat broke out across his forehead; his round face was slowly turning a deep crimson. "I would never do that!"

"He's right." Irma was now talking into the microphone. "Mr. Arbuckle and I was just talking. He was a perfect gentleman. And then we spotted the. . ." Irma stopped abruptly. Her eyes slammed shut and she stood there, head down, staring at the floor.

"Spotted what? What did you see?" Cal asked.

"Sorry, Mr. Arbuckle. Sometimes I can be a real dope."

Fatty had hoped for enough time to take care of his "situation." But when she had started to run for the house he had to stop her, grabbing for her arm. She was younger and quicker and all he had managed to do was rip her sleeve. The thing that had upset her the most about this incident was the damage to her dress. When he promised to not only replace it but throw in another with matching shoes and evening bag, she agreed to give him half an hour to take care of things.

"I think I know where Lily is," he slowly told the crowd.

"Well, for God's sake tell me," Judith demanded. "I've spent days putting this party together and now, maybe, some of the evening can be salvaged."

"If one of the men will go with me," Fatty suggested, "we can escort Lily . . ."

"Anything. Do whatever you want. As long as she's not been kidnapped."

"No, I can assure you she hasn't," Fatty told her.

"Fine, then." Judith McKeon pivoted around on the heels of her practical shoes, annoyed, and marched out of the room. "Just like that old cow," she muttered to herself. "Selfish, ungrateful . . ."

"Mr. Means?" Fatty said. "If you would be so kind as to come with me."

"And just what are the rest of us supposed to do?" Bing asked.

"Eat, drink and be merry. Isn't that why we're here?" Fatty asked.

"I suppose it is," the crooner answered. Then, turning to Cal, he said, "Play something light. How about a Charleston?"

"Sure thing, Mr. Crosby."

As the music started up again, Means and Arbuckle headed through the ornate doors. When they had crossed the patio and stepped into the plush grass, Means asked his companion, "Why me?"

"Because we are two of a kind, I suppose."

"How can you say that? Before tonight, we've never met."

"Not face to face, you're right about that. However, I am very well acquainted with your reputation, Mr. Means. We both have scandalous backgrounds. And it's that fear of being disgraced again that puts us on our best behavior."

Means stopped dead. "So, if each of us in on his best behavior, then it stands to reason we are the most honorable of all the men—or women—here."

"Exactly. Now, follow me. I want to show you something."

The men continued walking in the direction of the jagged shoreline. The only light guiding their way came from the full moon.

"There." Arbuckle pointed. "See her?"

Means studied the area he was being shown. After a moment he was able to differentiate between rock, sand, water and a human form. He gasped. "Is that? No . . ." He leaned as far as he dared. "It can't be."

"I spotted her while talking to that girl with the band. Of course she went all hysterical. She even started to run back into the party. Well, I wasn't even sure it was Lily down there . . ."

"And you couldn't afford another scandal, now, could you, Mr. Goodrich?"

"Come on," Fatty said, removing a cigarette from a silver case. "We both know I can't use my real name if I want to work in the movies. The Hays office saw to that."

"Cleaning up Hollywood. There's a good one for you," Means said. "The town's crawling with hookers and drugs, bootleg hooch—"

"Men like William Randolph Hearst who flaunts his mistress, men who think nothing of the lives they ruin. No, nothing matters to them except money," Fatty said with contempt. "You certainly are aware of the kind of diseased vermin making huge profits in the film industry, Mr. Means. So you can certainly understand why I tried delaying Irma's exit."

Means nodded. "Well, I guess we should get down there and see if that is in fact our hostess before worrying about what decisions need to be made."

"How do we do that without causing a riot?" Arbuckle asked. "You're the investigator. The ex-FBI man. What do we do?"

"We're not alone in our need for propriety, Arbuckle. Why, just from the misfortune that has befallen the two of us, every single person in that house knows how easily their careers can tumble down around them and their families. We have to go back in there and stoke that fear."

It was as if they had all forgotten about Lily completely. When the two men entered the grand ballroom, not one guest turned to ask them what had become of her. The music was loud, the glasses were full and the majority of voices were competing for attention. Gaston Means walked the length of the room alone without attracting one glance.

When he had come to what looked to be the library, he was met by a butler.

"May I help you, sir?"

"Please get Miss McKeon for me."

"Certainly, sir." The elderly man bowed and slowly, as if each step caused pain, walked out of the room.

She must have been just down the hall, because Judith McKeon returned within a moment.

"Well? Where is she?"

"I assume Lily . . . Mrs. Armstrong-Smith has a gardener on the premises? A caretaker?" Means asked.

"Yes, William. He lives in the cottage up the road."

"Call him. I need his help."

"May I ask . . ."

"You may not. Call him and tell him to meet me by that dead evergreen near the cliffwalk. Tell him to bring a lantern and a rake."

"Fine."

"Oh, and Miss McKeon," he said, looking up at the tall woman, "I'll need you to stay close by."

She glared down at him as if he were an imbecile. "I live here, Mr. Means. Where else would I go?"

❁ ❁ ❁

"That's her, all right," William said as he watched Means drape Lily's body with a tablecloth. "I kept telling Mrs. Armstrong-Smith that she should put a fence up along here. But she'd just laugh. Told me it would detract from the 'wildness' of this place. Can you believe that?" he asked, eyeing Arbuckle as he approached. "Wildness? After all the money she poured into this property? After the landscapers and architects, builders, fancy artists? There ain't nothin' wild left out here except maybe that water down there."

"Thank you, William," Means said when Arbuckle was standing next to him. "Please, don't say anything to alarm the staff. We'll have Miss McKeon send for the doctor who will in turn, no doubt, send for the police."

"Whatever you say, Mr. Means. But I want it on the record that I warned her many times. She was very headstrong; she didn't listen to many people."

Means nodded, watching Fatty bend over to lift the cloth from Lily's face. "I'll make sure the authorities are made aware of your concerns."

"That's all I'm asking, Mr. Means." William removed his cap from his jacket pocket and pulled it down over his thinning hair. "That's all I'm asking." Satisfied that he was blameless, William quickly walked back to his cottage.

Fatty stood up. "She fell, then? But I don't understand why . . ."

Means waited until William was out of sight. "That's what I thought at first. And that's exactly what I want William to believe. At least for the time being. But if you'll look closely at her neck you can see the bruises."

Fatty slowly lowered his hefty frame again. Means held the lantern closer to the body. "Well, I'll be. You can see the imprints of hands, right there, plain as day."

"The person who did this had to be very strong."

Fatty wheezed as he stood up. "How do you know that?"

"Well, not only did they strangle Lily but they dragged her body all the way out here. How do you suppose they did that? Without being seen?"

"What makes you so sure she didn't come out here on her own? Maybe she just wanted some fresh air."

"Not likely. She'd be getting ready for her party. You know how much she looked forward to these productions of hers. Besides, did you happen to notice she only has on one shoe? And her stockings are worn away only on the heels."

"So? Maybe she didn't have new stockings for the party. And her other shoe probably came off when she was thrown into the water."

"No, if I'm not mistaken, that's it over there."

The two men walked toward the object Means pointed out. Holding the lantern close to the ground, it was easy to see a black velvet pump half buried in the soft earth. "Whoever killed Lily had to be strong enough to drag her out here."

"I don't like the way you're looking at me, Means." Fatty was angry. "I thought we were in this together."

"Relax, I didn't mean that to sound like an accusation. I'm just thinking out loud."

"So what do we do now? We have to go back in there."

Means looked toward the mansion. "And we have to convince everyone to trust us enough so they don't leave until we can figure out who killed Lily."

"Why does everyone have to stay for us to do that?" Fatty asked.

Means brushed off his jacket. "Because, Arbuckle, what we both fear the most will happen quicker than you ever imagined. If you thought you had troubles before, wait until you see what they do to you now. Both of us have been put through the grinder, had our reputations ruined. But somehow, we managed to make lives for ourselves again."

"Yeah, things are a helluva lot better than they were a few years ago."

"And I have the new book," Means said. "But this, getting our names connected to a murder? This would bury us alive! There'd be no coming back . . . ever."

Fatty didn't understand what Means had planned; all he knew was he was scared. "Okay," he said, "just tell me what to do." He reached in his pocket and pulled out a large handkerchief to blot the sweat.

"What time is it?" Means asked.

"I don't know." Fatty shrugged.

"But you have a pocket watch. There," Means pointed to the chain hanging from Arbuckle's gray flannel vest.

Arbuckle looked down, embarrassed. "That's just for show. I had to hock the watch years ago."

Means didn't care about his companion's sad financial state. "Well, I imagine we've only been out here for twenty minutes—half an hour at the most. From the sound of things inside, I don't think we've even been missed."*

When Irma saw Arbuckle enter the brightly lit room, she immediately thought of Lon Chaney. The way he'd contorted his face—his whole body— when he played the Hunchback of Notre Dame had given her the willies for days. His eyes bugging out that way. Poor Fatty, she thought. He looked so ill-at-ease that she felt deeply sorry for him. The lights made his skin look waxy. She stopped singing without realizing she had done so. And when she stopped, the band stopped. And when the musicians broke off so abruptly, everyone in the room froze.

It was Zelda Fitzgerald who came to life first. "So," she giggled, apparently drunk, "where is our little Lily? Our precious little flower? Our lovely, lost Lily?" Her laughter embarrassed practically everyone in the room.

Gaston Means walked onto the dance floor. "Gather around," he said. "I have an announcement."

"Oh, a game! We're going to play a game!" Zelda clapped her hands together.

"Hush," someone shouted.

"You wouldn't talk to me like that if Scott were here." She took another gulp of her drink and then retreated into a pout.

"But he's not, so kindly hush up," the same person told her.

Satisfied he had their attention, Means began. "First off, is Miss McKeon here?"

"I certainly am," she said as she walked over to stand beside him.

"Good. What I am about to tell you is very upsetting but I want you all to remain calm and quiet until I've finished."

Judith straightened her back and folded her arms across her chest. "Just tell us, Mr. Means, we're not children."

"Our hostess is . . ."

"Dead! I knew it!" Irma said.

The crowd ignored the singer and continued staring at Means as if she hadn't spoken.

"She's right, I'm afraid. Lily must have fallen. We found her body down in the water."

"How terrible," Judith said.

Disbelief ricocheted around the room, hitting each guest in their gut, then their heart. Shock, then commotion. "Dreadful!" "Unbelievable." "How very awful." "Poor Lily."

Fatty looked at Means, confused.

Means motioned for him to remain quiet. Then turning to Judith, he asked, "Do you have a guest list?"

"In my office. I'll go get it."

Several people asked the butler for their coats. Means hurried over to the servant and told him to stay where he was. "Listen. Please. No one can leave here yet."

"The party's over, as they say, old chum," Bing said, slapping the man on the back.

"The police have to be called," Means said. His words quieted the room.

"Then we should clear out so they can do their work. Write up their reports. Whatever it is they do." Dorothy Parker walked to the bar and sat her empty glass on a coaster.

Judith returned with the list and handed it to Means. He held it over his head. "I have the names of every person in this room and I'm going to check to see if we're all here."

An elderly woman wearing a diamond choker timidly asked, "But what does that matter? Lily had an accident and . . ."

"It wasn't an accident!" Arbuckle shouted from his side of the huge room.

"Is this true?" Judith asked.

"Well, possibly. Maybe. I believe her death was caused by someone other than . . . herself."

Fatty came closer. "He means she was murdered."

"I have to get out of here," W. C. Fields said. "I can't be associated with any of you. Look what happened to ole Fatty there. No, no, this would definitely ruin me. Excuse me, but I must be on my way."

"Sorry, Mr. Fields. That is precisely why you should not leave. We must all stay here and be accounted for. There is strength in numbers. If we all remain calm and vouch for each other, we're safe."

"Then tell me, my good man," Fields asked, looking down at Means with disgust, "why did you tell us Lily succumbed to an accident when in fact she was murdered?"

"I'll tell you why," Fatty said, "because he was a hot shot with the FBI, then a private investigator after he got involved in one too many scandals. Now he's looking to solve a murder—make the headlines and a new name for himself. Think all will be forgiven, Mr. Means? Think you can write a brand new book about the murder of Lillian Armstrong-Smith?"

Means was the confused one now. "No, why would you ask me that? I thought we had an agreement? An understanding of sorts."

"I did too until you lied to me out there, when you showed me Lily's shoe."

"What do you mean?"

"Oh, I know you think I'm just a big, fat, dumb clown. Everyone does. But I'm real good at what I do. I spent years practicing falls, tumbling, figuring out where arms and legs land when you chase someone. Hell, I did nothing else for hours at a time with the Keystone Cops. I'm a professional, Mr. Means, and damn good at what I do---did.

"The shoe you showed me was dug deep into the ground. If someone dragged Lily, as you assumed they did, her shoe would have slid off and fallen away—not pushed down into the soil. For the shoe to end up where and how we found it, would have meant one of three things: someone pushed her forward, she walked to that place willingly, or she was running away from her attacker. However, it was you who found the shoe, in the dark. Odd, considering I had been out on the grounds in the yard—on that very spot---earlier and missed it. Imagine! In the light of the full moon, I missed a silver object the size of a shoe, sparkling there—like a spotlight. Therefore, I can only assume you planted it yourself, Mr. Means."

Means fell down into a plush club chair forcing it against the wall. "All right, I admit I put the shoe there, but only after I'd stumbled over it earlier."

"Why would you do such a thing?" Judith asked, stunned.

Embarrassed to look the woman in the eye, he spoke slowly. "I needed to be believed."

"You mean admired," Fatty said. "You thought this was just the opportunity you needed to regain some credibility."

"Is that true?" Bing asked.

"Yes," Means said, still too cowardly to look up. "I worked for the FBI. I had respect, a position close to the president of the United States. The most powerful man in the world."

"And you brought disgrace down upon yourself," Bing ranted. "You brought disgrace to your office and your country. There is no one to blame for your misfortunes except you, sir."

"I know. Don't you think I know all that?"

"So," Judith said, "let me see if I understand this. You took Mrs. Armstrong-Smith's death as an opportunity to benefit yourself?"

Dorothy Parker sniffed. "Typical man, you'll always land on somebody's feet."

Judith McKeon shook her head. "Poor Mrs. Armstrong-Smith."

"Oh come now, you hated her . . ." Arbuckle's fat hand swiftly clamped over his mouth.

Means's head jerked upward to look at the secretary. "You did?" And then shifting his eyes to Arbuckle he asked, "How would you know something like that? Have you met Miss McKeon before this evening?"

"Well, yes, and . . ." He looked to the woman contritely.

"It's okay, Roscoe, I'm not ashamed of our friendship."

"Friendship? This is all so cozy I can't stand it," Parker quipped.

"Miss McKeon wrote me several letters while I was going through my ah, trouble."

"Fan letters?" Means asked.

"It started out that way," Judith told them. "I was infatuated with . . ."

"A star. It happens all the time," Crosby said. "But the papers, magazines, they were full of stories. All the gory details. Weren't you afraid you were corresponding with a murderer?"

Judith looked at Fatty adoringly, "Oh, no. I could tell Roscoe would never hurt anyone. He's a gentle, kind, sensitive soul."

"And you could tell all of this from . . . what?" Bing asked. "What ever led you to believe you knew this man so intimately . . . unless . . ."

"No! Don't even think it! Nothing happened between the two of us."

Means studied the guest list he had gotten from Judith. "I notice here that your name is not among those invited, Mr. Arbuckle,"

"And if you look closer, Mr. Means, neither is yours," Judith pointed out.

"I don't understand."

"I invited you: both of you. It was easy just to slip in a few extra guests, being responsible for the invitations and all. Mrs. Armstrong-Smith never saw what went out in the mail or what I didn't want her to know came back."

Dorothy Parker finished her martini, held the empty glass up to attract a waitress. "So why the invites?" she asked.

W. C. Fields laughed. "Life is certainly a stage and how we all do strut. Our little lady here set us up. We were all here for her entertainment. Isn't that so, my dear?"

"No. I just wanted to see Roscoe. I knew he'd never consent to meet me otherwise. So I spoke through Mrs. Armstrong-Smith. But it wasn't as if she would have appreciated a man like you," she said to Arbuckle. "Truth is, she always thought you were a killer."

"So knowing what her reaction would be at the very sight of me, you wanted to shock her? Upset her?" Arbuckle's face fell into a soft frown.

"It's terrible," Judith admitted. "I know it's unforgivable but, Lord help me, as much as I wanted to be with you, I wanted to see her uncomfortable more. I wanted to see her frightened."

Cal walked over, Irma trailing behind. "Miss McKeon, should I tell the boys they can pack up and go home? Or do we have to wait around for the police?"

Judith was glad for the interruption. "What do you suggest we do, Mr. Means?"

"Why in Sam Hill are you asking that imbecile?" W. C. Fields wanted to know.

"Because he's the closest thing we have right now to any kind of law."

"Law by association? That's rich." Parker laughed.

"Tell your band to hang around," Means addressed Cal, ignoring Dorothy.

"Sure thing." Cal turned to leave and Judith spotted the necklace around Irma's neck.

"Hold on a minute, you." She grabbed Irma by the arm. "Just where did you get those pearls?"

Means stood up and advanced on the woman, hoping to frighten her into an answer.

"Cal gave them to me. Honest! I ain't no thief, I'm a good girl!"

The bandleader started for the French doors. Means chased after him.

A group of drinkers sitting in lawn chairs laughed as Means shouted for help. It was Novarro who ended up tackling the man.

"Get offa me!" Cal shouted to the actor. Then to Means, "I found them. Honest, Mr, Means. Over there. I swear! Just go ask that guy." He pointed to the bartender stationed under a green awning.

"Bring him over here," Means told Novarro.

Grabbing the man by the collar of his tuxedo jacket, the actor dragged Cal across the lawn.

The bartender smiled, oblivious to the commotion. His attention had been focused on one of the attractive waitresses. "What'll it be, gentlemen?" he asked when he saw them.

"The gentleman here," Means said pointing to Cal, "claims he found a strand of pearls out here and that you can vouch for his story."

"Name's Howard Pearson, sir, and no, I'm sorry but I never saw any such thing. I'm afraid he's lying to you."

Cal's shoulders went limp. Novarro released his hold but stood close. "Come on, Howard, tell them how I found those damn pearls right over there." Cal pointed to a spot near the cliffwalk. "Ya saw me. I showed ya them. Ya acted like you didn't know where they came from, that ya'd never seen them before."

Howard rubbed his chin, the stubble looked like dirt stuck to his face. "Sorry, Cal."

Before anyone could stop him, Cal lunged across the bar and grabbed the bartender. "I thought we were friends here, Howard. Ya told me if I covered up for you, I could have the pearls for Irma. Ya told me . . ."

"Get him off me," Howard grunted.

Hearing the commotion, Judith McKeon came running, leaving the rest of the party inside, watching the scene as if it were a moving picture. "Howard," she said jerking to a stop. "I didn't know you were here."

"Isn't he one of the bartenders you hired?" Means asked.

"I called the agency and they sent over some people. I've used Howard in the past. There's never been any trouble before. We have a good working relationship."

Howard pushed himself away from the men. "Working relationship? Judith, we both know it was a hell of lot more than that."

Before she could speak, Means addressed the man. "Tell us how you would define your relationship with Miss McKeon."

"I have connections, know what I mean? I'm very popular with the upper crust, especially in these difficult times. Understand what I'm saying here? I can get alcohol—illegal hooch. High quality and lots of it. I've helped her out on more than one occasion."

"That's true," Judith said. "Mrs. Armstrong-Smith is very demanding and when she wants something I either accommodate her or I'm not only out of a job, but as she has threatened many times, never going to find work in this country."

"It's a big world out there, Miss McKeon," Means said, "and I'm sure an intelligent woman such as yourself . . ."

"You don't understand how influential Mrs. ArmstrongSmith is . . . I mean was. And excuse me, Mr. Means, but you of all people should understand how difficult it is to start over with a questionable reputation. It follows you everywhere. I've watched it happen over and over again."

Means nodded. "You're right; I do understand." Turning to Howard he asked, "So you've done some favors for Miss McKeon from time to time, and worked as a bartender at a few parties. That's all there is to it, then?"

"Yes," Judith answered. "That's all."

"And when did you last see the pearls?" he asked her.

"Days ago. In fact, Mrs. Armstrong-Smith was still looking for them earlier this evening."

"Cal, do you want to stick to your story or are we calling the police now? I think we can drum up a burglary charge if not murder."

"Okay, no police. I swiped them—so what? I didn't know they were hers. I didn't know who they belonged to."

"Explain," Novarro said, anxious to hear the man's story.

"I got here earlier this afternoon to check things out—set up. I saw the pearls on the floor in the hall. I picked them up, put them in my pocket, and gave them to Irma. Thought maybe I'd get lucky after we were done tonight."

"And if Irma got caught wearing them, she'd be the one in trouble, right?"

"To be honest, I never thought that far ahead. I had other things on my mind."

Arbuckle joined the group in the middle of Cal's story. "Let's go back inside," Judith suggested. "It's getting cold out here."

Means stood fixed in thought. "You never saw Mrs. Armstrong-Smith leave the house?" he asked Judith.

"No, I told you, the last I heard she was getting dressed in her room."

"What side of the house is your room on?"

"The opposite side."

"Why? Wouldn't she want you close by?"

"Yeah, you were always telling me what a tyrant she was," Fatty said.

"Precisely, that's why I insisted I be in the other wing. I needed some privacy. I do have a personal life."

"I'll say," Howard laughed.

Everyone turned.

"Shut up, Howard!" Judith snapped.

"Shut up! Go away! Be quiet! I'm sick of your orders, Judy. You can't treat me like that anymore."

Means saw his opportunity and sympathetically asked the man, "Like what, Howard? Does she treat you badly? Women can be so . . ."

"She's a bitch! She lies to me; she treats me like a dog."

"But you love her anyway, right?" Means asked.

"Yes, but she loves someone else."

Means turned to Arbuckle. "Did Miss McKeon ever confess her love for you in any of her letters?"

"Well . . ."

"Come on, man, no one can hold you responsible for what another person writes."

"Occasionally she would say something along those lines."

"And you told me you loved me, too," Judith said. "Tell them. Tell everyone now how much you love me and how we're going to be together. Forever! That's what you said . . . forever!"

"And just how did you expect that to happen, girlie, when you was with me?" Howard shouted. "All the time telling me how that bitch boss of yours was the only thing keepin' us from being together and now I find out you was writing this fat man, planning to be with him. But I was the one who got rid of . . ."

"Continue, Mr. Pearson," Means insisted. "You were the one who got rid of who?"

"No one."

"Call the police," Means told Judith.

She didn't move. It took a moment but when she spoke she erupted. "You, Howard? You killed Mrs. Armstrong-Smith?"

"For you, Judy. For us."

Howard jumped over the bar and started for the cliffwalk. Arbuckle and Novarro were on his heels. The smaller man tripped him and Arbuckle pinned him to the ground.

Judith ran inside for the phone.

"Gaston Bullock Means," he told the reporter. "M . . . e . . . a . . . n . . . s."

"I've heard that name before. Wait a minute. Don't tell me." The pretty young thing was anxious to get all her facts straight.

"I used to work with the president; I was with the FBI." He beamed.

"And now you've solved a murder!" she said.

"I guess I was just born to be of service to my fellow man."

"Well jeepers, Mr. Means, I can't thank you enough for talking to me. None of the other people at Mrs. Armstrong-Smith's party will give me the time of day."

"Don't mention it, my dear. Don't mention it."

DR. SULLIVAN'S LIBRARY

It was always there in the eyes. Close to the surface. And after sixteen years of looking into so many of them, ever respectful of each life spread out in front of him, he started cataloguing his patients.

Romances took slow, lazy blinks. Soulful eyes fringed with long ashes, usually. Smoky colored eyes hiding secret passion. *Biographies* were self-involved, so very insecure. Always looking for a mirror on the wall or rummaging through a purse for a compact. Wondering how they measure up, comparing everything they do to what the next guy's done. *Westerns*: Like an old Gene Autry movie, everything for them is in black and white. In their world, only two groups of people exist: good guys and bad guys. When they make a decision, they stick to it. No in-betweens—no going back. Intolerant eyes, opinionated, arched eyebrows. Now *Science Fictions* were the complete opposites of Westerns. Gullible, lonely. They joined support groups, tried every fad diet, sent hard-earned money or savings to televangelists. Contradicting what he'd originally thought to be the case, this group had the least imagination or creativity. It took a few years, but Dr. Maxwell Sullivan finally learned that those who lived, worked, and vacationed outside the box were *Mysteries*. Colored lenses covered their naturalness. They thought before speaking, took nothing at face value; whenever he ran into a wall, he was usually dealing with a Mystery.

As he flipped on the light, he perused his calendar, looking for his favorite type of Mystery. Not just a nice, uncomplicated Who-dun-it, no, today he desperately needed a *Thriller*.

"Mr. Hargrove, please, have a seat."

Sid Hargrove sat. The brown pin-striped suit jacket stretched across his broad shoulders. The white shirt looked as though he had just unwrapped it, fresh from the cleaners. His tie—art deco, a twenties kind of look. It all worked.

Dr. Max Sullivan sat behind his desk, facing the man. "So," he leaned back, studied the man a moment, then said, "tell me about yourself. "

"No."

"You are aware, Mr. Hargrove, that I've been appointed by the court?"

"Yes."

"So you're going to have to talk to me sooner or later. . . ."

"Look, I don't have a problem. This is all nuts. That ex-wife of mine, talk about your nut jobs, she was one of the biggest. But that was over twelve years ago."

"Then how did this domestic incident occur? Why were you at her home?" It was all there in the file, but it was better coming from the patient. Each word carried emotion. Each emotion carried clues.

"It wasn't anything like she told the cops. I have friends in the neighborhood. That's all. That's the only reason I was there at all."

"What about Jessica?"

"I get her on the weekends."

"And this 911 call was made on a Wednesday."

"I stick to the rules. I don't need no more judges telling me how much and for how long I gotta kiss that bitch's ass just to get to spend time with my kid."

"Your daughter's ten years old."

"Yeah. She's beautiful. And smart. Always on the honor roll. Amazing, isn't it, how something so beautiful can come out of a slut like her mother."

"So, if you were just in the neighborhood, how did you end up in your wife's—"

"Ex-wife."

Max leafed through the papers. "Judy. How did you end up inside her house, beating her up?"

"It ain't like she said."

He never flinched. Steady. He was lying, and damn good at it. According to the latest statistics, one in every twenty-five people have no conscience. The number was staggering, even to him. It was unbelievable that of the seventy-six patients he had seen in the last two years, three of them were cold. Unfeeling, uncaring, and detached. Experience showed him those three could not be reached. They'd play with him and he'd play right back, cashing their checks or the state's or the insurance company's, and try not to think about them once the hour was up. Three.

Two more to go.

❀ ❀ ❀

Madeline Whitney. History of manic depression, migraines, lapses in memory that she attributed to alien abductions. After their second session, he'd catalogued her as a *Gothic*. Easy to tears, drooping lids that half-covered gray eyes. Colorless, odorless, she instigated her own sadness and wore it like a coat of armor. Rusty armor. Even if someone pried her out of that suit, she'd crawl right back in. It was the only safe place she knew. Comfortable in the discomfort.

"Why did you cancel our last session?"

"I couldn't get out of bed. Look at my arm."

"What happened?"

"It wasn't there when I went to bed last night."

"Maybe you did it in your sleep. Sometimes my fingernail snags—"

"No. We both know it wasn't that."

She did it all for attention. We do everything for the attention, don't we?

"Madeline, does it sound logical to you that while you sleeping someone—"

"Or something—"

"—came into your house, walked into your bedroom without waking you, cut your arm and then just left?"

"Yes . . . it does."

He adjusted his glasses. "Do you remember when we talked about how normal actions result in logical reactions?"

Her neck seemed to suddenly be made of rubber, enabling her to lift her head even further from her rigid body.

"How many times must I tell you not to say my first name? To you I'm Mrs. Whitney. If we are to ever figure out how all these terrible things are happening, why I out of millions of people in this world have been singled out, if we are ever able to go to the authorities, you must remain objective. Professional. Please, I'm recording this session like all the rest, and if you keep crossing that line, that spiderweb line separating hired help from friend, we'll never be able to present an accurate, scientific thesis."

Six months he had been seeing her, and still she ranted. The more she spoke, the more anxiety filled each word. Breathing exercises hadn't worked, visualization, medication, nothing seemed to cut through her paranoia. He studied her eyes. The belief was still dominant. She took cover behind every strange word she uttered. And that total belief released her from any responsibility for her own actions. No fault ever landed on her doorstep. No fault equaled no guilt. The purity of her delusion made her almost perfect.

Almost.

Before making his decision, however, he had to see Owen Sawyer.

❋ ❋ ❋

Sunday dinner with the family.

"Max, sweetheart." She hugged him so tightly, her gardenia perfume fouled his collar. "I made your favorite. Are you alone?" Every week she asked.

Every week he was alone.

No need answering.

She took the bottle of wine he offered. "Daddy's in the basement. Fooling with those damned trains of his. Go have a visit while I finish up the salad."

As Max clomped down the wooden stairs, the sound of miniature wheels racing along metal tracks made him smile. The first train set had been one of those cheap things that circled the Christmas tree. No landscaping, no toy commuters, only one cardboard drugstore cut out from a box top and folded into shape. But it had hooked them. The next year, Max had bought a plaster house with money he'd saved from his allowance, with white glitter glued to the roof. To his eight-year-old eyes, it had looked like real snow and when the Christmas tree bulbs flashed on and off . . . wow. By the third year a real scale-model train looped and raced through station after station in the basement.

"Hey! Get in here, mister fancy doctor." Big Max held his arms open. Max smiled and carefully gathered the frail man into a hug. "You look good, Pop."

"Liar."

"Do I look like I'm lying?" He stepped back to give his father direct access to his eyes.

"All's I can tell you is, never play poker. They'd cut you to pieces and then play with them pieces until there weren't nuthin' left."

"Nice image, Pop. You always did have a way with words."

He shrugged. "It's a gift."

Max dragged a metal stool over to a spot next to his father. Big Max lifted an engineer's cap off the desk behind him and pulled it down onto his son's head. Forty-five years old, and Max still got a kick out of it.

It was nice. The two of them sitting together, the aroma of meatloaf spicing the air around them. As Max gazed across the large table covered with green felt and miles of track, some peace started to filter down through his tension. But then Big Max had to go and spoil it.

"How's it comin'? You know. How much longer 'til you decide somethin'?"

Owen Sawyer twitched. When he was in the office, Max made sure this patient stretched out on the couch, otherwise, once that foot of his started shaking, furniture rattled, lamps flickered—it all made Max slightly nauseous.

A *Travelogue*. Just as a joke to himself, Max had likened this particular patient to a travel book only because of his constant movement. When they'd met for the first time, Sawyer had rocked back and forth in his chair for the full hour. The even, incessant, maddening motion had started an end table vibrating, causing a vase to finally crash to the floor. Traveling. Unsettled.

But after six months of reading the man, Max had learned he was a total contradiction to what he'd originally thought. He'd never seen such a calm person. Dead calm inside. Thoughtful, even, emotionless. Secrets lived deep down inside that psyche. So deep that Max hadn't been able to shine the tiniest bit of light on any of it in all the time he'd been working with Sawyer. And he'd worked especially hard with the man. But something else bothered him . . . something he'd never mentioned to a colleague or noted in his file. Owen Sawyer frightened him. Max struggled with himself, re-examined his compassion, fought this irrational fear. But then he had his own breakthrough and reclassified Sawyer as *True Crime*.

By the time Sawyer was fourteen, both of his parents were also in therapy. For his fifteenth birthday, he decided to treat himself and stole both his brother's car and his nineteen-year-old girlfriend and headed for the liquor store. When the clerk refused to sell either of the teens alcohol, they'd beaten the man and grabbed all the beer they could carry in addition to one hundred seventeen dollars from the register. It only took the police an hour to track down the car and haul the two off to jail.

In and out of juvenile court, Sawyer had developed a cocaine habit that never went away. Today, at forty-two, he worked as a dishwasher at a cafe one town over. Married twice, divorced twice, no children. Apparently no one could stand the man.

"What would you like to talk about today, Mr. Sawyer?"

"You know what, Doc?"

"No, what?"

"I don't know a damn thing about you."

Max scrutinized Sawyer's wet grin. "You're not paying me to tell you—"

"You're supposed to make me feel better, right? Talking to you is therapy?"

"Yes."

"So, spill your guts. Ahh, come on, Doc. I could use a good laugh. It'll make me feel better. Promise."

Those eyes. Calculating. Trying to undo him. Make him doubt himself. Max felt his face flush with hatred for Owen Sawyer.

☆ ☆ ☆

Time was running out. As Max watched the timer count down one last minute on the treadmill, he wondered what the hell he was going to tell his father. Or even worse, how would he handle his mother?

Heading for the locker room, his only thought was of a hot shower. Clear his head and his body. Almost there, he spotted the vending machine and was struck with the urgent need for a soda. Unzipping the pocket of his sweatpants, hoping to come up with exact change, he caught parts of a conversation between two women coming from somewhere around the corner.

"That slimy sonofabitch. I'd like to hang him up by his balls. And while he's squirming up there on that meat hook, screaming for me to let him down, I'll ask him, calmly, if he's sorry for all the shit he's put me through."

"That's so mean."

"Whose side are ya on, here? You know all the crap he's pulled on me."

Max thought he recognized one of the voices.

"Imagine it, the bastard's hangin' there, beggin', and I tell him to bite me. No mercy for that fuckin' creep."

"Yeah, he deserves whatever he gets. More, even."

"But he begs. An' keeps on cryin'. And I say, 'No. Never. You lose.' An' I start cuttin'."

Laughter and then she saw him. "Oh, Dr. Sullivan, I didn't know you were—"

"Jeanine, hi."

"Kelly, this is Dr. Sullivan. Dr. Sullivan, this is my friend Kelly."

"Hi." He gave her a quick smile.

"The boss," Kelly said. "I've heard a lot about you."

He didn't ask what she'd heard because he was looking at Jeanine, wondering how she could be smiling so sweetly at him now, when just a second ago she'd been so brutal, so crude.

"I've never seen you here before," his receptionist said demurely.

"I joined last week."

"Well, I'm sure it's just to stay in the shape you're in; you certainly don't need to lose one pound."

"Thanks." Was she flirting, he wondered.

"And your hair," she tucked a damp curl behind his ear, "it looks sexy all messed up like that."

Yep, she was flirting.

"Jeanine, where's my three-o'clock?"

"She just called; she'll be fifteen minutes late."

Max snapped off the intercom. Passive-aggressive. He of all people should know what his patient was doing. But waste aggravated him the most. And the older he got, the less forgiving he became of those who wasted his time. He'd have to work on that, especially in his profession.

He got up to tell Jeanine to charge Mrs. Hornberger for the full hour plus an extra hundred to teach her a lesson. As he opened the door a crack, he stopped.

"You know the rules, Mr. Hargrove. Your appointments are always on Tuesday. Today is Thursday—"

"Get out of my way, you dumb bitch. I need to see the doctor and I'm going in there."

Max pulled the door open enough so he could watch what was happening.

Jeanine threw her stapler at the back of the man's head and then raced around her desk. "What did you call me, asshole? Who the hell do you think you are?"

Like a whip snapping, Hargrove turned and slapped Jeanine across the face. "I'll have your job for what you did. I'm bleedin' here."

Max stood fascinated, hoping Jeanine didn't need rescuing—not just yet.

"You like to beat up women, don't you? I type up all the Doctor's reports and I know all about you. I've dated bums just like you. You're weak. Just an overweight, stupid, fucked-up bully!"

Hargrove's face reddened. It was glorious to watch. This bout with Jeanine would do him more good than months of therapy. Max almost rushed in when he saw the man make a move toward Jeanine, but then realized she was all over him. She pulled her arm back and whacked the man across his pock-marked cheek. The sound was thrilling.

"That's it, lady, you're dead."

Jeanine grabbed her letter opener. "A threat? You assaulted and then threatened me! Now you can either get the hell out of here or wait while I call the police. What'll it be?"

"Sullivan!" Hargrove shouted. "Doctor Sullivan!"

Max hesitated long enough to give the impression he'd been clear on the other side of his office, seated behind his desk when the commotion started.

"What?" He even managed a look of surprise at seeing Jeanine holding a long, silver letter opener up near Hargrove's neck. "What on earth—"

"Either you fire this whore, or I'll have your license. She should never work in a doctor's office. With sick people. Fragile people. . . ."

No apologies. Jeanine stood defiant. "Fragile, my ass!"

And that's when Maxwell Sullivan knew he was in love.

❀ ❀ ❀

Sunday dinner with the family.

"Max, sweetheart." She hugged him close. No gardenia perfume this week, his mother's cheek felt slick and smelled of suntan lotion. A sure sign she had been working in the garden before starting dinner.

"I'm making lasagna. Hope you're hungry. Are you alone?" Expecting no answer, she turned back to the stove.

"No, Mom, I'm not." Max waved for Jeanine to come into the kitchen from the living room, where he'd left her.

Gracie Sullivan turned around to see her son standing next to an attractive redhead.

"And who have we here? Come on, don't be shy." She held out her arms.

Jeanine obliged with a polite hug. "Hi. I'm Jeanine. Max's secretary. It's nice to meet you, Mrs. Sullivan.'

"Let's have a good look at you."

Max watched as the women sized each other up and was surprised that his mother's premature familiarity wasn't putting Jeanine off in the slightest. In fact, she seemed amused. Good. Today had to go well.

"So? Where have you been keeping her, Max?"

"Be gentler, Mom, this is only our sixth date and if you keep this up, it'll be our last."

"Oh, no, I don't think so. She seems pretty sturdy to me."

Jeanine smiled.

"No, honey, go down and say hi to your father. Dinner will be ready n twenty minutes. Jeanine, come help with the salad. We can talk."

"Yeah, honey," Jeanine said, sarcastically, "run along."

"Okay by me."

The first thing Max noticed as he walked down the basement steps was the silence. No trains, no whistles.

"Hey, Pop, ya down here?"

"And where else would I be?"

As he came around the corner, Max saw his father stretched out on the brown-and-orange tweed recliner his mother had bargained for, twenty years ago in a garage sale. The large chair practically swallowed his old man up. Big Max was wearing a maroon cardigan instead of his favorite B&O sweatshirt. Max realized for the first time how few strands of hair were actually still attached to his father's shiny head. He looked so old. Max hated this.

"Come on, Pop, let's try out that new engine I got you last week."

"Not now. I'm tired, Max. Sit, talk to me."

Max sat.

"I thought I heard another voice upstairs."

"Yeah, I brought a date—Jeanine—for dinner. You'll like her."

"Is she anything like that Sarah girl? So much blond hair and pale skin. Ahh," he waved his hand, as if trying to dismiss the memory, "too weak, too pale, no character. You need a woman like your mother. . . ."

"I know, Pop, I know."

"Do you?" Big Max's eyes brightened. "Do you really understand how important a strong woman is? For sure one of the biggest assets you'll ever have in our business."

"Jeanine has been working in my office tor almost a year now, but I never really noticed her until a few months ago. She's great."

"So, ya screwed her yet?"

He never changed. Sick, healthy, old or young, his father was crude. It didn't matter if they were in front of hundreds of people or sitting together with the trains, the old fart was always blurting out something that made Max hate being related to such an asshole. But every wave of anger was immediately followed by one of guilt. And here he was again, trying to ride it out, back to shore, where he could regain his balance until it happened again. And it always did.

'No, Pop, I haven't screwed her."

"Why the hell not? You have to establish who's in control from the beginning, Power, Max, how many times do I hafta tell you? It's all about power. Running a business, keeping a broad . . . ya gotta stay strong. In control."

Max nodded.

"Are you listening to me, son?"

"Yes." How could he not be listening? Big Max was shouting. Always loud. Max took after his mother, if he had to liken himself to either parent.

"Dinner!"

Big Max stood up. "Let's go and have a look at this girl. See if she's got what it takes."

"I really love your mom, you know? And your dad's a sweetheart."

Ten more dates and he still wasn't sure. Being in love was great, but he did have a business to run.

"Isn't it fun that my birthday falls on a Sunday this year? That way we can have dinner with your folks . . . oh, did I tell you she called?"

"My mother called here?"

"Yeah, she and your dad have a big surprise. Do you know it is?"

He knew exactly what was going to happen, but he said, "Haven't got a clue."

"Really?" She cocked her head in that little-girl way that he found so endearing.

Forcing himself back to work, he asked, "Is my one-thirty here yet?"

"I'll go check."

"If he is, could you stall for a few minutes? I have to make a call."

"Sure." She threw him a kiss before closing the door behind her. Quickly he dialed the phone. "Mother, pick up. Mom? Are you sure it's time? I really like this one; I hope you're right. I don't want to scare—"

Gracie picked up on her end. "Stop worrying. Trust me."

"Trust you? That's what you said last time. With Brenda. Remember?"

"Let it go, Max. So I made a mistake—one time. Believe me, Jeanine is going to love her present. This will be her best birthday ever. One to remember. One that will change all our lives."

"If you say so."

"Why are you doing this to me?"

Jack Beckley fought against the duct tape fastening him to a splintered chair.

"Shut up!"

Big Max snapped the hedge clipper. Jack screamed as his right index finger dropped onto the concrete floor.

"Hold on!" Gracie ordered. "You're going to spoil everything."

Max parked next to his mother's black Mercedes.

"Why are we out in the middle of nowhere? Wait a minute." Jeanine grinned. "Is this part of my birthday surprise?"

Max leaned over and gave her a serious kiss. "I hope you like it."

Jeanine looked through the windshield. "But everything's closed up out here."

"You'll see."

Max got out of the car and walked around to open her door.

🕸 🕸 🕸

"Listen . . . I think I hear a car door," Gracie said.

Jack prayed somehow the cops had gotten wind of his situation. "Over here! Help me!"

Max led Jeanine to a side door of the old depot.

"Watch your step."

"Are you really sure this is the right place?" Jeanine asked, more confused than ever after hearing some commotion from inside.

"I'm sure." Why hadn't they gagged him? Amazing. Thirty years in the business, and still so sloppy.

Once inside, the couple headed for the single light in the back.

"Surprise!" Gracie and Big Max yelled.

Jack's eyes bugged out when he saw her. "Jeanine? Baby? Oh, thank God it's you."

It took Jeanine a moment for her eyes to adjust to the light from the lantern on the floor. It took another moment for her to recognize her ex-boyfriend.

"Jack? Why are you . . . ? Mrs. Sullivan?"

"Come here, birthday girl," Big Max said "I got somethin' real special for you. Asshole, imported from Newark. Special delivery."

"We picked it out ourselves." Gracie laughed at her own joke.

"See? I remember," Max said, "from that first day we bumped into each other at the gym. You were so upset. Because of him." Max kicked Jack in the shin. "I'm never going to let anyone hurt you again. Ever. "

"You know these people? For Chrissake, Jeanie, look what they're doin' here."

Big Max held out a power drill. "Too serious. Is this a friggin' party or ain't it?"

"Noooooo!" Jack blacked out before the drill went completely through his thigh and into the chair.

Max watched Jeanine closely, waiting for her to crack. To scream. To run. But she didn't. Overwhelmed by her strength, Max knew the time was right and lowered his weight, balancing on one knee. "I have a surprise for you, too, honey."

The birthday girl turned toward the diamond ring.

"I want you to marry me, be my wife. My partner."

"Isn't it all too perfect?" Gracie asked. "Just like Big Max and me. Living together, working together. Now we'll all be one big, happy family. . . ."

"Max? I don't understand. Your parents are psychiatrists, too?"

"They're talking about the family business—not my practice. That's just something to do until I found the right person. I thought it would be a partner to work with. To train so when Mom and Dad retire . . ."

"Boca Raton. It's gorgeous there," Big Max said.

". . . but I never dreamed, I'd find someone like you."

Gracie smiled proudly. "I took the business over from my mother. She started it right after Daddy was killed. It was just for revenge that first time, but she found she was good at it. And she really loved the work."

"What exactly is 'the work'?" Jeanine asked.

"Ma was a . . . cleaning lady, That's how she thought of it."

"But instead of using a mop, she used a .45, some wire . . . whatever it took," Big Max said with admiration. "She was somethin' else. You remind me a lot of her."

"And your dad?" she asked Max.

"Oh, he takes a contract now and then, but mostly he keeps books, makes contacts, sets up appointments."

Gracie walked over to Jeanine, putting an arm around, said, "Look, we both know women are stronger, more thorough. Aren't you sick and tired of kissin' ass?"

Jeanine nodded, still fairly stunned by the turn of events.

"Do you love my son?"

"With all my heart."

"And isn't it great how easily you can resolve your anger right now? This very minute." Gracie nodded toward Jack. "No such thing as therapy in my world. Give back as bad as you get, that's what Ma used to say. Plus there's lots of money in our line of work, travel, fancy clothes. You get to meet more than a few very interesting people. So you have to clean up a few messes, get your hands dirty every now and then, but the benefits are far greater than the actual work."

Jack moaned and the foursome looked over in his direction. Max joined the women. "In case I have to remind you, Jeanine, I love you very much."

Big Max shouted across the room from his position next to Jack, "So, what do you say, kid? Wanna join the family?"

"Would I be replacing you, Big Max? Staying put in the office while Max gets to have all the fun?"

"No, I've got just the right person to fill in for Dad," Max told her. "Mr. Sawyer."

"Owen Sawyer? Wednesday? Four o'clock Mr. Sawyer?"

"Yes."

Jeanine frowned, thinking a moment. "But he's so . . . so . . . oh yeah, he'd be perfect."

"Good, that's all settled," Big Max said, "so can we please finish up here and go get some dinner?" He handed the drill to Jeanine. "There ya go, hon. Enjoy. But remember, this is a gift. After this you only do it for money. After all, it's a business."

She stood there looking from the drill to Jack, then from Jack back to the drill. "I still can't believe you did all this for me. It's the best present I ever got." Taking care, she pressed the tool into Jack's right shoulder, waiting for his reaction before she squeezed the trigger.

"Don't do it! Come on, Jeanine, you can't really be this angry just because of a few smacks now and then. We had some good times. Remember?"

"I remember the black eyes, two loose teeth, five stitches, and most of all the—"

Her coldness suddenly made him angry. "You deserved all of it—"

"—abortion. I remember how you said I didn't have to go to a real doctor, Jack." She pressed the trigger and the drill bit dug into his shoulder, chewing up his flannel shirt as shreds twisted and reddened with blood.

Now his face. She came at his eye, oblivious to the screams. Long, raw strings of agony.

"You know, Jack, I do think this will make us even."

Max watched, overcome with love. Everything was going to change now. His life in that office, that suffocating, ugly office was over. What a fool he'd been looking for his partner among the dark patients, the damaged. He'd wasted so much time searching all the wrong shelves. Jeanine was a *New Age* book, enlightened. Willing to try new and exciting lifestyles, an unconventional outlook on life. And those eyes. Clear, wide, and that complexion—except for the blood spatters—so smooth and clean . . . she was inspiring.

THE HOUSE OF DELIVERANCE

First it was food.

To hell with all the psychiatric logic from Dr. Phil and suffering looks from Butch. A bag of Chips Ahoys or a plate piled high with meatloaf, mashed potatoes, gravy and biscuits, a slice or two of chocolate cake for dessert, were the only things that comforted Opal. Potato chips with lots of onion dip. Ice cream sundaes, barbecue ribs, cheese in a can, popcorn with lots of butter and salt. It took more and more to help her get over what had happened to Brenda.

And she was getting there. In her own good time, in her own way. But soon she couldn't button her blouses, so she got stretchy T-shirts. Big ones. And pants with ten percent spandex, elastic waistbands—all in dark colors. She was fine with it.

Hamburgers with extra cheese, king-size orders of fries, pizza, fried chicken—anything fried—Twinkies Oreos, and doughnuts.

She was getting better . . . until her blood pressure skyrocketed, which led to migraines, shortness of breath, and backaches.

That's how she started taking pills, Diet pills from the drugstore, not the real ones the doctors prescribe. And she started losing weight. *There*, she thought, *is everyone happy now? Will you all leave me alone?*

But Timothy Bridgeman was out there somewhere having a life. Last she heard, he was interning down at Children's Hospital, and Brenda, sweet, beautiful Brenda, was still suffering so.

After a month her clothes got baggy. Another month and little lines around her mouth deepened, skin on her neck sagged, and she swore, if there was anyone around to swear at, that her knees had dropped close toward the floor. Looking in the mirror made her depressed. What had been the point? She'd forgotten. Besides, Butch never took her anywhere. It didn't matter what size she could squeeze into or even if she bought all new clothes.

"You're no good to anyone anymore," Butch shouted one evening during a commercial break from his basketball game. He shouted all the time; it was his normal tone with her now.

"What am I supposed to do? The police still haven't arrested that bastard. We've given them—"

"It's been more than three years. Stop waitin', 'cause nothin' ain't never gonna happen. Never! Get over it, will ya?"

"For your information, Mr. Smart-Ass, it's been two years and three months. Shows how much you care about your own daughter. What kind of a man are you, anyways? Our only child was violated by some punk who thinks he's better than us. He has to pay for what he done. Any normal parent, any parent who loved their kid at all, would want to kill Tim Bridgeman."

"Brenda's fine. Stuff like that happens in college. First time a kid's been away from home, booze, parties, hell, it happened to—"

"Rape's rape. It don't matter if you're on a date, or drinkin'—none of it matters. Brenda said she told that son of a bitch to stop. She swore she screamed for him to stop. Over an' over again, but he wouldn't listen." Why couldn't Butch get it through his thick skull that the law had been broken the moment Tim Bridgeman had turned into an animal?

"Yeah, well, all I know for sure is it come down to his word against hers. There never was no evidence. How do you figure that one out, Einstein?"

Their arguments always brought them back to that question. Truth was, Opal didn't know how to explain the absence of any semen or bruises on Brenda's body. And in a town, especially one as small as Atlas was, no one put up much of a fight against the family who ran the whole damn place. Certainly not her loser husband.

Butch stood in the doorway holding his beer can in one hand and a cigarette in the other. "Now listen up 'cause I don't wanna have to talk about this no more, woman. Your daughter needs you even if she ain't livin' here now. An' I'm sick an' tired of bein' the husband an' father of them poor Decatur women. I need you to straighten up. Do somethin' with yourself. Stop embarrassing this family. Get off your fat ass and go see Dotty. Or call up Rita—it's Thursday—play some bingo like you used to."

Opal sat in her chair across the room from Butch. The double-wide had been used when they bought it, but the furniture was new. Well, it had all been clean and pretty six years ago—before all this shit started.

Opal reached for a pill and studied her sorry excuse for a husband. "Just like that. You want me to get up and act as though nothing happened to Brenda. Geez, Butch, if only I could be as cold an' uncaring as you. Wouldn't that be dandy if the whole world could be as carefree an' happy as you? Tell me how to do that, Butch, an' I'll do it. For Christ's sake, just tell me how you manage to get up every day, go to work, an' not think about what Bridgeman done to your daughter? Your only daughter? Your little girl!"

He walked over to the ashtray on the end table next to her chair and put out his cigarette. Then he looked at her long and hard. After a moment he shook his head as if she were too pathetic to spend any more time with.

As he walked out of the room, Opal figured that the twenty pounds she'd lost with those big pills she'd been swallowing weren't making her feel any better about anything.

And that's when she found religion.

It hadn't come all at once like in some flash of silver, with Jesus standing in front of her wearing a robe trimmed in blue. It hadn't even come in a dream or a vision. No angels appeared at the foot of her bed like they had to Dotty, her neighbor on lot number six. The psychic at the fair she'd gone to years ago when Brenda was in sixth grade told her she'd never have any other children. She'd been right, Opal had known it the very instant she heard the words. But this wasn't nothing like that either. It happened in that quiet way life has of unraveling while you're working so furiously to tie everything up all neat and pretty.

And it happened at the House of Deliverance.

There it stood, but you had to look hard to find it. An old, run-down wooden building, off of Highway W, near a creek. Opal, who'd been living in Atlas for more than half of her forty-four years, had never even noticed it before. Until that day—that beautiful, glorious, sunlit day when she made a wrong turn.

"I have half a mind just to call the sheriff sometimes an' have him repossess your license," Butch was always threatening. "What are you thinkin'?" he'd ask if she got lost. "Hell, Opal, you never go anywheres to get lost. Take your head out of your ass sometimes, will ya?"

So it wasn't unusual, even though she was alone in the car, that she winced at the realization she was lost. But later, after much reflection, it became clearer than a glass of Stoly that destiny had been steering her Buick.

Sunflowers bloomed everywhere. Big flowers, standing as high as a grown person, and as she walked through the field they seemed to nod at her. Guiding her toward the front door.

There were no other cars around and it wasn't until she got closer that she noticed a small gravel-covered parking area in the rear of the building. Golden letters on the door were worn, the L in DELIVERANCE missing altogether. A small side window was broken, frosted over with cobwebs. But there didn't have to be anything fancy here, it was in the air. In the ground. Opal could feel it. This was a place where the Almighty Himself visited from time to time. She was sure of it.

There were eight rickety stairs; she counted each one before starting to turn the rusted door knob, wondering all the while if she was trespassing.

"No, this is meant to be."

"Can I help you?" a man with movie-star-blue eyes asked as he opened the door.

"I'm . . . I was just drivin' . . ."

"And you got lost? Ain't that what you're going to tell me, my child?"

"Well . . ."

He slicked a piece of hair behind his ear and she could see the gold pinkie ring shine. That had to be a real diamond, she thought. Why, a man as handsome as he was surely had to be one of God's chosen.

His laugh made her feel giddy. "Why, if I had a dime for every person who come to my door askin' directions, I'd have enough money to put a new roof on this old place."

"But I don't think I'm lost. Not really," she said. "In fact, now that I'm standin' here, I think I was meant to make your acquaintance on this particular day."

"And in this particular way?"

She wasn't sure if he was making fun of her or just being friendly, so she didn't answer.

He didn't seem to notice her confusion. "Well, Miss . . ."

"Mrs. Decatur."

"Well, Mrs. Decatur, care to have a look around? Since you made the trip anyway . . . on purpose or not. The Lord is always workin' out there in His mysterious ways, ain't He. We just have to relax and go along for the ride. Watch that step there."

For a moment Opal thought about saying no, getting back in her car, hightailing it home to . . . Butch. Oh yeah, Butch. Picturing him sitting in his big ol' recliner, spewing advice at her. No, she realized in that same moment, this was a better place for her to be.

"Thank you," she said, and walked through the door.

She hadn't expected much and the inside of the building met her expectations. There were no stained-glass windows, no golden trim anywhere. Not even a piece of carpet on the floor, Plain. Everything was so plain. Which made it all seem truer. Truer and more real than anything she'd known during the last few years.

As they stood in the middle of the large room, he introduced himself. "I am Reverend Hempel and I welcome you to the House of Deliverance." His hands waved through the air gracefully, like one of those magicians on TV who made whole airplanes disappear.

She nodded, glad to meet him.

"We're a small but close-knit congregation."

"Baptists?" Opal asked.

"No."

"Lutheran, then?"

"No. We're what you might call . . . seekers. The Johnsons were Catholic and the Quick family were Methodists, once upon a time."

"And now?"

"Just like the Bible says, Genesis 37:15: 'Behold he was wandering in the field—'"

"Just like me . . ."

"—'and the man asked him, sayin', What seekest thou? And he said, I seek my brethren.' They've all come to us because they were disillusioned, either with their faith or their way of life. Lookin' for others like them, lookin' for something more."

"Seekin' the truth."

"Exactly, Mrs. Decatur."

"Opal. I prefer Opal, if you don't mind."

"Now, Opal, why would I mind you treatin' me like a friend?"

He guided her to one of the pews and she expected to feel the roughness catch her skirt as she slid across the seat. But instead it was smooth, worn from years of use. Reverend Hempel walked across the wooden floor to the front of the room, climbed the single step, and reached behind a worn tapestry to flick a light switch.

The room was suddenly awash with the most comforting glow Opal could remember ever experiencing.

"There now, that's better," Reverend Hempel said. "Now you can get a real good look at our little church."

As he walked back toward her, she was able to see—really see—a crudely carved cross hanging in front of the tapestry. The contrast of reds in the fabric against deep mahogany made her feel calm. As she took in the entire room, there seemed to be enough space to seat maybe fifty people at the most. The windows, four along each wall, had been painted over with some sort of yellow glaze. The whole place felt holy. She wondered if she was having one of those epiphanies like Bobby Jo Winkelbauer was always talking about every time Opal went into the Kroger.

"It's glorious" was all she could say.

Reverend Hempel slid across the pew in front of her and stopped when he was positioned to her left. Then he turned around, rested his right arm across the top of the wooden bench, and put his feet up. "So you feel it, then?"

Suddenly Opal wanted to pour her heart out to this man. "If you're talkin' about the Holy Spirit, then I truly do. I felt Him while I was sittin' in my car and I'm sure He guided me up those steps and—"

"Right into the House of Deliverance."

Opal nodded so vigorously her glasses almost shook right off her face.

"So," the reverend began, "tell me, Sister Opal, what are you seekin'?"

That was all she needed. Someone to ask and be prepared to listen to her. And everything came tumbling out. She told him about her sweet, beautiful, smart Brenda and how that fuck—only she didn't actually say the F-word— Tim Bridgeman had ruined her sweetness. She cried when she got to the part about how crazy it was making her, but when he asked how her husband, Brenda's daddy, was handling everything, well, she got mad. Real mad.

"He acts as though nothin's happened. Like Brenda was askin' for it or somethin'. Are all men like that, Reverend? Because I pray God they ain't."

He nodded. "Yes, I'm sorry to say, it's been my experience most men react with anger. I try to counsel 'em, point out how all that rage just hurts their family even more."

"Well, it sure ain't that way with women. Every single one of my girlfriends want to go after Tim Bridgeman an' cut off that prick of his—pardon my French. But it's the God's honest truth, Reverend. I can't live with all this bitterness churnin' through my insides an' I can't live with my husband who won't hear me. He plain don't care."

"Now, I'm sure that's not true. He's just tryin' to be strong for you an' his daughter. You know, the reason men get so angry is because they think it's their job to protect their women. Mr. Decatur probably feels he let you all down."

Opal considered the idea and then dismissed it. "No, sorry, Reverend, you just don't know Butch."

"Well, that can be fixed. How about you two come back for Sunday services an' we'll all have a talk after the sermon. When everyone's gone home. Private. How does that sound?'

"Real good."

"What's wrong with our church? We belonged to Good Shepherd since before Mama died. I like it there. We know everyone. I feel comfortable—"

"You say hi to maybe four people, grumble, sit in your seat, an' fall asleep during the sermon. Every single one of 'em. You been doin' it for years, Butch."

"An' I like it that way. The Lord an' me, we got a deal, I give him an hour on Sunday and he keeps the devil away from me the rest of the week."

"Well, He sure did a piss-poor job of keeping the Bridgeman kid away—"

"Hey!" He pounded his fist on the table. The ketchup bottle tipped over and dropped to the floor. "I don't never wanna hear you talk about the Almighty with such disrespect again. Understand?"

"Sorry. But how can you sit there, actin' like everything's fine with the world. 'Cause it ain't, you know?"

"Don't you never let up, Opal? I'm sick an' tired to death of this. You got one song an' sing it mornin', noon, an' night."

"Come to the House of Deliverance with me, Butch. Meet Reverend Hempel. You'll see. It's different there."

He stopped chewing his dinner. "An' that will get you off my back?"

She nodded.

He gulped down the last of his sweet tea. "All right, you win. But just this one time."

Sunday finally came. Opal had told Brenda all about the church and Reverend Hempel, going on and on about how the Spirit had touched her in that little wooden house surrounded by sunflowers. How maybe if Brenda came with them, she'd feel it, too. But no amount of talking could persuade her daughter. Maybe next time.

She rushed to the bathroom, where the light was better, making sure her makeup was just right for the second time in ten minutes. The Mary Kay lady had shown her how to apply Bewitching Bisque foundation, but she could never get it to look like it had the day she purchased the products now stashed under the sink.

Butch came around the corner dragging his feet. He heaved a long sigh. "Let's go. The sooner we get outta here, the sooner we can come back."

Opal stopped what she was doing; after twenty-four years of marriage, she knew enough not to leave the house without looking her fashion reject of a husband over—real good. From his John Deere cap down to that Kmart plaid shirt he insisted was his favorite color, to his grass-stained boots, Butch wasn't fit to be seen.

"You're not wearin' those clothes. I laid out your gray suit on the bed. Go put it on."

He stood there, all dumb and disgusted like an overgrown ten-year-old. "Do I hafta ?"

"Wasn't it you who got all mad at the thought that I might be disrespectin' the Lord? Well, how do you think He's gonna feel if you walk into His house without givin' one tiny thought to your appearance? Cleanliness is next to godliness, Butch. You standin' there, lookin' like that, puts you next to a garbage man, not our Heavenly Father."

He didn't have an argument for that one. Slowly, grumbling as he went, he returned to the bedroom and put on his suit.

The church seemed even smaller than she remembered. But then there were sixty-one people crammed inside—Opal had counted. The windows were open and a cool breeze brought in the fragrance of wildflowers as Reverend Hempel preached his sermon. Several times she looked over at Butch, just to make sure he was still awake, and each time was surprised to see his eyes not only were opened but actually focused. And she couldn't help wondering, as she followed along with the hymn, if she was witnessing a miracle.

After he finished, Reverend Hempel turned the floor over to some woman named Alma Monroe. This was usually the place where Opal expected to hear an announcement of a prayer meeting or bake sale. At least that's the way it was done where she came from. But instead, the elderly woman just stood there. Gathering her thoughts? Opal wondered. But after two minutes passed, there was no witnessing, no speaking in tongues, just this woman in her very pink floral dress (with matching hat) standing there, smiling peacefully.

The longer it went on, the more uncomfortable Opal got. "What do you suppose is goin' on here?" she whispered to Butch. When he didn't answer she nudged him in the ribs.

He shushed her. Just like he did when he was all involved watching one of his football or baseball games.

She couldn't believe it.

Trying not to turn her head too much—heaven forbid she appear rude—Opal pretended she was checking the shoulder of her dress for lint. This maneuver enabled her to catch glimpses of most of the people near her out of the corners of her eyes. They, like Butch, sat mesmerized.

Opal was confused. Hurt. A little angry. What the hell was she missing?

The silence hummed in her ears. No one moved. Not the baby in her little seat propped up next to her mother, not the teenager who had been trying to get the attention of a brunette across the aisle. No coughing, no shuffling of feet. It was downright creepy, that's what it was.

Then the woman smiled. A big grin that made everyone respond with a smile of their own. Butch sat there, happier than she'd ever seen him in . . . never! She'd never seen him like that. Opal joined in, not knowing why but wanting to feel what everyone else was feeling. Needing desperately to feel something.

Reverend Hempel stood beside the woman the whole time. He was smiling now, too. A few more minutes passed, and then at last—at long last—he put his arm around her and bowed his head. She followed his lead. The congregation took their cue from her, and a prayer, like thousands of others Opal had heard or recited, was offered up.

There was no collection plate passed around. No woeful tales about the church needing this or that and how everyone had to dig deep and help. It was all about feelings.

At first Opal worried she didn't have any. That maybe she wasn't this caring, kind person she'd always told people she was. Especially when Butch wouldn't stop talking on the drive home.

"I ain't never experienced nothin' like that. I felt it, Opal. Right down to my sorry soul. I felt the Spirit in that church, just like you said. Hey, wanna go to the Waffle House?"

"What about your game?" she asked.

"Everythin's different now." He took his right hand off the steering wheel and squeezed her knee. "Everythin'."

Butch had meant what he said. Everything was different from that day forward. He was kinder, sweeter, more thoughtful about Opal's feelings. He hardly ever watched TV; all his spare time was now spent at the House of Deliverance, talking to Reverend Hempel privately or sitting in on Bible groups. He couldn't get enough.

At first Opal was thrilled. She'd have dinner waiting for him after work— they actually ate together now!—he'd help her clean up, and they'd drive down to the House of Deliverance together. Oh, she never told him she hadn't felt what he had that first Sunday. Why would she? He had never been happier.

Or more talkative.

"It's not like that bein'-born-again crap," he told her. Again and again. "It's like the Lord is swirlin' around inside me. Liquid gold, lightin' up every part of me. Warm. Peaceful. Hell, you know what I mean. I don't hafta tell you, do I?"

She'd shake her head every time he asked. "You sure don't."

After a month or so of going to that place every single night, Opal asked why they couldn't just go on Sundays. When he made a face, she added, "And maybe Wednesdays for Bible study? Isn't two nights a week enough?"

The old Butch would have told her *he* was the boss. *He* was the one who went to work every day. *He* was the one who paid the bills. All she had to do was obey *him* and she was doin' a piss-poor job of it. Instead he told her, "Whatever you feel is right for you, sweetheart. Go with your heart an' you can't go wrong."

Who was this man? How could there be such a complete change in such a short time?

"But if you don't mind, I'll probably go visit with Reverend Hempel by myself sometimes. Or we could have him over here, to supper now an' then."

Ah, there he was. She was relieved to see Butch was still in there, that he hadn't been possessed or turned into some kind of robot like the women in those Stepford movies. Still getting his way, only now he was taking a more Christian route.

She replied in kind. "Whatever makes you happy, darlin'."

The next Sunday she invited Reverend Hempel to come for supper on Thursday night. Butch had "suggested" she do it three times during the preceding week. "Could you make that meatloaf of yours? An' a cherry pie for dessert?'

When the reverend shook her hand after services, he accepted her invitation gladly. "Nothing I like better than to visit with my flock in their homes. It makes me feel like family."

When Thursday, came she had set the alarm to get up earlier than usual. It would take all morning to clean, find and then wash the good dishes, buy groceries, and vacuum. The afternoon was spent making that damn pie Butch was so set on, throwing a meatloaf together, ironing her blue dress, and fixing her hair. She had just finished making the iced tea when Butch drove up with Reverend Hempel.

Dinner went well. Compliments flew; Opal was happy that all her efforts had been appreciated. While she cleared the table, the menfolk strolled into the living room and patiently waited for her to make coffee. As she scooped up vanilla ice cream and plopped it on top of the warm pie, she felt ashamed of herself. Well, just a little bit. Looking around the corner, she caught a glimpse of the reverend and his kind face. Why had she felt so threatened? she wondered. She peeked over at

Butch, who sat smiling, softly conversing, and she thought what an ungrateful woman she was. Here she had what every woman in America wanted—or so she'd been told in thousands of articles and *Oprah* shows. Here she had a man who loved her. Who cared about her. Who always came home to her every night after work, except when he was at church. Church. How in the hell could a person be jealous of God? Maybe the devil was getting ahold of her soul. Maybe she had better start trying to change, like Butch had.

She loaded the silver tray saved for special occasions and holidays, and proudly carried it into the living room.

"And so, Butch, that's why—" Reverend Hempel stopped short when he saw Opal. She thought she would drop everything from the abruptness.

Guilty. That's how they looked at her.

Butch jumped up as if he'd been caught doing something nasty. "Here, let me help you with that."

All she could say was "Thank you."

Something was different. She'd suddenly gone from being the gracious hostess, wife of Butch, to the intruder. The outsider. She resented feeling unwelcome in her own home. They ate the pie, drank coffee, but within ten minutes of taking the last bite, Reverend Hempel looked at his watch and said, "Opal, this has been a truly delightful evenin', but I'm afraid I have an unfinished sermon layin' on my desk back home. Butch, could I impose upon you one last time to drive me back?"

Butch jumped up like he'd been sitting on a spring. "No trouble. My pleasure." He kissed Opal on the cheek and the two of them were out the door before she could even stand up to say a proper goodbye.

After the car had pulled out of the driveway, all she could do was shake her head. "Now what was that all 'bout?" she asked herself.

"I don't know, but I'm sure as hell gonna find out," she answered.

It took about two weeks. But when Butch came home from church especially late one night, Opal knew the time was as right as it would ever get.

"Okay. What's goin' on between you an' the reverend, I mean. Whisperin' that way when he come for dinner. You got secrets you're keepin' from me, Butch, an' I don't like it. Not one bit." She stood with her hands on her hips, strong. "Just look at yourself. Always in such a damn hurry to get down to the House of Deliverance that you run straight from work. No time to change into clean clothes. What kinda respect are you showin' the Lord by enterin' His house lookin' like a bum anyway? None of it makes any sense."

He'd barely managed to get through the door. Tossing his jacket in the corner, he slumped down into his chair. "Are you talkin' about sex here? Is that what's goin' round in your crazy head, Opal?"

"Don't be stupid, Butch! I noticed somethin' fishy goin' on that night the reverend come for dinner. It's that church. It's done somethin' to you and I don't like it. Not one bit."

He cocked his head. "I ask you to come every time I go—"

"Listen to me now. I am referrin' to that dinner weeks ago. I walked in an' you clammed up soon as you seen me. It was downright weird. Like you two had some big secret."

"We was talkin' about seekers. You know how he goes on."

"No, he never talked to me in whispers like he done you. So . . . are you gonna tell me or not? What did he say?"

"He told me somethin' that stuck in my head, Opal. It was so powerful I couldn't talk to no one about it."

"Not even me, Butch? Hell, I'm your wife. Been for more than twenty years. You can tell me everything."

Butch thought it over and then, suddenly, started to cry. All she could think to do was go to him, hold him, and tell him everything—whatever those things were—was all right.

"I've been so uncarin' to you. To Brenda. My own daughter! I'm so ashamed, Opal. Reverend Hempel told me that in Isaiah, the Bible says: 'Learn to do well; seek judgment, relieve the oppressed.'"

"I'm sure it does, darlin'." She patted his shoulder and could feel his body shaking.

"I've turned my back on my beautiful Brenda when she needed me most. I didn't relieve her of any pain and I didn't even try to seek judgment by gettin' that bastard Bridgeman hauled into jail for what he done to our baby."

Opal wanted to fall to her knees and give thanks. Finally! At long last, hallelujah, her prayers had been answered! "But I fixed everything, Opal. You'll be proud of me now. Brenda's gonna respect her daddy again an' the Lord will forgive me. I know He will."

She pulled back from him, squinting to get a good look into his eyes while she asked, "An' just how'd you do all that?"

"I wasn't at church tonight, or last night. Or even last week. I been plannin'."

"Plannin' what, Butch?" She was afraid to know the answer and yet she felt her heart race, excited to hear more.

"First I had to get me a gun. Wallace down at work had one he sold me real cheap. Then I had to watch Bridgeman till I was sure I could get him alone."

"An' just where were you tonight, Butch?"

"Out in the wood, buryin' his sorry ass."

Opal fell back. "He's dead?' she whispered.

"As a possum all stiff by the side of the road. An' you know what, honey? I feel like celebratin'. I feel born again."

The Lord certainly does work in mysterious ways, Opal thought.

The sunflowers had long since gone to seed since that first time she'd driven out there and found religion by mistake. As she walked up the stairs now so familiar to her, she could hear someone inside.

"Reverend? Is that you?" she shouted through the locked door.

The bolt turned and there stood the man who was going to set her free. Free at last!

"Why, Opal Decatur, what a nice surprise. Come on in."

She shuffled toward the front of the room. "Reverend, I've come to confess somethin' an' I need you to hear me."

He followed her but then stopped and sat in the front pew. "Now, Opal, you know we're not that kind of church. There are no confessions here. Jesus loves you. Pray to Him. You don't need no one else."

"Oh, I guess I didn't—"

"Come sit next to me. I can see you're upset about something. What is it?"

She sat down but kept a bit of distance between them. "So, if I tell you somethin' in confidence, just to ease my own soul, you might have to pass it on? I can't count on you to keep it private?" she asked.

"Depends, I guess."

"On what?"

He pursed his lips. "Well, I guess on the seriousness . . ."

"Butch killed Tim Bridgeman."

Reverend Hempel looked like he was the one who had been shot. Stunned is what he was. Sitting there dazed until she asked, "Are you all right?"

"I . . . well . . . I . . . are you sure about this?"

"Positive." He'd never know how sure she was. No one would ever know that she'd gone out after Butch left for work that day and looked for herself. Yep, right where he'd told her it was. A sloppy grave, just the kind Tim Bridgeman deserved.

"Well, I'll have to call the police. Yes." He stood up, walking quickly toward the back of the room. "That's what I've got to do. Can't have this black mark on my church. No, sir. Can't have this. Not while I'm in charge." He was still muttering when he got to his office. Forgot all about Opal and her husband. Just like she'd hoped he would.

Maybe she should try traveling next. See the world, well at least Disney World, and get away from all her busybody neighbors. For a while there they had so much to talk about, Opal couldn't blame them much. What with the police coming for Butch, hauling him away like that. Then there was all the business about digging up Tim Bridgeman's body and, of course, lots of juicy stories about Reverend Hempel and the House of Deliverance. Like he was a saint or something when all he did was make one phone call. Attendance was up so much there was a building fund to pay for an addition. And she'd even seen a commercial for Sunday services on Channel 10.

Religion had never really taken hold of Opal Decatur, but still she had to admire how the Lord had managed to clean up all the dirt—make things right. Of course, getting rid of Butch and Bridgeman couldn't make up for all her suffering . . . Brenda's, too. Nothing could. But it was a start.

AND THEN SHE WAS GONE

"High risk lifestyle, my ass. I supposed she thinks them dudes over to the firehouse are high risk, too? They out there cause they bein' paid to be out there. They gets to wear them uniforms, all clean an' nice, a fancy place to live for a few days a week. They don't live in them houses every day, ya know? And the food. You ever been 'roun one of them station houses when it's dinner time?"

"No, and I know you ain't, neither," Rita shot back.

Victor acted like he hadn't heard her, but she knew it was only an act.

"Well, it's like Christmas every damn day. But you think they eat it later? No way, they just cook them up some more."

Rita leaned back in the front seat, fishing around in her purse for the lipstick she'd bought last Saturday, waiting for Victor to finish griping. He was always carrying on about how much everyone in the world had except for him.

"An' po-lice? How can you say that's high risk when them muthas carry guns, for Chrissake? At least they got a fightin' chance. But miners . . ." He shook his large head back and forth slowly, ". . . now there's some high risk for ya. All the trouble them poor suckers havin' down in some hole in some shanty town? Goin' down into hell wearin' raggedy clothes, their lungs all black. Hardly makin' no money at all. Now that's what I consider high risk."

"Well, every one of them jobs, every single one of them is high risk, no matter what you think."

Victor jammed his right hand on the horn, yelled out the open window of the limousine, "Yo! Shit for brains. Ya retarded or somethin'?" then continued the conversation. "You're right, Rita, that's my point. We takin' all the risks while every asshole out there looks at your sorry ass thinkin' how dangerous ya got it when that ain't the truth, at all."

Victor and Louie lived in their own macho world, stumbling through days drunk and coked up. Somehow they had convinced themselves that the girls they sold day after day, night after night, were safe because of them. Cared for. Even loved.

"Me and the King, we knows how to work it. First we check out the Johns, an' then deliver you real classy, first class in a lim-o-seen. We always pick ya'll up later, don't we? Have you or any of my other ladies had to wait in the cold? Or the rain? No street corners, no alleys for my girls. Clean sheets, clean business, that's how I does things."

"She musta been talkin' 'bout them girls, the ones on the corners with their tits hangin' out, those girls that ain't lucky like me an' Tanya or Contrille," Rita lied.

"Yeah, maybe."

Victor stared straight ahead and Rita looked at his profile against the tainted glass. No hat for this limo driver, he wasn't anyone's servant. Victor had what the girls all called the three B's. He was bi, black and bald. Handsome, vain about how he looked. A large diamond stud glistened in his earlobe. It had been the first thing Victor had bought himself with the first dollar he'd earned pimpin'. Only Victor didn't never call it pimpin', he considered himself a "business man." His girls were his "staff" and the Johns, they were "clients." His motto: "If ya thinks proud an' walks proud, you is proud," would have been engraved on a plaque, hanging on his office wall . . . if he had an office.

"So where are you supposed to meet her?"

Rita put her lipstick back. "Look, I don't hafta go . . ."

"Oh yes, you do. I tol' you it's good PR."

"For Chrissake, PR for what? We're fuckin' breakin' the law here. We're doin' shit here that makes me an' you, both of us lowlifes."

"Lowlifes is somethin' you're puttin' on yourself there. Now, you're gonna meet her at her hotel an' do that interview."

Rita glared out the window, wondering how the hell all the decisions she'd made in her life had led her here? Sitting next to this jackass, ridin' in this stinkin' limousine, livin' an' workin' in fuckin' Hollywood, California? Why was she bein' punished just for bein' a little stupid?

"Did you brush your teeth?"

She turned and gave him a big toothy grin.

"Ya got on that underwear I bought ya?"

"What the hell does that matter?"

"It's respectable. It'll make ya feel like a lady."

That one cracked Rita up. "Lady, my ass."

Victor squealed to a stop for a red light. "An' don't go be talkin' trash like that. We want this Miss Whatzername to take notice of Victor's work force."

The light changed and he turned onto Sunset Boulevard.

"It's just that I hates that bitch. I hates everything about her."

"You don't even know her, baby."

"She comes into the diner the other day swishin' her Louis Vuitton like she owns the place and every damn thing in it. Tanya an' I sit there askin' each other just who the hell does this bitch think she is?"

Victor patted the bag in Rita's lap. "You got your own Vuitton, girl, so what you gripin' about?"

"I seen you, Victor. Me an' Giselle watched you sneakin' out of that Chink girl's apartment, buyin' this here knock off. Who the hell you think you're foolin'?"

If he hadn't been driving he would have hauled off and smacked her. But instead Victor just gritted his teeth. "No one knows the difference."

"I do. Giselle do. Even that stupid bitch Connie do."

"That Daisy Mae from Buttfuck Nebraska? I'll have to teach that hillbilly somethin' about respect."

Shit. Now Victor was mad and Rita's big mouth would probably be the cause of Connie getting knocked around. The poor kid couldn't help being so ignorant. Rita never told anyone how much she liked the girl . . . especially Victor. She was smart enough to not let him know she had feelings for anyone or anything. And now she was even smarter, sitting back and letting his anger run its course.

He pounded the steering wheel several times, hollered about how ungrateful every single one of his whores were until Rita couldn't stand it anymore. "Look, you want me to do this interview thing? So, tell me what to say."

That got him going. There wasn't anything Victor loved more than talkin'. Talkin' *at* her, talkin' *to* her, repeatin' every word, turning them over and inside out, sure she'd die without his expertise on everything in the whole frickin' world. That and money. Victor loved to hear himself talk and he loved money. The only thing Rita wasn't sure of was which he loved more.

Liz Petkus didn't think Rita would show. As she sipped her water she wondered if the coffee shop was too casual. She'd rethought her choice of meeting places for days. The first place she's considered was far too formal, too intimidating. The second place, too dirty. The last thing she wanted was for the hooker to think she was treating her with contempt. Even choosing her clothes had seemed difficult. After three changes she finally settled on jeans and a blue pullover sweater. A watch was the only jewelry she wore but it was the Rolex her father had given her when she'd graduated from film school. And now here she sat, so very proud of herself, making notes for her first documentary.

She checked the clock on the wall, behind the counter. If Rita didn't show up she would order lunch without her. She was starving.

"Are you sure I can't get you anything?" the waitress asked for the second time in ten minutes. "How about some iced tea, at least? A cocktail? Maybe some soup to start off with?"

The soup sounded good and Liz was just about to give in when she saw Rita walk through the door.

"My friend just arrived. Give us a few minutes."

The waitress was one of those too-much women. Too much bleach on her too short hair. Too much shiny lips gloss making her lips look way too big. Too much perfume, too much cleavage and way too much glitter on her claw-like fingernails. When she turned to look over her shoulder and saw Rita strutting toward the table she asked Liz, "That's your friend?"

"Yes, you know her?"

"I don't associate with her kind."

"Well, it's a good thing then that I'm only asking you to bring us some lunch and not be our friend, isn't it?"

Rita smiled as the waitress huffed off. Sliding across the black plastic seat of her side of the booth, she wiggled out of her jacket. "Tiffany givin' ya trouble? 'cause if she is, I'll tell Victor an' he'll—"

"No, it's okay."

"If that old queen been insultin' ya, Victor'll have to have a little talk with her, know what I'm sayin'?"

"Queen? That wasn't a woman?"

Rita laughed. "Nuthin's what you think it is in movieland. This here is Oz, Dorothy, an' that bitch is the Wicked Witch."

Liz hated feeling naïve, it shifted power to Rita and she had to stay in control if the project was to get done.

Liz leafed through notes scribbled on a yellow legal pad.

Rita sat across from her, calm, hands folded on top of the table.

Liz glanced up. "Are you hungry? Should we talk now or while we eat, or after . . ."

"It don't matter to me. But I gotta be out front at two. Sharp. Victor's drivin' me to a date at LAX, some dude has a two-hour layover an' wants to spend it with me." Rita smiled proudly.

"Okay, that gives us almost two hours."

"For what, exactly? When you made this date . . . an' it is a date . . ."

"Don't worry. I'm going to pay you for your time," Liz assured her.

"Good." Rita held out her right hand. "Two hours, two hundred."

"Now? Before we talk?" Liz asked.

"Get business outta the way first. That's how it's done."

Liz pulled out her checkbook.

"Cash," Rita said. "How dumb are you, anyway?"

Liz counted out two hundred dollars, leaving her with only thirty in her wallet.

After counting the bills again, Rita stuffed the money down inside her cowboy boot. Then she straightened up, folded her hands and asked, "So, what you need?"

Tiffany came back and threw down two menus. After they ordered Liz started right in. "I'm making a documentary about working girls, such as yourself. I want to find out how you got hooked up with Victor, why you . . . need him. What makes you . . ."

Rita played with a small pearl button on the cuff of her blouse, listening until she couldn't take anymore. "That the best you can do, girl? You tellin' me you takin' up my time askin' the same tired ass, bullshit questions everyone been askin'?"

"I know there've been documentaries abort prostitution . . ."

"Bet your sorry little self they done hundreds an' thousands of 'em. All the time showin' some bitch with her eye swelled up, dirty alleys, cars bouncin', parked on some street while they tape gruntin' and groanin'. An' every time they say, 'never-before-seen footage, shocking, the untold story.'" For the last part Rita sounded as good as Barbara Walters ever had. "I seen 'em, you seen 'em. Everybody who's got a TV set seen 'em. They be on the news, HBO, Showtime, all over every channel. So why does a girl like you from the middle of nowhere—"

"Lincoln, Nebraska. Then on to Iowa City where I studied film. I graduated at the top of my class, with honors, I am working on a grant, now. I think I know what I'm doing just a little bit better than some—"

"Hooker? Whore? Will it make you feel smarter to think I'm not as good as you? I can be anyone you wants me to be. You wants a druggie? I'll shake all over, scream for a fix. You wants me to tell you I come from a home where my Daddy raped me? Beat me? I'll gets me some scars to show you. I can be anybody you wants. But you. Look at you." Rita sniffed like she'd just smelled a pile of shit. "Just startin' out, tryin' to make a name for yourself. For the life of me, I can't figure out why you don't wanna do somethin' better. Why you wanna waste your time an' film on the same ol' crap?"

Liz didn't get angry. How could she? The woman sitting across from her had just said everything she'd been thinking for months. But she'd kept it to herself. Her first important project and it had come too easy. Late at night, when she sat up, doubled over with doubts, a thought had started taunting her. Asking her if maybe her father had pulled some strings? Her idea wasn't original. She knew it then and she knew it for sure now.

"Okay, let's suppose someone dropped a camera in your lap. What would you make a film about?" she asked Rita.

Their burgers arrived and Rita took a big bite. After a few moments of chewing and thinking she said, "The men. I'd tell the truth about them."

"You mean pimps? It's been done."

Rita nodded. "They likes to think of theyselves as royalty, you know?"

"I've seen films about the Pimp Ball. That big party they have, all of them arriving in limos, dressed in the ugliest suits, girls catering to them, fussing over them like they're movie stars."

"An' why you think that is?"

Liz shrugged. "I don't know' I've always wondered why anyone needs them for anything."

"It's the fear. They have the fear."

"Fear of what?" Liz asked.

"Bein' nobody. They knows they can't make it without us girls an' that scares 'em. Scares 'em big time. Then they pass the fear down to us. All the time sayin' how worthless we is, how we'd be nowhere without 'em."

Liz wiped ketchup from the corner of her mouth. "Work with me, Rita," she said. "Help me. Instead of interviewing you, I'll use you behind the scenes. I'll pay you a salary, you can be my production assistant."

"Uh-oh, here comes the fear again," Rita said.

"What do you mean?"

"I'm afraid you couldn't pay me enough to make it worth my while. An' Victor would never let me do anything like that. Are you crazy? He'd kill us both."

Liz tried to understand how one minute this woman could seem so educated, so self-assured, and in a heartbeat collapse into helplessness.

"You think Victor would kill someone? For real?"

"I ain't sayin'; I just knows better than to cross Victor." Rita picked up her burger and continued eating.

When Victor came to pick her up, King Louie was sitting in the back seat of the big black limo. The gaunt, pale pimp thought of himself as a full-time rock star and a part-time "businessman." He had a cell phone in one hand and a glass of champagne in the other. When she got into the front seat, Rita ignored their passenger.

"So, what happened? You didn't tell that bitch too much, did ya?" Victor asked.

"What kind of a fool you take me for?" Rita worked up an innocent look.

"I'm just lookin' out for you . . . an' all my staff. A man can't be too careful in this line of work."

"I know," Rita assured him, "I know you is."

King Louie snapped his phone shut. "I don't like this. Not one single, tiny bit."

"Shut up, you hillbilly," Victor shouted. "We needs to show our respectability. Rita show up there all classed up, no boobage hangin' out. She look like a model. Better than any those bitches in them magazines. Good enough to be in the movies. No damaged merchandise here, just prime cut— Grade A. Did you tell that woman you went to college? Do she know that? You tell her no one makin' you do nuthin' you don't wanna do? You what they calls a free agent. I just actin' as your manager, so to speak."

"I told her," Rita lied.

"Good."

King Louie pushed forward, stuck his face closer to the back of Rita's head. "We gonna be in her movie, then? All of us?"

"Maybe. She still got a lot of interviewin' to do."

"You sure she's gonna make us look good?" Louie asked. "Not like some derelicts in them cheap-ass pornos. Make us look respectable. High class?"

Rita stared straight ahead. "Sure."

"Say you love me," the John demanded as Rita spanked his fat ass.

"I loves ya, baby. I loves ya soooo much it makes me wanna hurt a good an' hard."

"I still don't believe you."

Rita picked up the magazine spread out on the night stand. He wants Halle Berry, she thought, he gonna get her. Rolling the magazine tight, she smacked his butt until he screamed. "Does ya believe me now, sweetheart? Can you feel the love?"

She waited for an answer but he was too busy jerking off. It was times like these that she felt so totally in charge of her life. Better than any big shot CEO. Just this dip shit an' her in one of her best rooms in the Beverly Hills Hotel. Five hundred dollars stuffed deep in her bag. Thirty minutes of workin' off the anger. That same anger those Botox wives carried with 'em to their fancy psychiatrists. It don't get much better, she thought.

Lifting herself off the bed she stood in front of her date, letting him take in her nudity. "Are we done or do ya wanna fuck me?"

As he laid there, she could see where the sprayed-on tan had dripped down his left thigh. "No, baby, we're done. That was great. I'll call Victor next time I'm in the neighborhood."

"You do that."

She slowly walked across the room to the glorious bathroom. After emptying a bottle of bath salts into the tub she lowered herself into the hot water and settled in for a leisurely soak.

Winter in Hollywood. Plastic Christmas trees, plastic snow, plastic credit cards makin' everybody nice an' happy.

It was always about the money. She mentally calculated. The money she'd taken from that Petkus chick topped off her private account at fifty grand. Victim, my ass, she laughed. Victor an' his idiot friend might scare the other girls but Rita was different. Rita had a plan and stayed focused. Rita was goin' to Paris. Get herself a little place, buy some new paints, study real hard. They liked black girls over there. Color didn't matter in gay Paree.

She looked out the window at the lush surroundings, everything seemed to be washed with gold today. The jasmine scented room made her feel as though she was on an island planted in the middle of a sea bluer than blue. No need to rush. The dirt bag in the other room had an appointment and the room was hers for the rest of the day . . . or until Victor called.

She was thinking how she needed a pedicure when her cell phone rang. Then a knock.

"Should I answer it?" he asked from the other side of the door.

"Would you be sweet an' bring it in to me?"

Half dressed, he skittered across the tiled floor with the phone held at arm's length like it was a snake. "Cool ring tone. Prince rules."

What a dip wad, she thought. "Thanks."

He stood there for a moment, waiting for her to flip the phone open. Before speaking she dismissed him, watching him practically skip out of the room.

"Hello, Victor."

"I'm comin' for ya. Be out front in five."

She laughed. "Hell, I'm not even dressed here. You're gonna hafta give me—"

"Get your bony ass downstairs or I'll give ya up to the cops. Does ya want that? Does ya wanna end up in fuckin' prison?"

"Is this another one of your lame jokes?"

"Listen up. That white girl? The one makin' the movie?"

"What about her?"

"She got herself killed, stupid bitch."

"What that gotta do with me?"

"They found her in your crib, spread out on your bed. Dressed in your Gucci."

"God damn."

"Why'd ya'll go an' tell that cunt anything? Anything at all?" King Louie whined. "She was our ticket, man. Our free pass."

"What the hell you talkin' 'bout?"

"The cops have her for the crime, let her put in the damn time. How dumb are ya, man?" Louie reached up to rap his partner on his shiny skull.

Victor grabbed the man's wrist, nearly snapping it in two. "How many times I gotta tell ya? Never touch me. Never!"

"Alls I'm sayin' is we don't owe that bitch nuthin'. Not one fuckin' thing."

"She's one of my girls an' I takes care of my girls. That's what Victor do. Besides, she innocent. You knows that as well as I do."

"Who the fuck cares?" Louie smiled, wiping at his nose. The doper was always wet somewhere. "She takes the heat off us, keeps the cops off our ass."

"How do you figure?"

"What the hell do ya mean, how do I figure? What's wrong with you, man?"

"Rita knows lots of stuff that could get both of us locked up for a long time. Stuff worser than some murder. Stuff that gets ya killed in the joint."

Louie squinted up at his partner, "Murder's the worse. Dude, ain't nuthin' worse than that."

"Ya think?"

Rita was waiting in front of the hotel when Victor pulled up. Her hair, limp on her head, damp; she held a pair of gold metallic stilettos in her right hand. In her left she swung the tote bag containing her bra and panties as well as the usual. When she saw the limo pull up she ran, beating the doorman to open a back door.

Trying to be calm, Victor waved. "Fuck."

"What?" Rita asked from the back seat. "What now?"

"That's Freddie. You know, Four-Way Freddie?"

"From Glendale?" Louie asked. "So what?"

"So he seen Rita, all undone. An' he gonna remember, 'specially when he looks at TV, sees the news. Make him put two an' two together, know what I'm sayin'?"

"I ain't done nuthin', Victor. Ya believe me, don'tcha?" Rita asked, trying to hold it together.

"'Course I do, baby."

"So where we goin', then?"

Louie looked up, suddenly aware he was in a moving car. "Yeah, man, where we goin'?"

"We gotta stash Rita someplace safe."

"But Victor . . . I . . ."

"Shut up, girl, I knows what's best. Just trust me."

Now he'd gone and done it. Asked for the one thing she'd used up long ago. The one thing she didn't have to give. Not to him—not to anyone. Trust.

"'Course I do, Victor."

He braked for a red light and that's when she jerked open the back door.

Louie opened his door, unsure what to do.

As Rita cut through a parking lot she could hear Victor shouting for her to come back.

The good thing was, Rita didn't have any friends. She hung out with Victor's girls, but they didn't count. And she liked it that way. No family, no friends. No one cryin' or bitchin'. No guilt, no waitin' round for some half-assed promises to be kept that tender lovin' relatives or best friends passed out like they was free samples down at the grocery. She considered herself smart and lucky. Most the time. But now . . . well . . . she wasn't feelin' neither. There was no one to trust. Nowhere to go. No one to help her out. An' that sucked royally.

Her hair had dried and now stood out all kinky. Ducking into a gas station bathroom, she washed her face, pulled off her skirt, took a pair of shorts out of her bag and yanked them on. She'd left her shoes in the limo but always kept a pair of Nikes with her. Bending she hastily tied the laces. Without make-up she could pass for someone at least five years younger than her twenty-four years.

Now what?

She stood there, listening to voices outside, traffic, stood there just wondering. Then a knock at the door.

"Are you almost done? My kid's gotta go."

She'd have to leave sometime. Might as well be now.

A cab rolled by and she waved for it to stop. The driver, a burned-out hippie type, smiled. When she got in, he turned down music coming from some Moldy Oldie station. "Where to?"

She had no idea.

He patiently waited for her to say something but after a full minute he asked, "Just get into town?"

What was wrong with her? Lying was her business. If they gave out trophies she'd be in the fuckin' Hall of Fame.

A car honked but the driver ignored it, still waiting. "I bet you're an actress," he finally said. "We get busloads of 'em every day. Come to La-La Land to get a million dollar contract. Right?"

"No."

"Then you gotta be a tourist. Here to look at all the stars."

"You're good. Damn good." The bullshit kicked in and she smiled. Thank you, Jesus.

"So, what do you wanna see first, then? I can be your guide." He leered at her from the front seat. "Show you what's what, if you know what I mean."

She watched him lick hit fat, ugly lips and POW! Just like that, she was back in charge. "Sure." This could buy her time 'til she figured something out. "Maybe I can show you a few things, too." Flash them pearly whites, she told herself, an' keep movin'. Use the dude to hide behind. Douche bag wanna play the big man, let 'im.

He must have heard her stomach growl. "How about some lunch for starters? There's a great place over 'round Hollywood and Vine called Joseph's Café. Greek food. Sound great?"

"Let's do it."

Rita expected it to be like in one of them black an' white movies Victor was watchin' all the time. She really thought when she walked into the restaurant there'd be a newspaper on the counter with them big ol' black headlines. And those headline would be about that Petkus chick gettin' murdered. And there'd be a TV up over the bar or in a corner. They'd shoot a closeup of an anchorman, lookin' real serious, talkin' 'bout the murder. An' neighbors she might recognize from her building. All sayin' what a surprise it was they didn't hear nuthin', considerin' a woman was bein' murdered.

But it wasn't like that, at all.

"By the way," the cabbie extended his hand, "name's Perry."

"Rita," she said as he held the chair out for her.

Before the waiter could say anything Perry waved him off. "The lady and I will need a few minutes. But while we're decidin', you can bring us a couple of beers."

"Ain't you drivin'?"

"It's okay," he said. Then to the waiter, "Two Buds."

He started telling her about every fuckin' thing on the menu like he had the damn thing memorized. While she pretended to be listening her eyes kept track of every part of the room. How long did she have, was all she could wonder. How long until Victor or Louie went to the cops to cover their own be-hinds?

Perry was still yappin' when the waiter came back. She just nodded when he asked if it was okay for him to order somethin' foreign.

Then he stood up. "I gotta go wash my hands. This town's a cesspool, know what I mean?"

"Sure do."

He hadn't even cleared the dining area when she heard a rapping on the window near her. Then another, until she was curious enough to walk over to have a look.

"Yo, Rita."

The sun was bouncing off the glass and she couldn't get a really good look.

"Come outside."

A lot of men in Hollywod had long hair but not like his, the Beatle cut was his trademark.

She tried shushing him through the glass, but he kept calling for her to come out. Jumpin' up an' down like a fool idiot. The waiters outnumbered the customers, and those not in the kitchen were real busy ignoring her. So, she grabbed her stuff an' took off. Weird as he was, Rita knew she could trust Crazy John Lennon.

But by the time she hit the sidewalk, he was gone.

"Over here."

Rushing past the large window of the café, Rita ducked behind the bushes where Crazy John was hiding.

"You're in big trouble, Rita."

"No shit. Tell me somethin' I don't know, fool."

"That's why I ran over here soon as I saw you go in there. Don't worry— I'm gonna take you home. To my house. You'll be safe an' I got something really, really important to show you."

She'd never thought he had a home—well, not a real one. Now she tried picturing him in a regular house with furniture an' shit. Hell, the only time she ever saw him was on Hollywood an' Vine, where he was all the time cleanin' an' polishin' that star they laid down in the sidewalk for John Lennon. She and some of the girls had even started calling him Crazy John Lennon after a while 'cause that's all he ever talked about. A crazy fan but nice enough. Just some poor bastard with nothin' better to do, who'd never done nothing' worse than smile at her. Soon she started looking for him when she had a date nearby. She'd even make Victor stop so she could bring him coffee or a taco every now and then, thinking poor ol' Crazy was homeless.

"How far is it?"

"Long Beach."

He had to be kiddin'. "How the hell we suppose to get there? That's all the fuckin' way over there somewhere."

"Don't worry. I have a car."

A car? Who the hell was this maniac? "You got a car? I'm supposed to believe you got a house an' a car? All to yourself?"

Before she had a chance to get an answer he was slinking off toward a parking lot.

What else could she do but follow? Hell, man had wheels an' a place to crash. Best offer she'd had all day.

Then Crazy John Lennon all of a sudden straightened up all proud like an' took a set of keys out of a front pocket of his bell bottoms. Three keys, all attached to a chain with a small guitar made up of letters spelling out the word: IMAGINE. Then he put the biggest one of them keys into the lock of the whitest, sleekest sports car Rita had ever seen.

"Oh man," she whispered, "you gotta be shittin' me."

"Here we are." He pulled into a circular driveway.

"I still don't get it," Rita said. "You live all the way out here? You got beach right outside your back door an' you get in your fine car an' drive all the way to Hollywood for some ol' piece of sidewalk?"

"No, I do it to honor the greatest human being to have lived in my lifetime. I owe him that, at least."

"You don't owe no one nuthin', baby."

Crazy John unlocked the front door and Rita felt like she was in one of them magazines all 'bout style the movie stars have in their houses an' clothes—shit like that.

"Come on, Lovely Rita Meter Main, I'll give you the tour."

"How many times I told you not to call me that?"

"Eight times. You told me eight times."

"So why you still call me that, then?"

"It fits."

The formal living room was painted white. A white piano was the only piece of furniture and it stood in the middle of the room.

"John Lennon once owned this," he told her.

Dumbest thing she'd ever seen. A whole room just for one lousy piano. She was not impressed.

They walked down a long hallway and then he stopped.

"Before I open this door, I have to tell you I've never shown this part of my collection to anyone. Ever. You're the first."

She didn't know how to feel about any of it.

He took out the keychain again and inserted a small gold key into the lock. When he opened the door, Rita couldn't help but be impressed. Even if she didn't know what the hell she was lookin' at.

The room was huge. And like everything she'd seen so far, it was white. Walls, carpet, every shelf, even the two leather chairs. Glass had been mounted in front of every shelf. Dude lived in a fuckin' museum.

"Let me get this right so's I understand what's happein' here. You drive me all the way out to fuckin' Long Beach to show me all this very important shit while I'm runnin' for my life. My fuckin' life! You get that? Tell me I have this wrong. Tell me you're not standin' there in them raggedy old clothes—"

"Vintage, they're vintage clothes. From the sixties. And they cost a hell of a lot more than any of the knock-offs you wear."

"Well excuse me all to hell." She shook her head, still not believin' all this crap. "So, you're standin' like an idiot in some vintage clothes, expectin' me to cream my pants because you showin' me a buncha posters an' ol' records? Shit, I wasn't even borned when that Lennon dude got hisself shot. Am I supposed to care? You crazy, man. Really crazy if you think I care 'bout any of this shit."

His hands started to shake. "No, you're crazy," he said. "You're looking at a collection any museum would kill to have. You're standing in a house worth more than two million dollars; that you got to in a car driven by a genius. A brilliant man who would have been kind and loving to you, like I'm trying to be."

He walked over to the other side of the room. Behind a portrait of John Lennon and Paul McCartney was a safe. Crazy John twisted the dial and reached in. After closing it back up he walked over to her and handed her a plastic bag.

"What's this? More of your sixties shit?" she could tell she was pissing him off and didn't care one bit.

He bit his lip, trying to hold back anger caused by her disrespect. "No, it's a present . . . it's your freedom."

She held the plastic bag up and immediately recognized the Rolex. The one that Petkus bitch had been wearing. It wasn't easy to forget somethin' as big an' expensive as that. No way.

When she started to open the bag he jumped at her. "Don't touch it! It's got prints on it. I bagged it—like they do on CSI. You can take it to the police."

Rita didn't like what she was thinkin'. Backing away she threw the watch to the floor. "*You* killed her?"

"No, listen, that's not what happened. Why would I kill someone I don't even know? I'm a pacifist . . . like John was . . . like he wanted the world to be. Love, baby. Peace and love." He made that dumb-ass peace sign. It was the first time she realized how small his hands were. How gay he looked.

Bending to pick up the watch, still sealed in the sandwich bag, he took her arm and led her out of the room.

"Where ya takin' me?"

"To the kitchen. I'm, thirsty."

"So you saw Victor? You saw him kill that dumb bitch?"

Crazy John poured her another glass of iced tea. Carefully, up to the top line of the design on the crystal. Then he put a slice of lemon in the glass, carefully, so as not to splash on the white counter top.

"Like I said, I was down, cleaning the star and I saw Victor and that friend of his . . ."

"King Louie?"

"Skinny? Sounds like a real shit-kicker."

"Yeah, that's him."

"They were talking real loud. I couldn't help but hear. And then that woman shows up. I didn't recognize her. Figured her for a tourist until I saw her holding up a recorder, asking questions like she was interviewing him."

"Bet Victor ate that up."

"No, he seemed upset. Louie tried calming him down but Victor got angrier, especially when she kept calling him a pimp. It was getting dark and they started pushing her. Louie on one side, Victor on the other. I looked down for a minute, one tiny minute . . . and then she was gone. They all were. Victor came back after about five minutes; Louie was running after him, brushing his pants off."

"An' they was nowheres near my apartment?"

"What's your apartment got to do with anything?"

"Victor says they found her in my place. In my fuckin' bed, for Chrissake."

"You must of heard wrong. After I was sure they were gone I went down the alley. First I spotted her watch by the dumpster and then I see her foot sticking up. Carefully, I picked up the Rolex, figurin' it would nail those bastards."

"You see the news?"

"Yeah. Why?"

"An' they don't say she was found in my place?"

"Rita, Lovely Rita, where are you getting all this from?"

"So Victor lied. Why he do that?"

"'Cause you're holdin' out on him. Something about you cheating him out of money that belonged to him. 'Cause he wants to teach you and the other girls a lesson."

Rita hugged her bag close. It never left her side. It held her life, her fortune, her fifty grand. How the hell had Victor found out?

Crazy John asked if she wanted another glass of tea.

"No. I gots ta figure this out."

"What's to figure? You take the watch to the police, they have Victor's prints on it . . ."

"How do you know that for sure?"

"I watched them grab her, the way they led her down the street, they have to be there."

"You go, then, you so sure. Why I have to be involved at all? You go, Victor don't know you. You just a witness. A rich, white witness. Everybody believe you."

A phone rang from somewhere in another room. Crazy John held up a finger, cutting her off. "I gotta get that."

After he left, Rita crept behind, listening, trying to figure out who was tellin' the truth an' who the hell was jerkin' her around.

There was an office at the end of a long hallway, carpeted in white shag. That ugly shit oughtta be burned, she thought. As she stood close to the doorway she heard Crazy John yelling something about money an' promises. Rita leaned in closer.

"I delivered—you owe me, man. I'm not takin' no more crap from you, understand? I've carried you long enough. You an' Victor better be nice to me 'cause I got something here that can put both of you away. All I gotta do is make one call to the cops."

Liar. So he did know Louie. Was there one fuckin' man alive who didn't lie?

"That's better. You want the big rush—you pay. Good. I'll bring the stuff by around six."

Drugs. That was the only thing she wasn't into. King Louie was all the time tryin' ta get her high, but she told him to blow the blow out his ass.

Rita didn't move fast enough. The door opened and she stood, frozen. "You dealin', an' you dealin' ta Louie? Is that what's happenin' here?"

"Come on, whose side are you on? I keep you safe . . ."

"An' just why you be doin' all this for me? Just 'cause you queer for some dead Beatle? Is that it?"

His fist went into her face before he realized what happened. Just a reflex. But when her head hanged against the wall, she dropped hard. Blood spattered across the glass of his autographed White album, hanging beneath a single spotlight.

The sun was shining brightly, making John Lennon's star at Hollywood and Vine almost glow. But then he was one of God's favorites.

A grubby family of tourists walked over the star, Crazy John swore as they left dirty marks behind. "Have some respect, here!" bending down he squirted Windex across the metal and rubbed.

"Calm down." It was a cop. "We've been getting complaints. You harassing the tourists again, John?"

"No, man, I wouldn't do that. Love and peace. That's what I'm about. You know that, Pete."

"Yeah, I know what you're about. I heard you were down at the station yesterday. Word is you had some evidence regarding that girl found in the dumpster? Better watch out or Geraldo will be coming out here, making you famous."

Pete laughed.

Look at him, one of the little piggies they sang about. And now ol' Crazy John was their hero. Brilliant. Bringing that watch in himself really made him look like a concerned citizen. John Lennon would have approved big time of the way he tried to help Rita out. No kissing up to the establishment, just one on one. Love and peace. But maybe this one time, just to get the piggies looking the other way so he could keep his sources from drying up.

"Have you seen this girl?" Pete held up a picture of Lovely Rita.

"Rita. Wow, I used to see her around here almost every night. Then all of a sudden—nothing. One minute here, and then she was gone."

"Well, if you see anything, hear something, let me know, will you? Some of Victor's girls got together a reward for information. They're scared. You know how dangerous their line of work is. Hookers get thrown away all the time."

"Yeah, I'll let you know, Pete."

As the cop walked away, Crazy John looked at the flyer the cop had given him. Ten Thousand dollars. Shit, he'd made more than that just yesterday. But it wouldn't last long. No one had any idea how much money it took to keep up the house, the collection . . . his life's work.

Love, love, love. All you need is love.

And Lovely Rita's fifty grand.

WINNING TICKET

Everybody has a nickname. Oh you can sit there and shake your head, swear up and down that you don't and never have, but you'd be wrong.

There's the obvious ones: Jimmy No Thumbs or Bobby the Nose. And schoolyard names like the one we gave Peggy in second grade, after she had an accident: Pooh-Pooh Pants. Almost all the time, these kind of labels hurt or at least make you tear up from humiliation. But in real life, grown-up places, everyone has a moniker they're not even aware of.

That girl doing your nails watches you chewing on a fat wad of gum and to her you're Cow Lady. The waitress who has had to take your steak back twice and withstand a lecture when your martini arrived without three olives probably thinks of you as Big Mouth Dick. Neighbors talk behind your back, across the fence or down the hall. You're Cat Lady, The Dork in 3B, Bimbo or maybe, because of all the complaints they've lodged with management when you play "Love me Tender" or "All Shook Up" one too many times, you've been christened: Elvis.

So I didn't feel particularly guilty thinking of him as Liver-Spot Lou. Come on, the guy was covered with 'em. From the top of his bald, sweaty head to the knuckles on his pale hands. Don't get me wrong, he was an all right dude. Every night he'd come pushing his wife (Baby Betty) in a wheelchair. They made a perfect couple, both all smiles and bundles of fat packed into matching sweat suits. Probably in their late sixties, their routine was always the same.

Night owls. I've wondered about that. Maybe they couldn't sleep or lived nearby. Most of the seniors clear out by ten, but not Lou and Betty. He'd push her over to the penny slots—Double Diamond—and that's when the fussing would begin. This usually lasted ten minutes or so. First he'd have to drag aside the stool blocking their way, then position her in front of a machine. She'd want her coat off if it was winter or her sweater on if it was summer and the AC was cranked up. Then he'd waddle off to get her a cup of coffee. When he was satisfied she was situated, he'd take care of himself. Off with his coat, drape it over the back of her chair, pull over a stool, fish in his pocket for his wallet and then . . . finally . . . they were set to play.

A five was what they'd start with, feeding it into the blinking slot. It didn't matter if the machine's max was two dollars or one, they would always play the minimum—twenty cents—and take turns pushing the Bet button. I'd keep an eye on them and when their cups were empty, I'd stop by.

"Hi folks, how's it goin'?"

She'd look up and smile, waiting for him to answer. "Fine."

"Need anything?"

It was always the same: "Two coffees--one black, one double cream and sugar."

"Sure thing." I could feel him looking as my butt and I walked away. But I figured, what the hell, as long as he didn't touch.

After I came back with their order, he'd grin and tip me a buck. She'd slurp the coffee like she was in the Sahara and it was the last swig from her canteen.

It went on pretty much like that for a couple of years. Betty got larger from month to month. I didn't know they made wheelchairs that big. And sicker. One night I noticed she had a small oxygen tank strapped to her back. It was in a black nylon case and if you didn't look close, it could have passed for a purse except for the thin, plastic tube running up into her nose.

I had to hand it to Old Lou, he never got impatient with her, always taking such good care. I used to tell Jones that if ever I got old and sick, God forbid!, I hoped he'd be there for me. He said he would.

So three years pass. I started working over at Caesars in the Sportsbook. Bigger tips, less mileage on my feet, nicer outfits, and the guys wanted to be left alone to handicap. Jones got me the job; he's a cashier, taking bets. At first I was nervous about how this would all come together—us living and working in the same spaces. But we were doing okay. No plans to get married, we'd both been there, done that one to death.

One quiet Thursday in February, I'm bringing a Lionel Richie wannabe a scotch when I see Liver Spot Lou pushing himself in a wheelchair across the casino. Imagine my surprise. The guy looked thinner, which was a good thing, but older by ten years instead of the three it had been since we'd last seen each other. As he struggled to get around a crap table I noticed he was alone.

Finally he got himself into the room and then he shifted into fussy mode . . . some things never change. Slowly he peeled his coat off, and I do mean slowly, carefully spreading it over the back of a chair. Next he reached down into a basket attached to the back of his ride and pulled out a racing form, laying it gently down on the small desk in front of him. Then began the process of getting out of one chair and into another. All the while he was blocking the aisle, but like I said, it was a quiet night and no one seemed to care. I must have delivered six drinks by the time he finally got himself situated in one of the cubicles. After he'd adjusted the light, smoothed out his paper, licked at the stub of a pencil, he waved at me.

"Well, long time no see, stranger," I said, wondering if he'd recognize me.

"I thought that was you. Since when have you been over here?"

"Oh, more than two years, now. So, how have you been?"

"Not so good. My wife died last spring."

I reached down to pat his arm. "I'm so sorry. She seemed like a real nice lady."

"She was my world. I don't know what to do with myself now."

I was never sure of how to act when someone poured their heart out . . . especially a stranger. And as he kept looking up at me, waiting for comforting words, a smile . . . something . . . I asked what he wanted to drink, dummy that I am.

"A beer. Please."

"Going for the hard stuff," I teased.

"What have I got to lose? I'm just putting in my time, that's all it's about now." He jerked a thumb toward the wheelchair. "Between the diabetes, high blood pressure, and my heart, I'm living on thirty pills a day. The sooner I can join Eleanor, the better."

Eleanor, so that was her name. "It's crazy that we've known each other for years and never had a name to put with the face."

He held out his hand. "I'm Bill."

"And I'm Lacy," I said, shifting the tray to my left hand so I could grab his fat fingers.

"You'll laugh, but Ellie used to nudge me every time we saw you sashaying toward us. She'd say, 'Here comes Legs.'"

See what I mean about nicknames? Well I'll take that as a compliment. I felt like a real shit for thinking of this sweet man and his deceased wife as two funny old people. Even though they could have been my grandparents I should have been more respectful.

"Legs? Well those damn outfits we had to wear were very skimpy."

"I didn't hear anyone complaining," he laughed.

"Yeah, well, the tips were good."

"So why are you at Caesars?"

"Ahh, you know, boyfriend works here, better benefits, more hours, boring shit like that."

"Just be lucky you have someone." He thought a moment, obviously about Eleanor and I watched his face collapse.

"I guess. Well, it's great seeing you; I'll go get that beer for you."

"Thank you."

And that's how it went for a few months. Bill would come in the same time every night. He'd handicap for three to four hours a pop—win a few, lose a few. I was really starting to like the guy. When he finished his last beer he'd always toss me an extra ten but before starting for home, he'd get real chatty. Guess the thought of going back to an empty house got to him.

Sometimes he'd tell me about his parrot, Garrett. He hated that bird, always complained how dirty the damn thing was. But Eleanor had loved it and since they didn't have any kids it was all the poor guy had left. Pitiful, huh?

The last time I saw Bill was the Tuesday before Easter. We were busy that night, spring breakers gawking, playing Daddy's money at the blackjack tables. They ran me ragged and tipped for shit, if at all. Big boys with pea brains, staggering around with their booze in those over-sized cups, waving 'em like banners of courage instead of neon signs that they're idiots who have never been away from home before. All us girls laughed at 'em.

Bill was getting comfortable at his usual table when I noticed him.

"Well where have you been? I was starting to miss my favorite customer."

"I ain't been feeling too good," he said, studying his race form.

"You do look a little pale, honey. Sure you should be out?"

"A beautiful blonde is paying attention to me, I'm fine. Could I have a beer, please? When you get a minute?"

"Sure thing." I patted his back. "Nice to see you, Bill."

He didn't seem to hear that last part, too wrapped up in his calculating, I guess. Horses—they always come first with these guys.

By the time I got back from the bar with his drink, I knew something was wrong and made a beeline for Jones.

"Ahh, sweetie?"

"Oh hey, Babe," he said from the other side of the counter.

"See that guy over there?" I pointed toward Bill.

Jones squinted. "The big dude stretched out across the table? Is he taking a nap?"

"I'm not sure. Can you walk over with me?"

"Sam!" Jones called to a guy behind him. "Cover me a minute."

No one seemed to notice a thing—business as usual in Bill's part of the room. Jones leaned over and shook him. "Hey buddy, ya okay, there?"

No answer.

Setting my tray down, I had a try, "Bill? I got your drink here. Wake up."

Jones pushed Bill back in his chair and that's when we saw blood at the corner of his mouth. No big deal, if you weren't looking closely you'd never notice. But still, it was scary.

"Go call nine-one-one and I'll stay with him," Jones said after checking Bill's wrist for a pulse. "Hurry."

"Is he alive?"

"Just barely. Now go!" he said in such a controlled voice, I knew he was trying not to scare away the customers.

But I could have told him he didn't have to worry. You'd be surprised at all the tourists that get caught up and forget to sleep or eat or take their medication. Vegas does that to people, it gets their reality all twisted. So seeing someone down, spread out on the floor isn't anything unusual for the regulars.

Within three minutes of making the call, I saw two guys come running toward us. The room was buzzing now but that didn't stop people from lining up to make their bets. The rest of the casino was oblivious to the commotion. Jones had gone back to his window and I stood watching with Bernie, the floor manager.

Poor ole Bill was wedged in there pretty good. I felt so sorry for him.

"Get back, let the guy breathe," one of the EMTs said. Then he looked at me. "You know this guy?"

"Kinda."

"Does he have any relatives nearby? Someone we should call?"

The other paramedic was still trying to get Bill to wake up.

I shook my head. "No kids and his wife's dead."

An oxygen mask was strapped across Bill's face while an IV got started. Things started moving fast then. They loaded Bill onto a gurney and raced out of the casino. I watched as they got swallowed up by the crowd.

"So, I heard about all the commotion today. You know the guy good, or what?" Darlene asked.

I was waiting for Jones in the hotel coffee shop. "Kinda. He was a regular, used to see him and his wife all the time when I was over downtown. She died a few years ago and now he's alone. Plays the horses all day. It's sad."

"Yeah, life will kick ya in the ass when ya ain't payin' attention," Darlene said. "It sure ain't fair—none of it. Ya waitin' for Sweet Cheeks?"

"Who?"

"The girls that work with Jones call him Sweet Cheeks and they sure ain't talkin' about the ones on his face." She laughed.

"And what do all of you call me?"

"Lucky, honey. Havin' a guy like that . . . I'd say you're pretty damn lucky."

I tried being polite but I was starving. When she finally got done with her patter, I ordered a bowl of chili and a Coke.

"What'll Sweet Cheeks have?" She winked and I wanted to hurt her.

"He told me not to wait for him."

"Gotcha." And she was off.

I'd only been waiting for twenty minutes when Jones arrived, pretty good for him seeing that punctuality isn't exactly his strong suit. And when he settled in, he was all business.

After he'd ordered I asked what was going on.

"Something happened."

"Good or bad? No, wait, maybe I don't want to know . . . do I?"

"It's your friend, Bill."

"Did you hear something?"

Jones scootched closer to me. "He's dead; I called the hospital and they said he was DOA."

My heart sank. "Aww, what a shame. But you didn't even know the guy so why would you check up on him?"

"In case they have any kind of caller ID I wanted the Casino's number to be on record."

"I still don't get it."

"I'll tell you in the car. Right now I need you to just eat your dinner and act normal."

"Why do I need to act? I am normal. Aren't I?"

He rubbed the stubble on his chin. "Just eat."

So I ate my chili as normally as I could. Jones wolfed down his cheeseburger which was normal for him. We didn't talk much, which was also normal for us. We've always been more physical that intellectual . . . if you know what I mean.

☣ ☣ ☣

On the way home Jones explained about the tickets. "Guys do it all the time, especially the cleaning crew."

"And it's legal? Even though it's on the floor doesn't mean it's yours. Someone else paid good money for those tickets."

"Listen. A guy comes to my window and places a bet. I give him the ticket. No record of a name, nothing—I just hand him the paper. When the winners come in, it's his responsibility to bring the ticket back to cash it in. Simple."

"How long does he have to do that?"

"A year."

"So why would someone throw away a winning ticket?"

"Oh, they don't do it on purpose," he said. "Mostly it's just because they're careless . . . or lazy. Maybe they read the numbers wrong, maybe they forget they bet on the horse. Some of these dudes make twenty bets a race and those bets are spread out over different tracks all around the country. It gets confusing. Half the time they don't even know what they have. Or maybe they've been on a losing streak and a few bucks here and there don't matter."

"But Bill was kinda busy, Jones. Fighting for his life--remember? And what do you do? You rob him?"

"Would I do a thing like that?" He seemed genuinely hurt.

"Well . . . I guess not."

"After they took him away, Bernie told me to gather up all his stuff and we'd send it over to the hospital. You know there was his wheelchair and all sorts of crap in that basket. Mostly junk. A bottle of water, magazines, a picture of some woman . . ."

"I bet that was Eleanor. You didn't throw it away did you?"

"Lacy, what kind of guy do you think I am? Have you ever known me to do anything mean or illegal?"

"No, honey, I'm just upset is all."

"So I was picking up his race form and inside was three tickets. For some reason I put them in my pocket. Weird, huh?"

"And that's when you called the hospital? If he was alive and well you would have taken the money over to him, right?"

"Sure I would have."

By this time we were in front of the apartment. I started to get out of the car but he grabbed my wrist. "Wait a minute. I want to talk here."

"Okay, okay, so how much are these tickets worth anyway?"

"The three of them add up to almost thirty grand."

I didn't know what to say.

"All long shots, can you believe it? The guy sure went out in a blaze of glory. Not that anyone'll ever know."

"And it's not as if he has relatives to give the cash to," I said, thinking about all that dough.

"Right." Jones kissed me. "Now you got the picture."

"So what next?"

"Well, that's what we gotta talk about. There's a catch but I think I figured a way around it."

We went to Bill's funeral . . . it was the least we could do. There weren't many people there. Bernie and three of us girls who had served Bill beers, Jones and his friend Sam from the sports book. An old woman who went to church with Eleanor came with her teenage grandson. The funeral director at the Palm Mortuary told me how Bill had made all the arrangements after Eleanor passed away because he wanted to be sure he got the plot next to hers at the cemetery.

When I told Jones what I'd found out he said, "See? The guy didn't need any money then and he sure doesn't need it now."

I did feel better seeing that he'd splurged on a really nice casket for himself—mahogany with a black velvet lining. The casino had sent over flowers and aside for the fact that there were only about a dozen of us, it was very nice as far as funerals go.

Another week passed before I bought the wig, a cute little red number, about three inches shorter than my own hair. Jones was at work and it was my day off so I took time getting dressed. I put on the jeans I'd gotten at Good Will over a year ago and this old sweater that had shrunk from way too many washings. I worked hard to be sure there was nothing new that could be traced back to me from one of those hidden cameras at the mall or a recent receipt. Jones laughed that I put so much thought into everything but I watch those forensic shows and it's always the tiniest detail that trips up an almost perfect crime.

I checked myself out in front of the bathroom mirror. "Pretty good, if I do say so myself," I told the reflection of the stranger staring back at me. Then I unwrapped the shoes I'd been saving for our vacation and hurried over to Caesars.

☆ ☆ ☆

I was nervous waiting my turn in front of Jones's window. He was busy with some blue-haired lady who wanted the whole betting thing explained to her . . . again. It gave me time to go over my check list. Fake ID—check. Jones's friend Pete had done a decent job. Tickets—check. The three winners were tucked deep inside my wallet. No jewelry—check. Nothing that would stand out or be recognized. Wig in place—check. My hair was pinned up so tightly under the red stuff that I was getting a headache.

Sweating bullets, I cursed out the reason I stood there like a freakin' idiot. The No Shittin' At Home rule as Bernie referred to it. Any employee found gambling at their workplace would be fired on the spot. But Jones and I agreed thirty grand was enough of a reason to take the risk. It would pay off all the debts we've accumulated and still have some left over for a down payment on the motorcycle Jones had been wanting. But when all the dust settled, we'd still need our jobs as well as references, we weren't talking millions but a fresh start.

"Calm down, it's simple," I could hear Jones's voice in my head. "So you hand over the tickets and I run them through for verification. When they come up winners and you have to fill out the tax forms, your name is Cheryl Dillon. Don't slip up!"

"Cheryl Dillon," I whispered to myself. "Cheryl Dillon from Tennessee."

I finally made it to the front of the line. Jones looked up at me. "Can I help you?"

He did it so good, like he didn't even know me . . . for real. I tried not to smile. "I want to cash in these tickets."

The guy working next to Jones smiled at me for a second and then went back to the customer he was helping. So far so good. I'd lowered my voice and even added in a little Southern drawl so he wouldn't catch on. I'm no Drew Barrymore but I felt as though I was getting ready to accept my Oscar until he stopped what he was doing and asked, "Don't I know you?"

"You from Nashville, honey?" I asked. "Cause if you are . . ."

"No, sorry."

The preppy in front of him chimed in, "Come on, if you want to get her number do it on your own time. I'm in a hurry here."

That's when I realized all the guy was doing was flirting with me.

"Well, congratulations," Jones said. "You've got some winners here. If you'll wait a minute I'll get my manager."

"Really? I can't believe it, I've never won anything!" Damn, I'm good.

We'd made sure it was Bernie's day off so I felt confident standing there, waiting. And I started to wonder why I had been so worried? People got paid big bucks every day. Now I was one of them, that's all.

I recognized the man as he walked toward me but I didn't know his name.

He'd only been at Caesars for a month or so and we never seemed to work the same shift. When he was closer I could read his name tag: Dave Mitchell.

"Looks like we have a big winner here," Jones told Dave and handed him the tickets.

"Twenty eight thousand, nine hundred, seventy-five dollars and thirty two cents. Is that right?" he asked Jones, turning the winners over in his hand.

"That's right."

We all stood there for a moment. Jones had this smile plastered across his face; I could see the sweat making his forehead shiny. I smiled and in my best Loretta Lynn voice gushed, "I'm so excited I can hardly stand it."

Dave smiled. "Well, Miss . . . ?"

"Dillon."

"If you'll follow me we'll go back to my office. I'll need you to fill out some tax forms."

"Sure thing." I looked at Jones and gave him a little wink. No one saw, I was sure. The cameras are overhead and even if someone caught it, I could always say I was just being friendly.

A big security guard appeared. Jones had warned me there would be security with that much cash. The three of us walked across the casino floor and down a narrow hall, back to this gaudy office with a cheap desk in the corner.

"Here you go, Miss Dillon," Dave said as he pulled out a chair for me.

"Well, aren't you sweet."

When we were comfortable—the two of us seated and the security guard standing by the door, Dave reached into his desk for the forms. He was five minutes into explaining how to fill them out and where I should sign when he got paged. "Sorry, I'll be right back."

The door had just closed when the guard walked over to me. "Okay, Jugs, what are you doin'?"

"Jugs?"

"It's a compliment. Don't get mad. All the guys call you that. Hell, look at yourself, you could be on a calendar or somethin'. We're always laughin' how a jerk like Jones ever got someone like you." He winked at me.

"Sorry," I said. "My name is Cheryl Dillon."

"Huh, no, if I'm not mistaken, your name is Tracy, Lacy, something like that. But you'll always be Jugs to me, I'd recognize them anywhere."

"Look . . ."

"No, you look, we don't have much time." He got closer. "Just keep doin' what you're doin' and ask for cash. Then say you want an escort to your car and you pay me there."

"Pay you? How much?"

"I'm not greedy. Twenty should do fine."

So here I am. Still at Caesars, still on my feet for eight hours, still with Jones. Pete the Creep, the guy who made up the phony ID for Cheryl Dillon, came crawling over to our place like the low life he is. He threatened to call the cops if we didn't give him a cut. Jones handed over five grand to shut him up. In spite of the glamour, Vegas is a small town and we can't afford to be banned from the casinos. Hell, we can't afford much these days. The money we have left isn't enough to pay the bills or get Jones's bike. The possibility of getting caught and having a record keeps me tossing at night.

But the thing that gets me the most is this nickname thing. I can't get past it. We all go along, minding our business, feeling safe, thinking no one notices us much. But really we've been branded—all of us. Oh sure, some of those names are cute and we know what they are and laugh. But some can screw a person up for life.

YOU WOULD CRY, TOO

Women had always shown her the way.

First it was Gramma. Her earliest memory should have been of her mother, she supposed, but Gramma was the first one to point the way. Every Saturday morning she'd come over to their house, arms loaded down with treats from the bakery across the street from her little apartment. Since Gramps had died, the only thing that seemed to comfort Gramma was food. Making holiday meals, checking out new restaurants in the neighborhood or hauling bags full of jelly donuts, coffee cake and cookies to her only daughter's house. And as the rest of the family sat around the kitchen table, stuffing their faces, Gramma and her little Susie set up TV trays and ate while watching the *Shirley Temple Theater*.

Little Shirley was cuter than cute and could do it all: act, dance and sing. Every little girl wanted to be her, and every mother wanted their daughters to be her, too. But five-year-old Susie Webster couldn't sing one song all the way through. She was clumsy, and especially had no interest in acting out stories with grown-ups. Whenever a stranger tried to talk to her, she'd get so shy it made her stomach hurt. Until that miraculous Saturday morning, right before Easter. Something happened that day while Susie and Gramma were watching, *Curly Top*.

A handsome man, wearing a suit, lifted his little "darling" up, sitting her gently on top of a shiny white piano. He had such a kind voice. And when he started singing to her, she smiled—such a trusting smile. Halfway through his song, Curly Top got up and began dancing across that baby grand. It made Susie want to dance on a piano too—if they had one. And whenever she thought back to the moment that started her on the road to success, Susie gave all the credit to Shirley Temple.

After weeks of nagging, she finally got her first pair of tap shoes. Not fancy ones like girls wore in the movies, but they fit and made a nice sound. Next came dance lessons. Twice a week Mom would pick her up from school and take her directly to Miss Shelly's.

A former dancer on Broadway, Miss Shelly had been in the chorus of *The King and I* and *West Side Story*. One time, for a whole week, she'd even danced with Sammy Davis, Jr. in *Mr. Wonderful*. But that was when Miss Shelly was younger and before her knees got bad. Now she owned and operated Miss Shelly's Dance Academy out of the spacious basement of her home.

After three years, Susie moved on to the School of Modern Technique, to study jazz with a little ballet thrown in to strengthen her legs and improve her posture. Soon she was riding the bus downtown, three times a week.

By the time she hit puberty, everyone was telling her to try her talent out in the pageant world. She was certainly pretty enough, a million times cuter than Sandra Dee, Aunt Audrey always said. When she came in third place for Miss Teen Syracuse, she wasn't too disappointed. As if she wanted to spend the next year wearing a silly crown or modeling or even being some kind of inspiration to someone? Get real.

And then she was watching *American Bandstand* one day and there was Lesley Gore. Singing with that great voice of hers, telling everyone they could go to hell, it was her party and she'd do whatever she damn well pleased. Talented, confident, no boy drummer or guitarist behind her . . . just dancers. Pretty girls doing the Mashed Potato, having a ball, oblivious to cameras and lights, even the live audience. Those girls got paid to just have fun. They didn't have to sing; they didn't have to talk to Dick Clark, try to sound smart and funny. All they had to do was wear groovy clothes and do the Swim or Twist. And, unknowingly, Lesley Gore had decided Susie's fate. The teenager would go to New York City and become a go-go dancer.

But first she had to kill Susan Ann Webster. Nothing exciting was ever going to happen to a girl who lived with her parents and dumb brother in Syracuse, New York. Movie stars did it all the time—threw away their old selves, picking glamorous new names that would look better on a marquee or stage bill. When she told Dad, he got all mad.

"You're a Webster and should be proud! Our line reaches back to Noah Webster. How many people can say that?"

She wasn't buying it.

He tried again. "As long as you're living under my roof, little girl, you'll do what I tell you. And I say your name stays. No changing."

"When I'm eighteen I can do whatever I want," she cried.

They didn't speak for days until her mother championed her cause. Finally, grudgingly, he agreed that she could be whoever she wanted to be, as long as she graduated from high school first.

With diploma in hand, Susie marched herself down to City Hall. The clerk smiled when Susan finished filling out the form, in duplicate, and signed it: Meadow Rose.

No more dance classes—she was as good as she'd ever get. All the has-beens who shouted at her to stand straighter or bend lower, had to realize that now was her time to be a somebody. Times were changing. And they were changing fast. She had to hurry so she wouldn't be left behind. But how to begin? Darlene Bellini, her best friend, was the angel who pointed the way next.

"Guess who just got a job at the Peppermint Lounge?"

"The same place Audrey Hepburn goes?" Meadow asked.

"And Judy Garland, Marilyn Monroe . . . all those famous people. Even Frank Sinatra. They all love Joey Dee's band."

"Who? For Pete's sake, tell me."

"Richie."

"As in your homo brother, Richie?"

"One and the same. He met this guy, Chad, I think they're dating or something. Chad knows the owner and got Richie a job bartending."

"So can he get us in? To see all the movie stars?"

"Even better! He'll help you get a job there—dancing. I told him how great you are."

"Me? At the Peppermint Lounge? The hippest club in the world?"

They jumped up and down, excited with their plan.

Confidence covered her like a shield as she strutted through the noisy station. She knew she looked cool and it didn't matter what anyone said. Meadow's white crocheted skirt matched her boots—a look she'd seen on American Bandstand. And the pink ruffled jacket was an exact copy of one Jean Shrimpton had worn. If people didn't like any part of her . . . they were just jealous.

A strong blast of cold air hit her as she walked up out of the subway. But she only smiled. Half a can of Adorn had made her pixie cut indestructible. "The Seven train will leave you off at Forty-second and Broadway—that's in Times Square, think you can remember that? Forty-second and Broadway . . . don't forget," Darlene had drilled her a million times. "And be careful," her mother had warned, always so afraid of everything. It wasn't as if Meadow lived in Hooterville! Syracuse was in New York, for cryin' out loud.

Dirty newspapers stuck to patches of crusty slush. Posters flapped, ragged, hanging limply from any surface a thumbtack could penetrate. Neon signs were crackling to life as the winter sky started to darken. Tires squealed at red lights, horns honked and everyone and their brother seemed to be shouting or screaming at each other. The super-charged city couldn't intimidate her, though, she would not be distracted.

PEEP SHOW 25c, LIVE GIRLS, HOT DOGS, PIZZA and CAMEL CIGARETTES. Ads for everything that could be sold—all larger than life. You could buy anything—and anyone in New York City. But Meadow found the commotion exhilarating, the grim a little dangerous, and the bright lights beautiful.

"Got any spare change?" A hippie wearing a heavy overcoat, his hair pulled back in a ponytail, held out his hand.

"Sorry."

He followed her. "Aww, come on, what's a quarter to a chick like you?"

If only he knew, she thought, feeling the subway token in her pocket and thinking of the two dollars in her purse.

"All I need is—"

—a job, she mentally finished his sentence. "Sorry."

He ran around to stand in front of her. The bottom of his right shoes flapped like it was clapping the sidewalk.

She stopped abruptly. "Please, stop bothering me; I don't have any extra change."

He shrugged and smiled sweetly, holding up two fingers in a V. "Peace." As he started to walk away, he shouted over his shoulder at her. "I hope you find some love today."

Her stomach growled but she ignored it.

Darlene had told her about a girl they knew from gym class, how she had ended up over on 44th in one of those horrible dives. Oh, she told everyone was an actress, but they all knew the truth. "She gets paid to show her private parts, up on a stage, in front of a whole room of dirty old men. You're way better than that," Darlene said.

"Hey, Sister Mary, got a light?"

The woman who stood in a doorway next to the Pussycat Club had her hair all teased up on top of her head like some exotic nest. Her fishnets were torn at the knees and the leopard print dress looked two sizes too small.

"I don't smoke. And why would you call me Sister Mary? Is it a religious thing or something?" Meadow hoped she didn't sound rude.

"Honey, all that white is fuckin' blindin' me."

"Well, at least I don't look like I just crawled out of an alley." Trying to be polite was obviously a waste of time with this girl.

"You don't have to go all ape shit on me, here. I was just kidding. Hey, don't walk away when I'm talkin' to you, girlie. Hey!"

One more block, Meadow thought. Just keep walking.

She'd been to the city for dozens of school trips: The Statue of Liberty, Empire State Building, every boring museum there was. With her family she'd come to see Technicolor movies on a big screen or meet relatives for some kind of celebration. There were a few dates when the guy had enough money to try to impress her at some fancy restaurant. But now she was by herself . . . on her own. And it felt great!

The cold wind cut through her nylons; her legs were getting raw from the chill. February was an ugly time in the city. After Christmas, when the earth was dirty with left-over snow, everyone seemed so angry . . . or sad.

Finally, there it was, the candy cane-striped awning she'd seen in so many pictures. She was really there and it felt delicious. Now where was Darlene?

A man opened the front door. "We're closed. Come back later."

"I'm just waiting for my girlfriend."

"Well it's pretty cold out here, don't wait too long or your boots'll crack." He winked and went inside.

"Ha, ha." So her boots weren't real leather. She picked her foot up to inspect the shoe. And maybe they were really, really shiny, but they looked good.

Meadow checked her watch. It was a curse to be punctual when the rest of the world was always running late. She got penalized every day. How many hours had she spent waiting . . . alone. In restaurants, theater lobbies, in front of stores, in the cold, the rain and heat that made her flip go straight.

"There you are," Darlene said as she rushed under the awning. "Always the first to arrive . . . Little Miss Perfect. Making all of us dumb slobs look stupid."

Meadow didn't respond, she was too busy looking at the stupid bow holding back one side of Darlene's long hair.

"So, why didn't you go inside?"

"They're closed."

Darlene tried the door; when it wouldn't open she knocked. No one answered so she pounded with her fist. "Hello!"

After a few more tries, she gave up.

"Now what?" Meadow asked. "I came all the way down here . . ."

A lock turned; the large door opened. A rush of British Sterling hit their noses. It was Mr. Wise-ass.

"We're closed."

"I'm Richie's sister," Darlene said.

"We got three Richie's workin' here."

"Richie Bellini," Meadow chimed in. "He's a bartender."

"The only Bellini we got is a Ricardo. That him?"

"I forgot," Darlene whispered to Meadow. "The idiot changed his name."

Meadow smiled. "That's him," she said.

"You don't know your own brother's name?" The guy looked amused. "I'll go get him." Then he stood back, holding the door open for the girls. "So come in, already."

"Thanks," they both said as they stepped out of the cold and into the dimly lit room.

"It's smaller than I thought it would be," Meadow observed. "It always looks so much bigger on TV or in the magazines."

"Don't we all."

It didn't matter that neither of the girls understood what the man said, they were in the Peppermint Lounge—that's all that mattered. They were breathing the same air Annette had! They were standing on the floor hundreds of famous feet had walked across. Meadow couldn't help herself and ran over to the bar, running her hand along its mahogany surface. Darlene stood in front of a mirrored wall, smiling and waving at herself.

In that light, the man looked old enough to take Geritol. He watched the two for a minute then said, "I'll go find Ricardo."

Meadow did the Watusi to the dance floor in the back. This was all too good. Her mind ran wild with possibilities. She'd start off as a dancer, get to know the band. They'd ask her to dance on stage and maybe someone like Lesley Gore would see her. Or someone from the Jackie Gleason show—and she'd get on TV. Then the movies! Elvis had those girls dancing around him in all his movies. She could do that . . .

"What the hell are you doing here?" It was Richie and he was pissed off.

Darlene looked mortified. "You remember Meadow? You've only met her like a million times."

"Sure." He nodded toward her then grabbed his sister by the arm. "What are you doing here and why did you bring her with you?" He must have thought Meadow couldn't hear their conversation, but she could.

"You told me that maybe you could get her an audition—to dance. She's really good and—"

"People come here to dance, not to watch dancers. And how old is she, anyway?"

"Same as me."

"Do you know what trouble I'd be in if Chad found out you were in here—both of you—underage kids? The police would come and haul us off to jail, if anyone told them. Are you stupid or what?"

"But you said—"

"Just go home."

Darlene was persistent. "No, you told me that they needed dancers—"

"Come back when you're twenty-one," he yelled over to Meadow.

Darlene started to cry from the humiliation.

"I'm outta here," he said as he walked away.

Meadow ran over to Darlene, hugging her friend. "It's okay, there're tons of clubs in New York. Let's go."

"Wait until I tell my mother how that jerk treated us."

Meadow coaxed her friend through the door. "My brother can be a real pain, too. Come on."

Snow was dotting the dark sky. The temperature seemed to have dropped a few more degrees since Meadow first arrived in the city. As the girls walked, they went over the scene at the Peppermint Lounge a dozen times. The whole situation seemed to get funnier as they looked at it from every angle. By the time they'd gone a few blocks, they were laughing.

The diner smelled like burnt chili, but they were super hungry and didn't care. Red, vinyl-covered booths sat empty, making it easy to get a seat that time of night. The place was usually jumpin', full of the theater crowd hoping to grab a quick bite before the curtain went up. The girls sat away from the door, hoping to stay warm. When the waiter finally came over, they ordered hamburgers, fries and Cherry Cokes.

"Lana Turner got discovered drinking a soda," Darlene said, dipping a fry in a blob of ketchup on her plate.

"But she didn't want to be a dancer. All she needed was a pretty face to get noticed. I have to find a job dancing somewhere—that's how people will see my talent."

"I know!" Darlene buzzed with an idea. "We'll go to Philly, where they shoot *American Bandstand*! Everyone in the studio and watching on TV will see you."

"Genius!" Meadow said. "Why didn't we think of that before?"

By the time they'd finished their hot fudge sundaes, they were planning what they'd wear on the train ride to Pennsylvania.

Meadow's spirits were high as she walked down Broadway toward the subway. It was only 7:30 but that time of year it always felt later. Mom had made her promise to call when she got to Aunt Audrey's apartment in Brooklyn. When was she going to realize her daughter was a woman. . . .

Arms clamped around her chest; Meadow tried to catch her breath but the cold air stung going into her lungs.

Someone was dragging her backwards. Her brain couldn't understand. What was happening?

He was laughing, pulling her along while she tried to stand up on her own. "Hey! Stop it!" she screamed. But he just kept laughing, a scary, nervous giggle.

When he threw her down, she could feel the wet alley beneath her. Something sharp tore at the back of her leg. Garbage was scattered everywhere, the smell made her gag.

Lights behind windows facing the alley illuminated faces of people inside. Some sort of store. She could hear voices inside and screamed, "Help me! Please help!"

His big hand clamped over her mouth. "Shut up." When he got closer she could see he was a kid, younger than her. While his hand squeezed her lips together, his other hand pulled her legs apart. She struggled but his knee came down, wedging between her thighs. Once his weight was on her, pinning her to the grimy alley, he clawed at her panties. Ripping them.

She punched up at his face.

They struggled. She rolled, frantically trying to get away, cutting her arms on bits of broken bottles. Why was he doing this to her?

When he had her pants off, he started tugging at her jacket. She could hear the fabric tearing. A button flew off, hitting a garbage can, making a dull clank.

No, no, this couldn't be happening. It wasn't real. No!

When she scratched his arm, he slammed her head into the ground. She couldn't black out . . . she couldn't let go . . . such fear . . . help . . . terror . . .

He started to unzip his pants.

She tried hanging on, forced her eyes to focus on his face, remember those bushy eyebrows, that big nose, that ugly coat.

"Hurry up or you'll miss 'em!" a girl's voice. "What you doin' in there?"

"None of your damn business."

She tried to scream, to bite his hand . . .

"All I know is you've been talkin' about this all day."

Couldn't she see what was happening?

"Are you coming or what?"

Meadow kicked, trying to get the girl's attention.

"I'm outta here," the girl finally said.

Oh, God, no one was going to help her . . .

And then he stood up, zipped his pants, straightened his shirt and ran away.

She laid still for a minute, taking inventory of the damage. Her tongue touched each tooth—all there. Her lips felt swollen, the bottom one cut, but she couldn't taste blood. She slowly sat up, touching the back of her head, checking both hands. No blood there either. Wobbling to her feet, brushing herself off, she whimpered from the fear. Her nylons were shredded, ground with dirt. She wiped off her legs with a hankie from her purse. He hadn't even tried to take her money. Her boots were scuffed. She inspected the back of her jacket, realizing she never wanted to wear it again.

It seemed to take forever to walk to the end of the alley, into the light. When she got there it was the quiet she felt. No one shouting, not much traffic, everything seemed to be waiting . . . but for what?

Had to get to the subway; had to get to Brooklyn. Should she tell Aunt Audrey? If she did would any of the family let her out of their sight ever again? She'd just say she fell; no real harm done. They'd believe her if she could get the panic under control. Stop thinking about it—about him. Happy thoughts. Luck had been with her; it could have been so much worse. Her lower lip trembled. Think about good things: Bobby Rydell, a brand new, baby blue convertible, root beer floats. But, like a broken record, she kept coming back to that maniac.

Almost there, keep walking, she repeated to herself, don't look at anyone. But when she passed an appliance store, closed for the night, bars over glass windows to protect the merchandise, she saw the crowd. Unable to stop herself, she slowed down.

Three TV sets, all tuned to the same channel, were on display. Ed Sullivan was introducing the next act. "Tonight, here on our stage—The Beatles!"

She recognized the plaid jacket in front of her and when he turned to say something to the skinny girl next to him, Meadow saw that big nose, too. But he was too mesmerized by the Beatles to see her. The fear charged her legs into a trot at first and then into a frantic run.

It was all anyone could talk about—the Fab Four. In a weird way she should have been grateful. If it hadn't been for the Beatles she might have been killed—or worse. But for a long time Meadow couldn't do anything but cry. His hands were clawing at her even when she just tried to relax, close her eyes for a few minutes. When she did manage to fall asleep, he was on top of her. She spent days in her room, always denying anything had happened in the city to change her. Always hiding how her hands shook. Never letting anyone know that she checked the locks every night—twice.

She broke it off with Jim, everything about him made her cringe. But they'd only been on four dates, so it didn't matter. When Darlene called, all excited that she had money saved up to get to Philly, Meadow lied, telling her that Dad wouldn't let her go. But she hadn't even asked him. At home with her family became the only place she felt safe and even they thought it strange how much time she was spending with them. Still so afraid, she couldn't stop crying.

What was she supposed to do now?

After a month all the frightened teen wanted to do was lie on her bed and listen to the radio. A man had tried to hurt her, but the Beatles and Ed Sullivan had saved her. A wash. The real hero had been that skinny girl in the alley, she reasoned. So she waited for another woman to save her—to show her the way.

And then she heard Lesley Gore sing . . .

"I'm young and I love to be young . . ."

She could feel her heart racing.

"...To live my life the way I want..."

That's what she had to do . . . live her life.

"You don't own me . . ."

Nobody owned Meadow Rose. She was young and had talent!

She walked quickly as she came into the light, up out of the subway. It was spring in New York and the air was warm but still she wore a sweater, buttoned all the way up to her collar bone. Not because she was cold but . . . careful.

The Ed Sullivan Theater was an easy walk. She'd come into the city early, sure to get to Aunt Audrey's way before dark. There was a line at the side door and she got in at the end. Auditions were starting at 11:00am. The June Taylor dancers needed two girls.

Note: On February 9, 1964, crime rates plummeted all over the U.S. between 8 and 9 p.m. when the Beatles performed for the first time on the Ed Sullivan Show.

GRANDMOTHER'S VILLAGE

Environmental Research International (E.R.I.) was financially distressed. Kelsey Turner was counting on #34 to do the proverbial trick. Max and Jeffery had projected the dig would yield half a million in profits, priceless historical artifacts, plus the added dividend of government assistance. Once #34 was listed as an authentic Indian Village, set right in the middle of the project, the surrounding area was planned for an independently owned, E.R.I. nature center, cultural museum and children's history workshop. Tourists would redirect through Washburn, North Dakota and E.R.I. would continually benefit. Television coverage, radio spots, Triple-A travel guides, the potential was endless.

As Director of Public Affairs for E.R.I., Kelsey was professional and efficient. As owner and chief stockholder of Hidden Treasures, Kelsey schemed, lied and plotted with privileged knowledge reaped from E.R.I.

She smiled at the thought of plastic souvenir teepees, T-shirts, toys and Indian dolls, all stamped with the Hidden Treasures logo. The site at #34 would permanently remind travelers of an ancient heritage, invoke national interest. So what if those travelers bought a few mementos of their trip and Kelsey Turner felt the extra income?

Now Mattie Tom was coming. The papers would report her arrival tomorrow. And, if the local press was hesitant, Kelsey had informed *World News* of the visit to #34 by an authentic Shaman. She nibbled a manicured fingertip, thinking how horrified Max would be knowing she had also called *The National Informer*, anonymously, with an outlandish story, the likes of which made the tabloid notorious.

After hearing Mattie Tom lecture in Grand Forks at the University, Kelsey had finalized her plan. The respected authority would stir up national interest, the dig would receive free coverage, and Kelsey Turner would get rich. Sitting back in her velour chair, smugly recounting that day's business, Kelsey wished she didn't have to wait until morning for things to start happening.

The intercom on the right corner of her oak desk buzzed. "Miss Turner?"

"Yes?

"A package arrived from number thirty-four. Should we send it to the lab or Mr. Lane's office?"

"I'll ask Max what we should do with it when he calls. Put it in his closet for now."

"Yes, ma'am."

Kelsey stood, listening at the door adjoining her office to Max's. She waited for her secretary to deposit the package and leave. Slowly opening the door, she walked to his storage closet and spotted the small, brown paper wrapped bundle on the green carpeted floor. Returning to her own office, she shook the box, deciding to inspect its contents personally.

Several burlap pouches, each stamped with large black letters: PROPERTY OF E.R.I., were unwrapped from their dirty newspaper. Two of the bags contained arrowheads and dirt samples. One heavy bag was filled with crude ornaments fashioned from beads and course thread. A particular necklace, combining blues, mauves and red stones, caused her to hesitate. She held it to the venetian blind for daylight reflection. Slipping it around her neck, she quickly re-packed the box, sealed it over with tape and returned it to Max's closet.

"Things get lost all the time," she told herself.

Rubbing the pendant between her fingers, she tucked it inside her silk blouse, where it rested heavily against her skin.

He ate the special: chicken fried steak. Fried between layers of soggy batter, covered a second time around with white, lumpy gravy, it tasted greasy, cold and wonderful. At home his diet was restricted. Here, he indulged himself. His reward each evening was to sit in this corner of Bobby's, watch the locals, catch what pieces of gossip shot his way and gobble down that day's bill of fare.

"Max, hey pal, how the hell's it goin'?"

"Bobby," he extended his free hand to the café owner. "The same. Slow . . . you know. What's new with you? Haven't seen you in weeks."

"Nothin'." Bobby laughed around the ever present match stick in his mouth. "My old lady's bitchin' she works too hard. Wonder how she'd like a fuckin' torch job." He winked.

Bobby Roy Jackson had been jailed for killing and burning his first wife in the garbage can out back. You could still see blood at the bottom of the barrel, if you had a mind to look. Bobby Roy always did have a bad temper.

"Them dumbass waitresses start bitchin', too. Just because they know I can't touch 'em. They take advantage."

Parole came after seven years of good behavior, the mysterious disappearance of the only eyewitness and with the condition that Bobby Roy keep his hands, and matches, to himself.

"I tell you, pal. Like them T-shirts say, 'Life's a Bitch 'n' Then Ya Die.' Should say, 'Ya Marry a Bitch 'n' Then *She* Dies." He grinned again, slapping Max on the shoulder.

"Guess so," Max agreed aloud, dissenting silently. His wife, Karen, was the joy of his life. But it wasn't fashionable to admit you loved your wife, especially one that had been around for sixteen years, but he did. "Yeah, life's a bitch, all right."

"Later." Bobby waved as he went to work the bar, delivering his punch lines and friendly handshakes.

Max wanted to finish his dinner and gin, get back to the house and sleep. Morning would bring the Indian and all that bullshit. He resented the interference. He realized, however, this far into the project brought irritability along with one of the longest dry periods this area had experienced in twenty-five years. It was great for the digging, torturous for the spirit. Time was slipping by; government funds were allocated for only six more weeks.

Once back at E.R.I., months would be spent compiling notes, preparing lectures. More months cataloging, writing papers, reports; this was the most important find in over seventy-five years. After all the facts were reported, the highway department would evaluate the data, deciding if asphalt should be laid or if #34 should be declared an historical landmark.

Wesley Douglas pushed through the smoke and men gathered in front of an electronic dart game, searching for Max. He enjoyed wearing the archaeological title and gear much better than the dirt and boredom which were, in fact, reality for the two men. His khaki shorts, matching shirt and sunburnt skin made him stand out among the denim-and-plaid crowd.

"Max, hey man, I've been lookin' all over hell for you."

"Here I am," Max said through a mouth full of steak.

"The Indian, Mattie Tom, she's here."

"Now?"

"Yeah, came hiking up an hour ago. Wanted me to take her to the site."

"Shit." His stomach bucked from Bobby's special gliding its way down to float atop greasy nerves. "What's going on now?"

"How should I know?" Wesley played stupid when asked for information and real smartass when showing off for town girls. He would dig and sift, minus his safari shirt, flexing for the crowd. Max often thought Wes' muscles resided beneath his straw, fried curls, most times covered with a beige pith helmet

"Okay, I'm done eating, anyway. Come on. My dinner's ruined."

"Sorry, shit. What was I supposed to do with the old broad? She just up and appears demanding we take her to the site. Now."

"She's in no position to demand diddly. Where the hell is Jeffery? I haven't seen him for hours."

Wesley shrugged.

The irritated man threw down enough money to cover his tab plus a generous tip.

Grit powdered the windshield as they headed out of town and back onto the trail leading to camp.

"What the hell's this broad here for, anyway?" Wesley asked as Max swung the jeep to the right, jerking both men.

"She's a Shaman, born in the area. Kelsey thought the local flavor would get us some support. She wasn't supposed to come until tomorrow, though."

"You mean, like a witch doctor?"

"Yeah, sure," Max sighed. "Jeffery thought she might help us identify some of the things we can't catalog."

Wesley stared. It infuriated Max how dense the handsome man could get. He was good at his job, however. The crew liked him; they worked hard under his supervision. He got down into the pits with the kids, lifted shovel for shovel, stayed until the last digger headed home. His brains might be small in comparison to his biceps, but then, Max and Jeffery filled in where Wesley left off.

Jeffery Roberts completed the team sent by E.R.I. to inspect land designated to yield Highway 45 through the southern tip of North Dakota. His specialty was field survey. His preciseness allowed him to come within small percentages of mechanical calculations. He was a walking, breathing computer and the most withdrawn, nervous, unlikable man Max had ever met.

Sliding to a stop across long grass fringing the crooked house, Max and Wesley could see a figure propped on tilted steps. The house, an abandoned cabin, was now being used for their sleeping and living comfort. The idea was to live as cheaply as possible while working on the dig which was located uphill and due north another two miles.

Mattie Tom sat, hands curled in her lap, a yellow, over-sized shirt draped to her knees. Max thought she looked wooden. A multicolored, beaded band strung around her head. Lacking traditional braids, her black hair lay in bangs then curled under, softly, in one length to her shoulders. She stared, not at the approaching vehicle, but at the sun nestled inside pink and orange clouds.

Max stepped down from the jeep, slapping his Levi's, patchy with dirt, as he walked toward the woman.

"Mattie," he called.

The Indian woman, older than Max by at least ten years, resented this thirty year old hippie-type treating her with so little respect. She was a spiritual leader, revered among her people for her knowledge of tradition. She was a teacher, a keeper of beliefs. Greeting the newcomer, she grunted without moving.

"I thought you were coming tomorrow," he said.

Sunlight caught Max from behind, haloing his face, outlining his bushy brown hair. Struck with fearful recognition Mattie Tom whispered, "It was you." Looking to Wesley, "And you. Is there another? A smaller man who also works on the digging?"

"Yes," they agreed. "Jeff. Jeffery Roberts. He's . . ."

"Five feet, seven inches. Short, graying hair, thick glasses that he needs for small details?"

"That's Jeff. When did you meet?" Wesley asked.

"We have never met . . . in the flesh. I saw three men in my dream. There was also a woman. She was crying, filled with such sadness. Is she here also?"

Wesley looked to Max, remembering the local women, visiting between heat spells, carrying covered casseroles, cakes and gallons of lemonade for the poor, hardworking young men. Catering to the minor celebrities who filled their hometown lives with exciting new discovering, none had ever cried, though.

"No."

"She will be here. We must go to the site, now. Tonight."

Max tried being diplomatic. "I don't want to offend, but why the rush?"

His ulcer burned and twitched at scraps of his undigested dinner. One screwup and the job would lose credibility, turn into a sideshow. He didn't want all their work chewed up by Highway 45. And yet, Mattie Tom could lend authority.

"Come inside, we'll make some coffee. We can head up to the site tomorrow, right after breakfast. I bet you're tired. It'll be dark in an hour or so. You won't be able to see a single thing."

"I did not come to see 'a single thing'," the Indian mocked. "I came to walk the ground, communicate with my ancestors. I didn't come to dig in the earth; I came to smell, embrace the essence of the village."

Years of rooting around in the dirt developed calluses over emotions. Facts outweighed abstracts. Yet inexplicably, Max understood what the Indian said. He had smelled the damp soil beneath the dust, relied on that untrained part of him more than even he knew.

"Start the jeep. We'll go now." Mattie Tom took small, scuffing steps, deposited herself on the red vinyl seat, staring ahead through bug-juiced glass.

The men rolled their eyes, then got into the vehicle. Max started the engine and steered toward the site. Trying for polite conversation, he rambled.

"This has been a very interesting project. We came across several eagle trapping pits. An interesting practice. The braves laying beneath branches, waiting to snare an eagle with their bare hands."

"Passage into manhood was a serious matter. Traditions were treasured throughout many generations, much as rare stones. It was a test, seeing who could grasp the greatest of all birds from the sky. Today, young men wear women's earrings, make-up, even clothing. There should be a test for them to prove manhood. They lack values."

"Ain't that the truth," quipped Wesley.

"Our culture is lacking in ceremony," Max observed. "The more I study different societies, the more I see what's wrong with our own. You must admit, though, that in spite of traditions and ceremonies, the Indian remained savage. They couldn't even get along with each other. Tribal wars. Murdering their own kind with no conscience whatsoever." The road was bumpy. Max wished for a Tums.

Mattie Tom was uncomfortable and insulted. It was the White Man's world which gave birth to such corruption. It was his world she was forced to live in, his world in which she felt alien. She knew the truth, had communicated with the spirits. They told her to perform the cleansing ceremony last night, rid herself of the evil trying to penetrate her soul. The spirits were her only friends. Even among her own tribe she was considered strange. A cultured, educated woman who played the teacher's role considered more appropriate by her people to be instructed by a man. The spirits were her guides, too. They demanded she come here this evening. She could not ignore their pleas.

Kelsey Turner locked her desk, looking forward to dinner at Buckinghams. New York suited her. Tomorrow would be exciting; she planned to have a front row seat. Should she wear her Calvins or Wranglers? Best to keep the image low key. When the profits started coming in, who the hell cared what she wore? Scratching a spot behind her left ear, she picked up her designer clutch bag.

"Good-night, Susan." She waved to her secretary.

"'Night, Miss Turner."

"See you Monday. Don't forget, I won't be in tomorrow. Remind Mr. Lane when he calls that I'll be at the site bright and early."

"Will do."

As they pulled up to the roped-off site, the three stepped from the raised chassis. One hour remained of late afternoon sunlight, one hour until complete darkness would shroud the sky, making all markers invisible. Strings and tools lay scattered. Mattie Tom walked quietly, her feet wrapped in soft moccasins fringed with turquoise beads. Her skirt swept tall grass as she stooped, inspecting the progress.

Max walked alongside the woman. "As you can see . . ."

"No words, please. I must listen. Can't you feel the great sadness?"

Wesley stood leaning against the jeep, unwrapped a stick of gun, rolling the foil between his fingers. It glittered, pretending to be something of value. He thought of the many artifacts found these past weeks. How future diggers might uncover items from his slice of time, thinking all of them priceless when, in fact, some would be as insignificant as the gum wrapper.

He could hear lectures filling universities of the future. "This McDonaldLand cup was a religious artifact. Once worshipped as the God of Happiness, Ronald McDonald's likeness was recreated on many household items. There were golden arched temples all over the world. Believers would travel to partake of the sacramental quarter pounder."

Shit, half the stuff they found, items indistinguishable due to deterioration or sheer lack of knowledge, were marked: RELIGIOUS ARTIFACT. Wouldn't the ancient ancestors have a laugh at a friggin' bedpan from some teepee being displayed in a museum, behind shatterproof glass, catalogued RELIGIOUS ARTIFACT? What the hell, who's to know the difference, anyway? He liked the work, the Indiana Jones image. It kept him outside, away from a suffocating office and cramped desk. Kelsey liked him, too, even let him buy into Hidden Treasures—and that wasn't all she let him into.

Wind pushed dry leaves across the dirt partitioned into sections. The warmth embraced the three, sensuously. Sun warmed their backs as they stood, each lost in such different thoughts.

"There," the Indian pointed. "It was there they decided to bury the dead.

The ones passing to the other world." She pointed past the site, up toward a mound covered with thick grass and a singular, rotting tree. Its trunk drooped over like a weathered, beaten old man. Branches scratched the earth, sifting beneath its exposed roots.

"We haven't gotten that far," Max explained. "Found the majority of items here. You really think there's something up there?"

She looked at him, disbelieving he would question her statement. "The spirits speak only truths."

She turned and started for the incline, some three hundred feet from the dig.

Max followed, waving to Wesley, "Come on. She says there's something over there." He had known last week something lay beyond the strings. Blamed the heat for sparking odd dread and depression whenever he looked over at the small hill.

"Sure 'nuff, boss." Wesley tossed the foil skyward then followed the two.

"I'm curious about the spirits you mentioned," Max said. "Do you have psychic abilities?"

"I am a Shaman. My father and his father, instructed me in the ancient ways."

"Isn't it unusual for a woman to be chosen?"

"I am the oldest of seven girls in my family. There has not been a male child born within our small tribe in several decades. You are correct, men are educated to carry on the tradition. However, in this case, I was the only one ready. I do feel a great responsibility and cannot allow the stories to be lost. Don't you agree that by learning of the past we can affect the future?"

She smiled at his curiosity. Perhaps she had misjudged this man. It felt good to be speaking without anger.

"I'm sorry if I seem rude," she went on. "Urgency overrides my manners. And, yes, I do possess some psychic ability . . . sorry, your name is?"

"Maxwell Lane. Doctor of Archaeological Studies. I, too, apologize for getting off to such a lousy start. You just took me by surprise, that's all."

Night slowly brushed clouds and sunlight from the sky. "This woman you spoke of before. The one you saw crying. Do you know who she is?" Max pushed his sweating hands deep into his jean pockets. The loose T-shirt flapped around his bony chest.

"No, I have never seen her before last night."

"Who?" asked Wesley, as he caught up to the figures silhouetted against the eerie sky.

"The woman in Mattie's dream. Remember, the one she saw crying?" Max said.

"Was she old or young?"

"Why do you wonder?" Mattie asked.

"Max." Wesley turned. "I forgot to tell you. Today some of the old guys were hangin' around. One got to talkin' about how his great uncle told him this spot was once called 'Grandmother's Village.'"

Sometimes his brain did function. When he relaxed that macho act, stopped trying so hard to impress, Wesley could be tolerable. Max looked to Mattie.

"Did you know that?"

Her head lifted to smell the wind. "I forgot." She meditated several moments. "Yes, it was an older woman I saw."

Max's good sense and practicality tried forcing all notions of spirits and foreboding dreams from his mind. Everything, he had been taught, had an explanation. Knowledge and techniques sooner or later exposed half-baked, far-fetched stories. But what about the crying he thought he had heard, days ago? It had taken three gin and tonics to smother the sobs that echoed in his ears.

No one spoke as Mattie Tom swayed her head from side to side in one gentle motion. No one noticed the mist seeping up beneath their feet. Darkness had come on quickly.

Mattie Tom chanted, singing her words. They were beyond the beams of the jeep's headlight so Wesley went back to get a flashlight. Then they saw the mist, rising up through tangled grass. This was a phenomenon neither man had witnessed before, especially not at this time of the year.

As the mist rose, apparently from the mound itself, Wesley grew frightened, Max more curious. It was only Mattie Tom who seemed not to notice, or care.

"A small fence, made of stone, surrounded this place," the Indian said. "It was here when they came. They did not know why. They built over where others had lived, and died. They did not care to know why the wall was built and suffered for their ignorance."

"A wall?" Max asked.

"There was part of a wall over there." Wesley pointed back to the edge of the site, past the jeep.

"There was one here, also," Mattie told him.

"What would be the significance of a stone wall?" Max asked.

"They thought it was to keep in the horses, the children, or to keep evil out. They were wrong." She turned and looked at Max. "It was to keep the sickness in, protect outsiders."

They stood transfixed in the summer darkness. Mists continued to roll, encircling the burial mound. Silence was more frightening than any sound.

Then Max saw something.

❋ ❋ ❋

Her table at Buckinghams was small, next to the men's room, and Kelsey Turner was pissed off. How dare they treat her this way! She'd get Gerald, the maître d'. God, look at that fat redhead with her fat neck. She shouldn't be allowed through the front door. She could get arrested for being such a cow, sitting in here, grazing, offending her fellow diners. Kelsey waved for Gerald, scratching her palm.

Nerves, she thought. I'll go home, grab a pizza. Tomorrow was too important to fuck up now. Waving to Gerald, just to get in her final words of complaint, she noticed several hives covering her hand.

"Did you hear that?" Wesley asked.

Max didn't answer. He was still looking at something on the mound.

"Where's this mist comin' from?" Wesley demanded.

"The spirits are unhappy," Mattie Tom said. "We are disturbing their land."

"What *is* that?" Max said, half to himself.

"Spirits, my ass!" Wesley snapped. "Look, we've been patient through this whole thing but you, lady, are full of crap. Spirits! And you, Maxwell, old boy, are losin' it if you think she's an expert on anythin' but bullshit."

Max wasn't listening. He had started walking toward the mound to try to identify what he was seeing. It was a . . . pile of something. Rags? Clothes?

"Where are you goin'?" Wesley demanded.

Max got closer, and as he did, he got a better view. "Good God!" he gasped.

Wesley and Mattie Tom came up on either side of him and stared.

"Jesus!" Wesley breathed. "Is that . . . a body?"

"It is," Max said.

"But . . . it's all . . . burnt."

"Not only that," Max said. "It's Jeffery."

Max sent Wesley back to the jeep to call the police.

"Tribal? Or the Sheriff? Or the State Police?" he asked.

"All of them," Max said. "Let them figure it out."

"Right."

Max turned, found Mattie Tom staring down at the body. The mist was swirling around them, remaining low to the ground. It almost covered the body. The smell of burnt flesh permeated the air.

Her lips were moving, but he couldn't hear anything. He assumed she was praying, silently. He decided not to disturb her.

He looked at the ground around the body. It was trampled with footprints. He wondered if the police would be able to tell anything from them.

"How do you know this is your friend?" she asked.

"There's enough of his belt left," Max said. "It's turquoise, so is the ring on his finger."

"But you cannot recognize his face," she said. "The ring, the belt, this could be anyone wearing those items."

"Look at his left hand, the one with the ring on it."

She leaned in closer. "He's missing a finger."

"He was born that way."

"But he was a good man?" she asked. "That's all that really matters."

"The best," Max said. "I don't know who would want to kill him."

Mattie Tom looked at him and said, "A not so good man."

"You don't think this could've been an accident?" Wesley asked.

"I know it wasn't," Max said.

"How can you be so sure?" Wesley asked.

"Jeffery didn't smoke," Max said. "He had no reason to carry matches. Look around the body."

"What am I lookin' for?" Wesley asked.

"There," Mattie Tom said, pointing, "and there. Are those . . ."

"Matches," Max said, "soggy wooden matches." He looked at Wesley. "That tell you anything?"

Wesley shrugged, looking agitated.

"Sure it does," Max said. "Bobby Roy, he's always sucking on match sticks and then tossing them around. Besides, he's got a reputation for killing people by burning them."

"One person," Wesley said, "his wife. That doesn't mean he killed Jeffery. Why would he?"

"I don't know," Max said, "we'll just have to let the cops sort it out."

"I don't think so."

Max looked at Wesley, who was pointing a gun at him and Mattie Tom.

"What the hell, Wesley—"

"Shut up, Max," Wesley said. "Just shut up. You talk too damn much."

"You?" Max asked. "You killed Jeffery?"

"No, I didn't kill him," Wesley said. "Pick up those matches. All of 'em."

There were three or four on the ground. Max bent over to pick them up. As he did the stench of burnt flesh got stronger in his nose.

"Give 'em here."

Wesley held out his free hand, gripped the gun tightly with the other. It was a .45, Max knew. He'd never seen Wesley with it before, but knew owning would feed his Indiana Jones image. He must have had it hidden in the jeep.

"Don't try anything."

Max was not brave enough to try anything against the loaded gun. He dropped the matches into Wesley's hand.

"Now what?" Max asked. "We die mysteriously, too?"

"Now, we wait."

"Wait?" Max asked. "You didn't radio for the police, did you?"

"An accomplice, most likely," Mattie Tom said. "Perhaps the man who did this." She gestured at the burnt corpse on the ground.

"He's probably the one who does the killing, right, Wesley?"

"Shut up." Wesley said. "Just shut up! Don't push me!"

Max wished he had the nerve to go ahead and push Wesley, who had probably never killed anyone, or even pulled the trigger of that gun, in his life.

But he didn't, so they waited . . .

Almost an hour later they heard the engine, then saw headlights as another jeep pulled into the site. During the time they'd waited the mist remained, hovering just above the ground, around their feet, neither fading nor increasing in density. Max's nerves were on edge. Mattie Tom seemed calm, and Max thought he could still see her lips moving silently.

The driver of the jeep killed the engine, but left the headlights on. Now the beams of both jeeps almost reached the mound.

"Wesley?"

"Up here!"

The new arrival made his way to the mound, carrying a flashlight. Wesley's flashlight was on the ground, giving them just a little bit of light.

Finally, the man arrived. Max could just make out the face of Bobby Roy, still sucking on one of his matches.

"Well, well," he said, playing the beam of his light over Max and Mattie Tom. "This the old Indian bitch?"

"Yeah," Wesley said.

"And my buddy, Max," Bobby Roy said. "Man, I'm sorry to see you here."

"What's this about, Bobby Roy?" Max asked.

"What's it always about?" Bobby Roy smirked. "What's it always about, Max? Money."

"Money? But how—"

"Hidden Treasures, baby," Bobby Roy said. "T-shirts, dolls, arrowheads—"

"Arrowheads?"

Max knew things had gone missing from the dig, there had even been some pilfering, but he wasn't aware of any large scale thefts.

"Don't strain yerself, Einstein," Bobby Roy said, "you wouldn't get it any more than yer buddy, there."

But Max thought he was getting it, and he looked at Wesley.

"This was your idea?" he demanded. "Stealing from the dig for profit?"

"Muscles here have an idea?" Bobby Roy interrupted. "Yer barkin' up the wrong tree there, boss. It was the chick, the one in New York—"

"Kelsey?" Max asked. "She thought this up?"

"She's one smart broad, knows how to turn a buck," Bobby Roy said. "Knew who to pick as a partner, too."

"What are you doin'?" Wesley demanded. "You're tellin' him too much."

"I don't think so, kid," Bobby Roy said.

"Whataya mean?"

Bobby Roy looked at Wesley.

"Come on, kid. They know too much. They gotta go, like yer other boss, there."

"You're gonna . . . burn them?"

"As much fun as that sounds, we ain't got the time," Bobby Roy said. He produced a gun of his own from behind his back.

"I'll do the old broad, and you do yer pal."

"I—I can't," Wesley said.

"Okay, I understand. I'll do Max and you do the broad."

"No, I mean . . . I can't."

Bobby Roy gave Wesley a disappointed look. "Okay, I'll do 'em both. Is it gonna bother you to watch?"

"Well . . ."

"Jesus, Wes," the other man said. "I'll take Max behind the mound and do him. Can you watch the broad until I come back? Then I'll pop her. Okay?"

"Yeah," Wesley said, "yeah, okay. I can do that."

"Jeez, I hope so." He pointed his gun right at Max. "Okay, boss, let's go."

"Wesley—" Max said, but Bobby Roy stepped forward and pushed him.

"Move, or I'll do you right here!"

Bobby Roy showed the way with his flashlight, waved his gun at Max to move. Max started walking. They circled the mound until they were out of sight of Wesley and Mattie Tom, who had never stopped praying to herself.

"Bobby Roy, you don't have to do this," Max said.

"Yeah, bro, I do."

"I don't think this is what Kelsey wanted."

"She wanted somebody who could do the hard stuff," Bobby Roy said. "That's why we're partners."

"And Wes?"

"He ain't no partner," Bobby Roy said, "but with you and Jeff gone, he might end up one. We're gonna need him to keep this dig goin'."

"Never happen. He can't handle it."

Bobby Roy prodded Max in the back with the gun barrel and said, "You won't be here to see one way or the other, so don't worry about it."

They walked a few feet more and then Bobby Roy said, "This is far enough. What's with this mist?"

"Don't know," Max said. "It seems to be coming from the mound."

"It don't matter," Bobby Roy said. "You want it standin' up or on yer knees?"

Max was about to answer when they both heard an inhuman scream from back the way they had come.

"What the hell—" Bobby Roy said.

They both forgot that Bobby Roy was supposed to kill Max and ran back to where they had left Wesley with Mattie Tom. Max was surprised to see the Indian woman standing and Wesley lying on the ground.

"What happened?" Bobby Roy demanded. "What the hell happened?"

"He is dead."

"I can see he's dead," Bobby Roy said, shining the flashlight directly on Wesley's body. "How?"

She shrugged. "The spirits."

"Spirits, my ass."

"Look at him," Max said. "Shine the light on his face."

Bobby Roy did as he was told. He got down on one knee and played the light over the dead man's face. The look on Wesley's face was one of pure horror, his lips snaked back over his teeth.

"Looks scared to death," Max said.

"Jeez," Bobby Roy said.

"Now look at me," Max said.

Bobby Roy turned, shining the light on Max over his shoulder and saw that Max had picked up Wesley's fallen gun.

"You don't have the balls," he said.

"Try me."

Bobby Roy stared at him a few moments, then laughed before dropping his gun.

Kelsey tried getting out of the ornate, claw-footed tub but spasms jerked her back into the scented water. She ripped at oozing blisters crawling up her arms, circling her wrists and swelling her fingers. She had to cool herself, relieve the fever. She tried again to gain her balance in the tub.

Reaching for a towel, she hoisted her raw skinned body from the polluted water, the soles of her feet burned, open now from the pressure of standing. She took a deep breath, tried to calm herself and lifted a leg over the porcelain side.

Her own blood and body fluids acted as a slick undercoating. As she grabbed at the towel rack it snapped under her rushing weight. Her head struck the toilet with such force that she was dead before hitting the floor.

Laying beneath her clean nightgown was the necklace found at site #34, the necklace she had stolen from her boss's office. Its tag, still inside the burlap bag, boxed up in Maxwell Lane's closet, could have given Kelsey some interesting data: Circa 1837, Mantan tribe. 98% wiped out in small pox epidemic.

As the Tribal police and sheriff led Bobby Roy away, arguing over who was going to get him, Max stood next to Mattie Tom.

"What will happen to your work now?" she asked.

"I'll have to get some new people involved."

"You should be very careful."

He shook his head, agreeing. "I've been wanting to ask you about the praying . . . or chanting, you were doing?"

She looked puzzled. "Praying?"

"Your lips were moving almost the whole time we were being held back there."

"Oh, I was talking to the spirit of Grandmother. She is the guardian of the Mantan people."

"And was she the one who killed Wesley?" he asked slowly.

"You said he was frightened to death."

"Yes, but by what?"

"By something he saw, I suppose." Mattie Tom smiled enigmatically, deciding maybe they didn't have to dig up the mound after all.

SISTERLY LOVE

Upon reviewing my life, which I do every birthday, I am not only amazed at all I've been through, but the order in which chapters have unfolded. Certainly not the way I thought they would or tried to make things happen.

Take marriage for example. When my friends were at that gushy stage, planning weddings and all conversations revolved around flowers, cakes and invitations, I sat by disinterested. I was going to stay single and have a career. A lawyer, I fantasized. Perry Mason was a big deal on TV back then. Oh sure there was his secretary, Della Street. Today she'd be referred to as his "executive assistant." She was smart, attractive and clever . . . for a woman. But I wanted to be the big cheese, wrenching a confession out of the killer, center stage on the witness stand.

In spite of my inflated expectations, however, I did end up married, and before everyone else in my crowd. But I remember walking down the aisle toward my husband-to-be thinking this will never last. I'll never celebrate a twenty-fifth let alone a fiftieth anniversary. So why did I do it? Well, it was the easy way out.

It was the easiest route away from my politely detached family. I wouldn't have to fight off any more horny, rude dates. And I did love Simon. But looking back, I see that I wasn't a fighter. I was a good, nice girl, the kind every mother wanted her son to marry. And when I'd get depressed through the years, there was comfort knowing all the girls who graduated with me went on to be teachers or nurses. Certainly not principals, doctors or lawyers. Not one in the bunch. Even the loud ones who carried picket signs and got arrested at sit-ins. In fact, they grew up to be the most traditional wives and PTA moms.

Then came children, homes with two-car garages, block parties, dogs and family vacations. I turned out to be everything I never wanted to be—and more.

Until the divorce.

After twenty-three years of marriage and all the restrictions that come with family life . . . I escaped.

Hallelujah! Now it was time to make all my dreams come true. There was enough time left to do everything I wanted. But what did I want? You can imagine my dilemma when I realized that my dreams had all changed. I no longer wanted to be a lawyer. At my age, lawyers now ranked one level above used car salesmen. I had lost all interest in learning to play the piano, read *Don Quixote* in its original Spanish, back-pack anywhere, and marry Paul McCartney.

But I could move and start over in a new place while I figured things out. So that's what I did.

To a little adobe house with a backyard view of mountains. The colors in Santa Fe are energizing. Just what I needed. But for the first three months all I could do was sit. I sat on the patio and read. I sat in front of the TV and stared. I sat in airplane seats going back and forth to visit the kids. I sat and made lists so I'd know what to do when I was tired of sitting.

Then one morning it felt like I had jumped out of an airplane, almost as if I were skydiving. Free falling with my arms open to everything and my heart pounding. It was exhilarating. Confidence overtook me and I knew I could do anything. All I had to do was grab, just reach out, grab, and I could have it all.

The kids were doing great, all three old enough to be on their own. Even if I'd stayed home and been the good wife and mother, I reasoned, they weren't coming home anymore to eat my meatloaf or sleep in their rooms. All residual guilt was completely gone after a year and I started writing again. I finished poems that had been lying in drawers for years. I kept a journal full of ideas for short stories, novels and plays. Words circulated from my imagination to paper. I was inspired. I was brilliant. I was more creative than I had ever been. Until one afternoon when my old life made a surprise visit. My sister called.

"Barbara? Oh, Thank God."

"Natalie? What's wrong? You sound terrible."

"Wendell Mead is back. In fact I can see him now, right from the bedroom window."

"Have you called the police?"

She clicked her tongue and then let out a long breath. That familiar irritability came through. "Of course I did."

I waited a minute, but she didn't say anything. "And? What did they say?"

"It's always the same bullshit. If he hasn't threatened us, there's nothing we can do. So we just sit here and wait."

"Isn't there a law or something?"

"The law making a pervert stay a thousand feet away was passed after Mead was convicted. Now they say it's unconstitutional to make him move. I am so sick of this crap."

"Maybe nothing will happen. You have to stop being so afraid, Nat."

"That's all you've got for me? Thanks." She broke down. "Look, I shouldn't have called. Sarah's going to be home soon and I have to clean myself up."

"She's walking home alone?" I asked, shocked that my sister would be so careless with her eight-year-old.

"Give me some credit, will you? The Allison kids walk her home, they're in eighth grade, there's a whole bunch of them and they watch out for each other."

"Natalie, Sarah needs you, not some neighbor kids. She needs her mother."

"Don't you think I know that?" She was angry now. "You know I have this condition. Just the thought of walking down the front steps and I break out in a sweat, start shaking so badly I can't drive. It's like I'm dying. Why can't you be more understanding and realize I'm sick?"

"This isn't about you, Natalie, it's about your daughter. You have to think about Sarah."

"Damnit, Barbara, she's all I think about. Not like you who left her kids . . ."

"Kids? Come on! I would never walk out on them when they were little. I never did. I stayed . . ."

"I don't know why I even bothered calling you. Everyone says you're crazy now; menopause fried your brain. Your own mother is embarrassed that you're living in some run-down place in the desert. She still can't understand why you left Simon."

I tried again. "Natalie, I've asked you to bring Sarah for a visit. Come out and see for yourself. I've got a guest room, you can stay as long as you want. And I didn't leave Simon. We got a divorce. Believe it or not—he wanted it too."

"You haven't heard a single word I've said. I'm in the middle of a crisis here. I can't just pick up and leave. Aw shit, I don't know why I talk to you."

I was relieved when she slammed down the receiver. Nat and I had never been close, but each time I saw her or we spoke, I hoped. Maybe, someday, when we were older or happier. But the horror of having her little girl, my sweet, dear niece, molested was destroying that hope.

Six months passed. No word from Natalie. I could have called. Maybe I should have called right back after she hung up that day. But the truth was I didn't want to. That reasoning had never been good enough before. There always had to be other people's feelings to consider. But finally I could afford to be selfish with my time. I was in a perfect place both physically and mentally. For six whole months it was paradise.

They say the two big reasons people curl up and die are heart disease and cancer. I suffered from neither. My doctor just shook his head and said he had only encountered one other case like mine before. Couldn't even bring himself to look me in the eyes when he told me I would have a few good months before the pain started. After that it would all be about pain management.

Another birthday. Reviewing my life I wondered if I had ever made a real contribution to the world. Raising two great kids—now wonderful, productive adults—should have been enough but I needed more. None of the short stories I had hopefully sent off to dozens of editors across the country had sold. One poem made it into the local paper, way back on page six, at the bottom, near an ad for plant food . . . and an item about a small child who had gone missing. As I cut it out, I noticed the incident had happened in Natalie's neighborhood.

"Natalie? How have you been?"

"Fine." Her reply was cold. She didn't ask how I was, never did.

"How's Sarah?"

"Fine." So unyielding.

"I called to ask you something."

That click followed by a heavy sigh. I always felt that I was bothering her, that she had so many more important things to do. Anything was better than to have to talk to me. "What is it?"

"Did you call the police on Wendell Mead that day?"

"That was months ago, Barbara. Why the hell are you asking about it today?"

"I came across an article. There's a little girl, Haley Bennet? She lives in your neighborhood."

"Three houses down. She's in Sarah's class."

"What happened to her?"

"No one knows."

"Have the police talked with Mead? He can't still be living across from you."

"He's not. And now that you're so interested, I never had to call the authorities on him again. He took off a few days after we talked."

"How's Sarah?" I asked.

"How do you think she is? Damnit, Barbara, it's as if you never had any kids of your own; you don't have a clue. Sarah's scared to death. She's convinced Mead grabbed Haley and has her locked up somewhere. I kept her home with me for a few days."

"That's not good."

"Do you think I don't know that?" she asked. "What kind of a mother would I be if I turned my only child into a frightened, house-bound neurotic. Heaven forbid she turned out like me. Right? Isn't that what you're thinking?"

It was exactly what I was thinking. "No. What does Ted say about all this?"

Natalie laughed. "The dotting daddy is way too busy with his new wife and their baby. No time for Sarah now. We're on our own—like always."

"No you're not. I'm here."

"Since when? When have you ever been there for me?"

And that's when I finally got it. Pow! A brick upside the head couldn't have done a better job of getting my attention. Nothing I would ever say could change my sister's dislike for me. Something had happened in our relationship that she couldn't forgive. I'd asked, I'd pleaded, but she would only shake her head at me and give a disgusted look. It was her secret and she was intent upon holding the injustice against me forever. So I decided . . . at last . . . at long last . . . to stop talking. And do something.

"Okay then." This time I hung up on her.

Two good months, that was the timeline I set for myself. Sixty days to find Wendell Mead and stop him from hurting my family or anyone else's. Consequences didn't matter now. I had spent a lifetime obeying rules, doing the right thing. Not one traffic ticket, never late for an appointment. Everyone's time was so much more valuable than mine. I crossed at corners, paid my bills on time . . . the more I thought about it, I made myself sick thinking what a meek, uncomplaining person I had become. But now I had a mission. I would find and kill Wendell Mead. It was so exciting.

The first thing I did was Google him. There were thirty-six websites listing sex offenses he had been convicted of, an article dating back to the first "incident" when he got into trouble for hurting a girl in his twelfth grade class during a picnic. There were photos and even a fan club. His parole officer was mentioned in one article, so I started there.

Claiming to be Mead's common-law wife, I figured there wouldn't be anything on record and if he asked why Mead had never mentioned me I would be vague and say our relationship had ended a long time ago. But now I was back because Wendell had some important papers I needed.

I don't know if he believed me or not but I kept whining and coughing, saying I was sorry to bother him but I was very sick. Throwing in a bit of the truth would make my story more believable, I told myself. After ten minutes I guess the poor guy figured I wasn't going away quietly so he said, "Look, I haven't seen Wendell in months. There's a warrant out on him and I'm officially off the case. Sorry, ahh, Mrs. Mead, but the man's a loser. Better off to be rid of him."

"Don't I know it. But I do need my papers for the insurance company. And I know Wendell keeps those kinds of things with him. So . . . can you at least tell me if his last address was on Tripp Street? That's what I have in my book and before I drive all the way out there, in my condition, I wanted to be sure."

"No, I have one after that." Paper shuffled. "Here, I'm not supposed to do this, but like I said, I'm through with him and I'm not telling you anything John Walsh wouldn't want plastered across America, right?"

"Right. And if it will make you feel better, just think of me as one of those concerned Americans calling an 800 number, okay?"

He laughed. "One sixty-two Oakhurst."

The police couldn't find Mr. Mead so how was I supposed to? I was in a funk for a few hours until realizing that I had one great advantage. This was all I had to do. Today. Tomorrow. Next week. Twenty-four hours for the next few months I was going to work on this. The police had hundreds of other cases. They had families, lives. This was my life now.

I spread out the city map. Oakhurst was in a nice part of town and ran through Oakhurst Village, an upscale subdivision. I was surprised. After getting dressed, I stuffed a picture of Wendell Mead into my purse but really didn't need it. I had been studying his face for days. He was an attractive man, not at all what you'd think a deviate would look like. He was in his early forties, someone I would have welcomed into my home. He had a degree in electrical engineering, a high IQ. In fact a link from one website went to Mensa. But many children had been ruined by his perverted behavior. I kept that in mind as I drove, wondering about therapists who worked with those kids trying to exorcise Wendell Mead from nightmares. And I thought of my poor niece, Sarah. Physical signs of her attack had healed over a long time ago. Left behind, however, was emotional devastation. Mead may have run from the neighborhood but he was still right there—in Sarah's bedroom, her bathroom, living inside every person in that house. All of them were trying so desperately to get some kind of normal back in their lives but that bastard wouldn't let it happen.

There was a FOR SALE sign in front of the sunny, yellow house. From where I sat out front, I could see expensive shades pulled over the windows. A real estate lady, wearing one of those horrible red polyester jackets, knocked on my window.

"Are you here for the open house?"

I thought a moment, wondering if I needed to come up with some sort of story.

"I'm setting up now; come on in."

A story had recently been broadcast about the dangers real estate agents faced. All alone in empty houses, meeting clients they've never met. Women were being raped—the men robbed and beaten. I imagine this person was relieved to see a "mature" woman that couldn't cause much trouble. Or maybe she was just the trusting sort, you know, the kind who claim, "Nothing like that would ever happen to me and certainly not here, in this place."

I started to lower my window.

She held up a box. "I have cookies. Come on."

The house was immaculate and again I was surprised. Conditioned by hundreds of episodes of cop shows, I expected to find garbage on the counters, dirty handprints on walls and carpet ripped up. But this place was beautiful.

I let her walk me through each room. We chatted about the color scheme while munching on chocolate chip cookies. When the time was right, I asked about the former tenants.

"Oh, just one—a single guy, worked at home, something to do with the internet. He had an office in the basement. Only lived here a few months. That's why everything is in such good condition."

"Do you mind if I look around on my own?" I asked, after we were back in the kitchen. "Just to get a feel for the place?"

"No problem. I'll be right here if you need me. Take your time."

The downstairs office kept calling me. It was a small room. Nothing hung on the walls, but a row of nail holes had been lined up along the back of the beige door. I looked in every corner, behind curtains, inspected every ceiling tile. A loose piece of carpeting caught my attention but it wasn't until I was on my knees pulling at it, that I saw a plastic bin under the stairs. When I lifted the lid, papers and maps exploded all over the floor. A large calendar had been pierced with nails and the holes matched the ones behind the door. I checked today's date. Nothing. But next Wednesday Mr. Mead had a dentist appointment. I frantically searched for a phone book, knowing that if Mead was like everyone else in this century, he had all his numbers in a cell phone and that phone was with him. But it was worth a try. No book. Ready to give up, I uncovered a small bulletin board, at the very bottom of the box, pinned with several business cards. One was from a dentist downtown. It was an appointment card . . . for next Wednesday.

I sat in my car with the motor running, studying Mead's photo. It was a cool, rainy day and I hoped he wouldn't be carrying an umbrella or wearing a cap that would cover his short hair.

The appointment time came and went. I was working up courage to go into the office and ask for Mr. Mead when I saw him walking toward me. There was a parking lot across the street; he apparently was on his way to his car. He smiled as he crossed in front of my car. I smiled back as I stepped on the accelerator.

He tried to crawl away when he realized I wasn't going to stop ramming into him, that this was no accident. It took three more times until I was sure he was dead. Then I shouted, "Someone call 911; I just killed a man!"

We're very pleased to have Natalie Wilson with us today. This is her first interview since her sister, Barbara, was sent to prison for killing Wendell Mead."

Natalie nodded.

"So, Mrs. Wilson, are you going to visit your sister today for her birthday?"

"Why should I?" Natalie asked. "She's nothing but a cold-blooded murderer. I don't want to have anything to do with her."

"Some people consider her a hero, you know. Members of the jury even made statements asking the judge for leniency. Taking out a pervert like Mead, keeping him from harming any other children. . . ."

"If you knew her like I do, you wouldn't think there's anything heroic about her."

The reporter's forehead crinkled with confusion. "Well, I do know she's very ill. That her prognosis isn't good."

"Her prognosis is a whole lot better now."

"I don't understand."

"My sister didn't have any health insurance after her divorce. She'd be dead now if she hadn't killed Mead. All her medication, tests, operations are paid for by the state. She's even in an experimental program and is receiving drugs you and I could never get."

"But she sacrificed herself for you and your daughter. And I for one feel it is more than fair that taxpayers of this state pay her medical expenses instead spending the money for a trial and prison stay for Mead."

"And where's Haley Bennet?" Natalie asked. "It's been almost two years and still no sign of her. Wendell Mead could have told the FBI where she is. . . ."

"If he knew," the reporter said. "There's no proof that he had anything to do with her disappearance."

"All I know is my sister took away any hope of questioning a man authorities considered a person of interest. She acted impulsively, with no consideration for anyone. She's always been like that. You just don't know her like I do."

An Afterword, with the Author

Christine Matthews has written short stories for many mystery anthologies, collaborated on several novel-length "cozies," and made a name for herself—a *different* name, as it happens—as a writer of horror fiction. She lives along the Mississippi with her sometime collaborator, Robert J. Randisi.

Perfect Crime Books ventured a few questions, and here are Christine Matthews's answers.

Q.: The first several stories in this collection are about a private eye—but she doesn't bear much resemblance to Kinsey Milhone or V. I. Warshawski. Can you tell us where Robbie came from?

A.: I'd been writing short fiction for years, mostly in the horror genre. When I was asked to try my hand at a PI story I said, "Thanks for asking, but no thanks." The only PI I was familiar with was Jim Rockford. But I was going through a strange time in my life and as they say, "write what you know." So I tried figuring out how to incorporate real life in PI fiction and sat down to watch *Donahue*. The topic that day was "Strange Occupations." On the panel was an attractive woman who happened to be a PI. I took it as a sign and started to write "Gentle Insanities." A lot of the dialogue is word-for-word true. And so Roberta Stanton was born.

Q.: Robbie has more than a little in common with many of your characters. They seldom seem to achieve redemption. Is it unfair to say they're maimed?

A.: To say my characters are maimed is perfect. But then, aren't we all? No one can get through this life free of pain or heartache. All my stories are portraits (in part) taken from my life or people I've known. I've been told I ask too many questions and some people are put off by that. But I hope it shows

I'm interested. If you take the time to get past all the cheery "have a nice day" crap, the real stuff comes out.

Q.: The settings around Omaha ring true. First-hand observation?

A.: Yes, I lived in Omaha for 13 years. I love it there. I'm originally from Chicago, lived a few years in St. Louis but back to Chicago. My son was ready to start school and we (my ex-husband and I) were looking to buy a house. We couldn't afford what we wanted and those we could afford were in bad school districts. Then a job opportunity came up and we went to check out Nebraska. My friends told us to have a good life in Colorado. None of us knew where Omaha was then. But it's a great city and has everything, on a smaller scale, that any large city has.

Q.: While a number of these stories have been published before, could you tell us something about the ones that appear here for the first time?

A.: There are two new ones here: "Sisterly Love" and "Grandmother's Village." The first one came about from my own relationship with my sister, which is up and down. I thought about how differently we would react to a family tragedy. One of us would retreat, the other would bulldoze for a resolution. And would that situation bring us closer or push us further apart? The second, "Grandmoher's Village," was first written as a horror story. My brother-in-law, an archeologist, had been on a dig where strange things were happening. He told me this story and I thought it was creepy. It never got published and ended up in a drawer. Years later I was asked to write a story for a Native American mystery anthology. I dug it out and re-wrote. Strike two—it didn't get published there either. But I like this story very much and was anxious to get it out of its drawer.

Q.: It's not a tightly kept secret that Christine Matthews is a pseudonym for your mystery writing. You also write as Marthayn Pelegrimas. What does Pelegrimas do that Matthews doesn't—or vice versa?

A.: My real name is Marthayn Pelegrimas and I started my career writing freelance articles, poetry and horror. I'd planned to keep my fiction in that genre until I was asked to write mysteries. Then I moved in with another writer, Bob Randisi. Editing as many anthologies as he does, there's usually a spot needing to be filled. One time it's a mystery, then a western, then something erotic—I love the challenge. But I always wanted to keep my real name for my first love—horror. Enter my son, Marcus Pelegrimas. A very talented writer who has had great success with urban fantasy. He's written western series, under Marcus Galloway, so he can keep Pelegrimas for horror. It got confusing having two M. Pelegrimases out there. And since he was born with the name and I married into it, he won. I now will have the Matthews name on everything I write.

Q.: You are well known for short stories. Are there novels we should know about?

A.: I've written three novels with Bob Randisi: *Murder Is the Deal of the Day*, *The Masks of Auntie Laveau*, and *Same Time, Same Murder* *. They're about a married couple, Claire and Gil Hunt. She's a home shopping host and he owns a bookstore. And I wrote one on my own, *On the Strength of Wings*. It's about an independent woman who travels west (against her wishes) and becomes strong in spite of herself. It's been re-released by Crossroads Press and is doing really well.

Q.: What are your next projects?

A.: I'm finishing up a novel that's taken me several years to write. *Beating the Bushes* is about two fathers who've lost children and the friendship that grows between them. Originally I wanted to write a literary story about what these men go through but it's evolved into a thriller. The next novel, *The Dead Hour*, is about out-of-body experiences. Kind of a paranormal, romantic, horror story. I'm trying to have that one done next year. But life and short stories get in the way!

*Available from PERFECT CRIME.

CPSIA information can be obtained at www.ICGtesting.com
Printed in the USA
LVOW03s2307060115

421813LV00005B/74/P